The Rustlers of

Zane Grey

Alpha Editions

This edition published in 2023

ISBN : 9789357933193

Design and Setting By
Alpha Editions
www.alphaedis.com
Email - info@alphaedis.com

Contents

Chapter 1

VAUGHN STEELE AND RUSS SITTELL

In the morning, after breakfasting early, I took a turn up and down the main street of Sanderson, made observations and got information likely to serve me at some future day, and then I returned to the hotel ready for what might happen.

The stage-coach was there and already full of passengers. This stage did not go to Linrock, but I had found that another one left for that point three days a week.

Several cowboy broncos stood hitched to a railing and a little farther down were two buckboards, with horses that took my eye. These probably were the teams Colonel Sampson had spoken of to George Wright.

As I strolled up, both men came out of the hotel. Wright saw me, and making an almost imperceptible sign to Sampson, he walked toward me.

"You're the cowboy Russ?" he asked.

I nodded and looked him over. By day he made as striking a figure as I had noted by night, but the light was not generous to his dark face.

"Here's your pay," he said, handing me some bills. "Miss Sampson won't need you out at the ranch any more."

"What do you mean? This is the first I've heard about that."

"Sorry, kid. That's it," he said abruptly. "She just gave me the money—told me to pay you off. You needn't bother to speak with her about it."

He might as well have said, just as politely, that my seeing her, even to say good-by, was undesirable.

As my luck would have it, the girls appeared at the moment, and I went directly up to them, to be greeted in a manner I was glad George Wright could not help but see.

In Miss Sampson's smile and "Good morning, Russ," there was not the slightest discoverable sign that I was not to serve her indefinitely.

It was as I had expected—she knew nothing of Wright's discharging me in her name.

"Miss Sampson," I said, in dismay, "what have I done? Why did you let me go?"

She looked astonished.

"Russ, I don't understand you."

"Why did you discharge me?" I went on, trying to look heart-broken. "I haven't had a chance yet. I wanted so much to work for you—Miss Sally, what have I done? Why did she discharge me?"

"I did not," declared Miss Sampson, her dark eyes lighting.

"But look here—here's my pay," I went on, exhibiting the money. "Mr. Wright just came to me—said you sent this money—that you wouldn't need me out at the ranch."

It was Miss Sally then who uttered a little exclamation. Miss Sampson seemed scarcely to have believed what she had heard.

"My cousin Mr. Wright said that?"

I nodded vehemently.

At this juncture Wright strode before me, practically thrusting me aside.

"Come girls, let's walk a little before we start," he said gaily. "I'll show you Sanderson."

"Wait, please," Miss Sampson replied, looking directly at him. "Cousin George, I think there's a mistake—perhaps a misunderstanding. Here's the cowboy I've engaged—Mr. Russ. He declares you gave him money—told him I discharged him."

"Yes, cousin, I did," he replied, his voice rising a little. There was a tinge of red in his cheek. "We—you don't need him out at the ranch. We've any numbers of boys. I just told him that—let him down easy—didn't want to bother you."

Certain it was that George Wright had made a poor reckoning. First she showed utter amaze, then distinct disappointment, and then she lifted her head with a kind of haughty grace. She would have addressed him then, had not Colonel Sampson come up.

"Papa, did you instruct Cousin George to discharge Russ?" she asked.

"I sure didn't," declared the colonel, with a laugh. "George took that upon his own hands."

"Indeed! I'd like my cousin to understand that I'm my own mistress. I've been accustomed to attending to my own affairs and shall continue doing so. Russ, I'm sorry you've been treated this way. Please, in future, take your orders from me."

"Then I'm to go to Linrock with you?" I asked.

"Assuredly. Ride with Sally and me to-day, please."

She turned away with Sally, and they walked toward the first buckboard.

Colonel Sampson found a grim enjoyment in Wright's discomfiture.

"Diane's like her mother was, George," he said. "You've made a bad start with her."

Here Wright showed manifestation of the Sampson temper, and I took him to be a dangerous man, with unbridled passions.

"Russ, here's my own talk to you," he said, hard and dark, leaning toward me. "Don't go to Linrock."

"Say, Mr. Wright," I blustered for all the world like a young and frightened cowboy, "If you threaten me I'll have you put in jail!"

Both men seemed to have received a slight shock. Wright hardly knew what to make of my boyish speech. "Are you going to Linrock?" he asked thickly.

I eyed him with an entirely different glance from my other fearful one.

"I should smile," was my reply, as caustic as the most reckless cowboy's, and I saw him shake.

Colonel Sampson laid a restraining hand upon Wright. Then they both regarded me with undisguised interest. I sauntered away.

"George, your temper'll do for you some day," I heard the colonel say. "You'll get in bad with the wrong man some time. Hello, here are Joe and Brick!"

Mention of these fellows engaged my attention once more.

I saw two cowboys, one evidently getting his name from his brick-red hair. They were the roistering type, hard drinkers, devil-may-care fellows, packing guns and wearing bold fronts—a kind that the Rangers always called four-flushes.

However, as the Rangers' standard of nerve was high, there was room left for cowboys like these to be dangerous to ordinary men.

The little one was Joe, and directly Wright spoke to him he turned to look at me, and his thin mouth slanted down as he looked. Brick eyed me, too, and I saw that he was heavy, not a hard-riding cowboy.

Here right at the start were three enemies for me—Wright and his cowboys. But it did not matter; under any circumstances there would have been friction between such men and me.

I believed there might have been friction right then had not Miss Sampson called for me.

"Get our baggage, Russ," she said.

I hurried to comply, and when I had fetched it out Wright and the cowboys had mounted their horses, Colonel Sampson was in the one buckboard with two men I had not before observed, and the girls were in the other.

The driver of this one was a tall, lanky, tow-headed youth, growing like a Texas weed. We had not any too much room in the buckboard, but that fact was not going to spoil the ride for me.

We followed the leaders through the main street, out into the open, on to a wide, hard-packed road, showing years of travel. It headed northwest.

To our left rose the range of low, bleak mountains I had noted yesterday, and to our right sloped the mesquite-patched sweep of ridge and flat.

The driver pushed his team to a fast trot, which gait surely covered ground rapidly. We were close behind Colonel Sampson, who, from his vehement gestures, must have been engaged in very earnest colloquy with his companions.

The girls behind me, now that they were nearing the end of the journey, manifested less interest in the ride, and were speculating upon Linrock, and what it would be like. Occasionally I asked the driver a question, and sometimes the girls did likewise; but, to my disappointment, the ride seemed not to be the same as that of yesterday.

Every half mile or so we passed a ranch house, and as we traveled on these ranches grew further apart, until, twelve or fifteen miles out of Sanderson, they were so widely separated that each appeared alone on the wild range.

We came to a stream that ran north and I was surprised to see a goodly volume of water. It evidently flowed down from the mountain far to the west.

Tufts of grass were well scattered over the sandy ground, but it was high and thick, and considering the immense area in sight, there was grazing for a million head of stock.

We made three stops in the forenoon, one at a likely place to water the horses, the second at a chuckwagon belonging to cowboys who were riding after stock, and the third at a small cluster of adobe and stone houses, constituting a hamlet the driver called Sampson, named after the Colonel. From that point on to Linrock there were only a few ranches, each one controlling great acreage.

Early in the afternoon from a ridgetop we sighted Linrock, a green path in the mass of gray. For the barrens of Texas it was indeed a fair sight.

But I was more concerned with its remoteness from civilization than its beauty. At that time in the early 'seventies, when the vast western third of Texas was a wilderness, the pioneer had done wonders to settle there and establish places like Linrock.

As we rolled swiftly along, the whole sweeping range was dotted with cattle, and farther on, within a few miles of town, there were droves of horses that brought enthusiastic praise from Miss Sampson and her cousin.

"Plenty of room here for the long rides," I said, waving a hand at the gray-green expanse. "Your horses won't suffer on this range."

She was delighted, and her cousin for once seemed speechless.

"That's the ranch," said the driver, pointing with his whip.

It needed only a glance for me to see that Colonel Sampson's ranch was on a scale fitting the country.

The house was situated on the only elevation around Linrock, and it was not high, nor more than a few minutes' walk from the edge of town.

It was a low, flat-roofed structure, made of red adobe bricks and covered what appeared to be fully an acre of ground. All was green about it except where the fenced corrals and numerous barns or sheds showed gray and red.

Wright and the cowboys disappeared ahead of us in the cottonwood trees. Colonel Sampson got out of the buckboard and waited for us. His face wore the best expression I had seen upon it yet. There was warmth and love, and something that approached sorrow or regret.

His daughter was agitated, too. I got out and offered my seat, which Colonel Sampson took.

It was scarcely a time for me to be required, or even noticed at all, and I took advantage of it and turned toward the town.

Ten minutes of leisurely walking brought me to the shady outskirts of Linrock and I entered the town with mingled feelings of curiosity, eagerness, and expectation.

The street I walked down was not a main one. There were small, red houses among oaks and cottonwoods.

I went clear through to the other side, probably more than half a mile. I crossed a number of intersecting streets, met children, nice-looking women, and more than one dusty-booted man.

Half-way back this street I turned at right angles and walked up several blocks till I came to a tree-bordered plaza. On the far side opened a broad street which for all its horses and people had a sleepy look.

I walked on, alert, trying to take in everything, wondering if I would meet Steele, wondering how I would know him if we did meet. But I believed I could have picked that Ranger out of a thousand strangers, though I had never seen him.

Presently the residences gave place to buildings fronting right upon the stone sidewalk. I passed a grain store, a hardware store, a grocery store, then several unoccupied buildings and a vacant corner.

The next block, aside from the rough fronts of the crude structures, would have done credit to a small town even in eastern Texas. Here was evidence of business consistent with any prosperous community of two thousand inhabitants.

The next block, on both sides of the street, was a solid row of saloons, resorts, hotels. Saddled horses stood hitched all along the sidewalk in two long lines, with a buckboard and team here and there breaking the continuity. This block was busy and noisy.

From all outside appearances, Linrock was no different from other frontier towns, and my expectations were scarcely realized.

As the afternoon was waning I retraced my steps and returned to the ranch. The driver boy, whom I had heard called Dick, was looking for me, evidently at Miss Sampson's order, and he led me up to the house.

It was even bigger than I had conceived from a distance, and so old that the adobe bricks were worn smooth by rain and wind. I had a glimpse in at several doors as we passed by.

There was comfort here that spoke eloquently of many a freighter's trip from Del Rio. For the sake of the young ladies, I was glad to see things little short of luxurious for that part of the country.

At the far end of the house Dick conducted me to a little room, very satisfactory indeed to me. I asked about bunk-houses for the cowboys, and he said they were full to overflowing.

"Colonel Sampson has a big outfit, eh?"

"Reckon he has," replied Dick. "Don' know how many cowboys. They're always comin' an' goin'. I ain't acquainted with half of them."

"Much movement of stock these days?"

"Stock's always movin'," he replied with a queer look.

"Rustlers?"

But he did not follow up that look with the affirmative I expected.

"Lively place, I hear—Linrock is?"

"Ain't so lively as Sanderson, but it's bigger."

"Yes, I heard it was. Fellow down there was talking about two cowboys who were arrested."

"Sure. I heerd all about thet. Joe Bean an' Brick Higgins—they belong heah, but they ain't heah much."

I did not want Dick to think me overinquisitive, so I turned the talk into other channels. It appeared that Miss Sampson had not left any instructions for me, so I was glad to go with Dick to supper, which we had in the kitchen.

Dick informed me that the cowboys prepared their own meals down at the bunks; and as I had been given a room at the ranch-house he supposed I would get my meals there, too.

After supper I walked all over the grounds, had a look at the horses in the corrals, and came to the conclusion that it would be strange if Miss Sampson did not love her new home, and if her cousin did not enjoy her sojourn there. From a distance I saw the girls approaching with Wright, and not wishing to meet them I sheered off.

When the sun had set I went down to the town with the intention of finding Steele.

This task, considering I dared not make inquiries and must approach him secretly, might turn out to be anything but easy.

While it was still light, I strolled up and down the main street. When darkness set in I went into a hotel, bought cigars, sat around and watched, without any clue.

Then I went into the next place. This was of a rough crude exterior, but the inside was comparatively pretentious, and ablaze with lights.

It was full of men, coming and going—a dusty-booted crowd that smelled of horses and smoke.

I sat down for a while, with wide eyes and open ears. Then I hunted up a saloon, where most of the guests had been or were going. I found a great square room lighted by six huge lamps, a bar at one side, and all the floor space taken up by tables and chairs.

This must have been the gambling resort mentioned in the Ranger's letter to Captain Neal and the one rumored to be owned by the mayor of Linrock.

This was the only gambling place of any size in southern Texas in which I had noted the absence of Mexicans. There was some card playing going on at this moment.

I stayed in there for a while, and knew that strangers were too common in Linrock to be conspicuous. But I saw no man whom I could have taken for Steele.

Then I went out.

It had often been a boast of mine that I could not spend an hour in a strange town, or walk a block along a dark street, without having something happen out of the ordinary.

Mine was an experiencing nature. Some people called this luck. But it was my private opinion that things gravitated my way because I looked and listened for them.

However, upon the occasion of my first day and evening in Linrock it appeared, despite my vigilance and inquisitiveness, that here was to be an exception.

This thought came to me just before I reached the last lighted place in the block, a little dingy restaurant, out of which at the moment, a tall, dark form passed. It disappeared in the gloom. I saw a man sitting on the low steps, and another standing in the door.

"That was the fellow the whole town's talkin' about—the Ranger," said one man.

Like a shot I halted in the shadow, where I had not been seen.

"Sho! Ain't boardin' heah, is he?" said the other.

"Yes."

"Reckon he'll hurt your business, Jim."

The fellow called Jim emitted a mirthless laugh. "Wal, he's been *all* my business these days. An' he's offered to rent that old 'dobe of mine just out of town. You know, where I lived before movin' in heah. He's goin' to look at it to-morrow."

"Lord! does he expect to *stay*?"

"Say so. An' if he ain't a stayer I never seen none. Nice, quiet, easy chap, but he just looks deep."

"Aw, Jim, he can't hang out heah. He's after some feller, that's all."

"I don't know his game. But he says he was heah for a while. An' he impressed me some. Just now he says: 'Where does Sampson live?' I asked him if he was goin' to make a call on our mayor, an' he says yes. Then I told him how to go out to the ranch. He went out, headed that way."

"The hell he did!"

I gathered from this fellow's exclamation that he was divided between amaze and mirth. Then he got up from the steps and went into the restaurant and was followed by the man called Jim. Before the door was closed he made another remark, but it was unintelligible to me.

As I passed on I decided I would scrape acquaintance with this restaurant keeper.

The thing of most moment was that I had gotten track of Steele. I hurried ahead. While I had been listening back there moments had elapsed and evidently he had walked swiftly.

I came to the plaza, crossed it, and then did not know which direction to take. Concluding that it did not matter I hurried on in an endeavor to reach the ranch before Steele. Although I was not sure, I believed I had succeeded.

The moon shone brightly. I heard a banjo in the distance and a cowboy sing. There was not a person in sight in the wide courts or on the porch. I did not have a well-defined idea about the inside of the house.

Peeping in at the first lighted window I saw a large room. Miss Sampson and Sally were there alone. Evidently this was a parlor or a sitting room, and it had clean white walls, a blanketed floor, an open fireplace with a cheery blazing log, and a large table upon which were lamp, books, papers. Backing away I saw that this corner room had a door opening on the porch and two other windows.

I listened, hoping to hear Steele's footsteps coming up the road. But I heard only Sally's laugh and her cousin's mellow voice.

Then I saw lighted windows down at the other end of the front part of the house. I walked down. A door stood open and through it I saw a room identical with that at the other corner; and here were Colonel Sampson, Wright, and several other men, all smoking and talking.

It might have been interesting to tarry there within ear-shot, but I wanted to get back to the road to intercept Steele. Scarcely had I retraced my steps and seated myself on the porch steps when a very tall dark figure loomed up in the moonlit road.

Steele! I wanted to yell like a boy. He came on slowly, looking all around, halted some twenty paces distant, surveyed the house, then evidently espying me, came on again.

My first feeling was, What a giant! But his face was hidden in the shadow of a sombrero.

I had intended, of course, upon first sight to blurt out my identity. Yet I did not. He affected me strangely, or perhaps it was my emotion at the thought that we Rangers, with so much in common and at stake, had come together.

"Is Sampson at home?" he asked abruptly.

I said, "Yes."

"Ask him if he'll see Vaughn Steele, Ranger."

"Wait here," I replied. I did not want to take up any time then explaining my presence there.

Deliberately and noisily I strode down the porch and entered the room with the smoking men.

I went in farther than was necessary for me to state my errand. But I wanted to see Sampson's face, to see into his eyes.

As I entered, the talking ceased. I saw no face except his and that seemed blank.

"Vaughn Steele, Ranger—come to see you, sir." I announced.

Did Sampson start—did his eyes show a fleeting glint—did his face almost imperceptibly blanch? I could not have sworn to either. But there was a change, maybe from surprise.

The first sure effect of my announcement came in a quick exclamation from Wright, a sibilant intake of breath, that did not seem to denote surprise so much as certainty. Wright might have emitted a curse with less force.

Sampson moved his hand significantly and the action was a voiceless command for silence as well as an assertion that he would attend to this matter. I read him clearly so far. He had authority, and again I felt his power.

"Steele to see me. Did he state his business?"

"No, sir." I replied.

"Russ, say I'm not at home," said Sampson presently, bending over to relight his pipe.

I went out. Someone slammed the door behind me.

As I strode back across the porch my mind worked swiftly; the machinery had been idle for a while and was now started.

"Mr. Steele," I said, "Colonel Sampson says he's not at home. Tell your business to his daughter."

Without waiting to see the effect of my taking so much upon myself, I knocked upon the parlor door. Miss Sampson opened it. She wore white. Looking at her, I thought it would be strange if Steele's well-known indifference to women did not suffer an eclipse.

"Miss Sampson, here is Vaughn Steele to see you," I said.

"Won't you come in?" she said graciously.

Steele had to bend his head to enter the door. I went in with him, an intrusion, perhaps, that in the interest of the moment she appeared not to notice.

Steele seemed to fill the room with his giant form. His face was fine, stern, clear cut, with blue or gray eyes, strangely penetrating. He was coatless, vestless. He wore a gray flannel shirt, corduroys, a big gun swinging low, and top boots reaching to his knees.

He was the most stalwart son of Texas I had seen in many a day, but neither his great stature nor his striking face accounted for something I felt—a something spiritual, vital, compelling, that drew me.

"Mr. Steele, I'm pleased to meet you," said Miss Sampson. "This is my cousin, Sally Langdon. We just arrived—I to make this my home, she to visit me."

Steele smiled as he bowed to Sally. He was easy, with a kind of rude grace, and showed no sign of embarrassment or that beautiful girls were unusual to him.

"Mr. Steele, we've heard of you in Austin," said Sally with her eyes misbehaving.

I hoped I would not have to be jealous of Steele. But this girl was a little minx if not altogether a flirt.

"I did not expect to be received by ladies," replied Steele. "I called upon Mr. Sampson. He would not see me. I was to tell my business to his daughter. I'm glad to know you, Miss Sampson and your cousin, but sorry you've come to Linrock now."

"Why?" queried both girls in unison.

"Because it's—oh, pretty rough—no place for girls to walk and ride."

"Ah! I see. And your business has to do with rough places," said Miss Sampson. "Strange that papa would not see you. Stranger that he should want me to hear your business. Either he's joking or wants to impress me.

"Papa tried to persuade me not to come. He tried to frighten me with tales of this—this roughness out here. He knows I'm in earnest, how I'd like to help somehow, do some little good. Pray tell me this business."

"I wished to get your father's cooperation in my work."

"Your work? You mean your Ranger duty—the arresting of rough characters?"

"That, yes. But that's only a detail. Linrock is bad internally. My job is to make it good."

"A splendid and worthy task," replied Miss Sampson warmly. "I wish you success. But, Mr. Steele, aren't you exaggerating Linrock's wickedness?"

"No," he answered forcibly.

"Indeed! And papa refused to see you—presumably refused to cooperate with you?" she asked thoughtfully.

"I take it that way."

"Mr. Steele, pray tell me what is the matter with Linrock and just what the work is you're called upon to do?" she asked seriously. "I heard papa say that he was the law in Linrock. Perhaps he resents interference. I know he'll not tolerate any opposition to his will. Please tell me. I may be able to influence him."

I listened to Steele's deep voice as he talked about Linrock. What he said was old to me, and I gave heed only to its effect.

Miss Sampson's expression, which at first had been earnest and grave, turned into one of incredulous amaze. She, and Sally too, watched Steele's face in fascinated attention.

When it came to telling what he wanted to do, the Ranger warmed to his subject; he talked beautifully, convincingly, with a certain strange, persuasive power that betrayed how he worked his way; and his fine face, losing its stern, hard lines, seemed to glow and give forth a spirit austere, yet noble, almost gentle, assuredly something vastly different from what might have been expected in the expression of a gun-fighting Ranger. I sensed that Miss Sampson felt this just as I did.

"Papa said you were a hounder of outlaws—a man who'd rather kill than save!" she exclaimed.

The old stern cast returned to Steele's face. It was as if he had suddenly remembered himself.

"My name is infamous, I am sorry to say," he replied.

"You have killed men?" she asked, her dark eyes dilating.

Had any one ever dared ask Steele that before? His face became a mask. It told truth to me, but she could not see, and he did not answer.

"Oh, you are above that. Don't—don't kill any one here!"

"Miss Sampson, I hope I won't." His voice seemed to check her. I had been right in my estimate of her character—young, untried, but all pride, fire, passion. She was white then, and certainly beautiful.

Steele watched her, could scarcely have failed to see the white gleam of her beauty, and all that evidence of a quick and noble heart.

"Pardon me, please, Mr. Steele," she said, recovering her composure. "I am— just a little overexcited. I didn't mean to be inquisitive. Thank you for your confidence. I've enjoyed your call, though your news did distress me. You may rely upon me to talk to papa."

That appeared to be a dismissal, and, bowing to her and Sally, the Ranger went out. I followed, not having spoken.

At the end of the porch I caught up with Steele and walked out into the moonlight beside him.

Just why I did not now reveal my identity I could not say, for certainly I was bursting with the desire to surprise him, to earn his approval. He loomed dark above me, appearing not to be aware of my presence. What a cold, strange proposition this Ranger was!

Still, remembering the earnestness of his talk to Miss Sampson, I could not think him cold. But I must have thought him so to any attraction of those charming girls.

Suddenly, as we passed under the shade of cottonwoods, he clamped a big hand down on my shoulder.

"My God, Russ, isn't she lovely!" he ejaculated.

In spite of my being dumbfounded I had to hug him. He knew me!

"Thought you didn't swear!" I gasped.

Ridiculously those were my first words to Vaughn Steele.

"My boy, I saw you parading up and down the street looking for me," he said. "I intended to help you find me to-morrow."

We gripped hands, and that strong feel and clasp meant much.

"Yes, she's lovely, Steele," I said. "But did you look at the cousin, the little girl with the eyes?"

Then we laughed and loosed hands.

"Come on, let's get out somewhere. I've a million things to tell you."

We went away out into the open where some stones gleamed white in the moonlight, and there, sitting in the sand, our backs against a rest, and with all quiet about us, we settled down for a long conference.

I began with Neal's urgent message to me, then told of my going to the capitol—what I had overheard when Governor Smith was in the adjutant's office; of my interview with them; of the spying on Colonel Sampson; Neal's directions, advice, and command; the ride toward San Antonio; my being engaged as cowboy by Miss Sampson; of the further ride on to Sanderson and the incident there; and finally how I had approached Sampson and then had thought it well to get his daughter into the scheme of things.

It was a long talk, even for me, and my voice sounded husky.

"I told Neal I'd be lucky to get you," said Steele, after a silence.

That was the only comment on my actions, the only praise, but the quiet way he spoke it made me feel like a boy undeserving of so much.

"Here, I forgot the money Neal sent," I went on, glad to be rid of the huge roll of bills.

The Ranger showed surprise. Besides, he was very glad.

"The Captain loves the service," said Steele. "He alone knows the worth of the Rangers. And the work he's given his life to—the *good* that *service* really does—all depends on you and me, Russ!"

I assented, gloomily enough. Then I waited while he pondered.

The moon soared clear; there was a cool wind rustling the greasewood; a dog bayed a barking coyote; lights twinkled down in the town.

I looked back up at the dark hill and thought of Sally Langdon. Getting here to Linrock, meeting Steele had not changed my feelings toward her, only somehow they had removed me far off in thought, out of possible touch, it seemed.

"Well, son, listen," began Steele. His calling me that was a joke, yet I did not feel it. "You've made a better start than I could have figured. Neal said you were lucky. Perhaps. But you've got brains.

"Now, here's your cue for the present. Work for Miss Sampson. Do your best for her as long as you last. I don't suppose you'll last long. You have got to get in with this gang in town. Be a flash cowboy. You don't need to get drunk, but you're to pretend it.

"Gamble. Be a good fellow. Hang round the barrooms. I don't care how you play the part, so long as you make friends, learn the ropes. We can meet out here at nights to talk and plan.

"You're to take sides with those who're against me. I'll furnish you with the money. You'd better appear to be a winning gambler, even if you're not. How's this plan strike you?"

"Great—except for one thing," I replied. "I hate to lie to Miss Sampson. She's true blue, Steele."

"Son, you haven't got soft on her?"

"Not a bit. Maybe I'm soft on the little cousin. But I just like Miss Sampson— think she's fine—could look up to her. And I hate to be different from what she thinks."

"I understand, Russ," he replied in his deep voice that had such quality to influence a man. "It's no decent job. You'll be ashamed before her. So would I. But here's our work, the hardest ever cut out for Rangers. Think what depends upon it. And—"

"There's something wrong with Miss Sampson's father," I interrupted.

"Something strange if not wrong. No man in this community is beyond us, Russ, or above suspicion. You've a great opportunity. I needn't say use your eyes and ears as never before."

"I hope Sampson turns out to be on the square," I replied. "He might be a lax mayor, too good-natured to uphold law in a wild country. And his Southern pride would fire at interference. I don't like him, but for his daughter's sake I hope we're wrong."

Steele's eyes, deep and gleaming in the moonlight, searched my face.

"Son, sure you're not in love with her—you'll not fall in love with her?"

"No. I am positive. Why?"

"Because in either case I'd likely have need of a new man in your place," he said.

"Steele, you know something about Sampson—something more!" I exclaimed swiftly.

"No more than you. When I meet him face to face I may know more. Russ, when a fellow has been years at this game he has a sixth sense. Mine seldom fails me. I never yet faced the criminal who didn't somehow betray fear—not so much fear of me, but fear of himself—his life, his deeds. That's conscience, or if not, just realization of fate."

Had that been the thing I imagined I had seen in Sampson's face?

"I'm sorry Diane Sampson came out here," I said impulsively.

Steele did not say he shared that feeling. He was looking out upon the moon-blanched level.

Some subtle thing in his face made me divine that he was thinking of the beautiful girl to whom he might bring disgrace and unhappiness.

Chapter 2

A KISS AND AN ARREST

A month had passed, a swift-flying time full of new life. Wonderful it was for me to think I was still in Diane Sampson's employ.

It was the early morning hour of a day in May. The sun had not yet grown hot. Dew like diamond drops sparkled on the leaves and grass. The gentle breeze was clear, sweet, with the song of larks upon it.

And the range, a sea of gray-green growing greener, swept away westward in rolling ridges and hollows, like waves to meet the dark, low hills that notched the horizon line of blue.

I was sitting on the top bar of the corral fence and before me stood three saddled horses that would have gladdened any eye. I was waiting to take the young ladies on their usual morning ride.

Once upon a time, in what seemed the distant past to this eventful month, I had flattered myself there had been occasions for thought, but scornfully I soliloquized that in those days I had no cue for thought such as I had now.

This was one of the moments when my real self seemed to stand off and skeptically regard the fictitious cowboy.

This gentleman of the range wore a huge sombrero with an ornamented silver band, a silken scarf of red, a black velvet shirt, much affected by the Indians, an embroidered buckskin vest, corduroys, and fringed chaps with silver buttons, a big blue gun swinging low, high heeled boots, and long spurs with silver rowels.

A flash cowboy! Steele vowed I was a born actor.

But I never divulged the fact that had it not been for my infatuation for Sally, I never could have carried on that part, not to save the Ranger service, or the whole State of Texas.

The hardest part had not been the establishing of a reputation. The scorn of cowboys, the ridicule of gamblers, the badinage of the young bucks of the settlement—these I had soon made dangerous procedures for any one. I was quick with tongue and fist and gun.

There had been fights and respect was quickly earned, though the constant advent of strangers in Linrock always had me in hot water.

Moreover, instead of being difficult, it was fun to spend all the time I could in the hotels and resorts, shamming a weakness for drink, gambling, lounging, making friends among the rough set, when all the time I was a cool, keen registering machine.

The hard thing was the lie I lived in the eyes of Diane Sampson and Sally Langdon.

I had indeed won the sincere regard of my employer. Her father, her cousin George, and new-made friends in town had come to her with tales of my reckless doings, and had urged my dismissal.

But she kept me and all the time pleaded like a sister to have me mend my vicious ways. She believed what she was told about me, but had faith in me despite that.

As for Sally, I had fallen hopelessly in love with her. By turns Sally was indifferent to me, cold, friendly like a comrade, and dangerously sweet.

Somehow she saw through me, knew I was not just what I pretended to be. But she never breathed her conviction. She championed me. I wanted to tell her the truth about myself because I believed the doubt of me alone stood in the way of my winning her.

Still that might have been my vanity. She had never said she cared for me although she had looked it.

This tangle of my personal life, however, had not in the least affected my loyalty and duty to Vaughn Steele. Day by day I had grown more attached to him, keener in the interest of our work.

It had been a busy month—a month of foundation building. My vigilance and my stealthy efforts had not been rewarded by anything calculated to strengthen our suspicions of Sampson. But then he had been absent from the home very often, and was difficult to watch when he was there.

George Wright came and went, too, presumably upon stock business. I could not yet see that he was anything but an honest rancher, deeply involved with Sampson and other men in stock deals; nevertheless, as a man he had earned my contempt.

He was a hard drinker, cruel to horses, a gambler not above stacking the cards, a quick-tempered, passionate Southerner.

He had fallen in love with Diane Sampson, was like her shadow when at home. He hated me; he treated me as if I were the scum of the earth; if he had to address me for something, which was seldom, he did it harshly, like ordering a dog. Whenever I saw his sinister, handsome face, with its dark eyes always half shut, my hand itched for my gun, and I would go my way with something thick and hot inside my breast.

In my talks with Steele we spent time studying George Wright's character and actions. He was Sampson's partner, and at the head of a small group of Linrock ranchers who were rich in cattle and property, if not in money.

Steele and I had seen fit to wait before we made any thorough investigation into their business methods. Ours was a waiting game, anyway.

Right at the start Linrock had apparently arisen in resentment at the presence of Vaughn Steele. But it was my opinion that there were men in Linrock secretly glad of the Ranger's presence.

What he intended to do was food for great speculation. His fame, of course, had preceded him. A company of militia could not have had the effect upon the wild element of Linrock that Steele's presence had.

A thousand stories went from lip to lip, most of which were false. He was lightning swift on the draw. It was death to face him. He had killed thirty men—wildest rumor of all.

He had the gun skill of Buck Duane, the craft of Cheseldine, the deviltry of King Fisher, the most notorious of Texas desperadoes. His nerve, his lack of fear—those made him stand out alone even among a horde of bold men.

At first there had not only been great conjecture among the vicious element, with which I had begun to affiliate myself, but also a very decided checking of all kinds of action calculated to be conspicuous to a keen eyed Ranger.

Steele did not hide, but during these opening days of his stay in Linrock he was not often seen in town. At the tables, at the bars and lounging places remarks went the rounds:

"Who's thet Ranger after? What'll he do fust off? Is he waitin' fer somebody? Who's goin' to draw on him fust—an' go to hell? Jest about how soon will he be found somewhere full of lead?"

Those whom it was my interest to cultivate grew more curious, more speculative and impatient as time went by. When it leaked out somewhere that Steele was openly cultivating the honest stay-at-home citizens, to array them in time against the other element, then Linrock showed its wolf teeth hinted of in the letters to Captain Neal.

Several times Steele was shot at in the dark and once slightly injured. Rumor had it that Jack Blome, the gunman of those parts, was coming in to meet Steele. Part of Linrock awakened and another part, much smaller, became quieter, more secluded.

Strangers upon whom we could get no line mysteriously came and went. The drinking, gambling, fighting in the resorts seemed to gather renewed life. Abundance of money floated in circulation.

And rumors, vague and unfounded, crept in from Sanderson and other points, rumors of a gang of rustlers off here, a hold-up of the stage off here, robbery of a rancher at this distant point, and murder done at another.

This was Texas and New Mexico life in these frontier days but, strangely neither Steele nor I had yet been able to associate any rumor or act with a possible gang of rustlers in Linrock.

Nevertheless we had not been discouraged. After three weeks of waiting we had become alive to activity around us, and though it was unseen, we believed we would soon be on its track.

My task was the busier and the easier. Steele had to have a care for his life. I never failed to caution him of this.

My long reflection on the month's happenings and possibilities was brought to an end by the appearance of Miss Sampson and Sally.

My employer looked worried. Sally was in a regular cowgirl riding costume, in which her trim, shapely figure showed at its best, and her face was saucy, sparkling, daring.

"Good morning, Russ," said Miss Sampson and she gazed searchingly at me. I had dropped off the fence, sombrero in hand. I knew I was in for a lecture, and I put on a brazen, innocent air.

"Did you break your promise to me?" she asked reproachfully.

"Which one?" I asked. It was Sally's bright eyes upon me, rather than Miss Sampson's reproach, that bothered me.

"About getting drunk again," she said.

"I didn't break *that* one."

"My cousin George saw you in the Hope So gambling place last night, drunk, staggering, mixing with that riffraff, on the verge of a brawl."

"Miss Sampson, with all due respect to Mr. Wright, I want to say that he has a strange wish to lower me in the eyes of you ladies," I protested with a fine show of spirit.

"Russ, *were* you drunk?" she demanded.

"No. I should think you needn't ask me that. Didn't you ever see a man the morning after a carouse?"

Evidently she had. And there I knew I stood, fresh, clean-shaven, clear-eyed as the morning.

Sally's saucy face grew thoughtful, too. The only thing she had ever asked of me was not to drink. The habit had gone hard with the Sampson family.

"Russ, you look just as—as nice as I'd want you to," Miss Sampson replied. "I don't know what to think. They tell me things. You deny. Whom shall I believe? George swore he saw you."

"Miss Sampson, did I ever lie to you?"

"Not to my knowledge."

Then I looked at her, and she understood what I meant.

"George has lied to me. That day at Sanderson. And since, too, I fear. Do you say he lies?"

"Miss Sampson, I would not call your cousin a liar."

Here Sally edged closer, with the bridle rein of her horse over her arm.

"Russ, cousin George isn't the only one who saw you. Burt Waters told me the same," said Sally nervously. I believed she hoped I was telling the truth.

"Waters! So he runs me down behind my back. All right, I won't say a word about him. But do you believe I was drunk when I say no?"

"I'm afraid I do, Russ," she replied in reluctance. Was she testing me?

"See here, Miss Sampson," I burst out. "Why don't you discharge me? Please let me go. I'm not claiming much for myself, but you don't believe even that. I'm pretty bad. I never denied the scraps, the gambling—all that. But I did do as Miss Sally asked me—I did keep my promise to you. Now, discharge me. Then I'll be free to call on Mr. Burt Waters."

Miss Sampson looked alarmed and Sally turned pale, to my extreme joy.

Those girls believed I was a desperate devil of a cowboy, who had been held back from spilling blood solely through their kind relation to me.

"Oh, no!" exclaimed Sally. "Diane, don't let him go!"

"Russ, pray don't get angry," replied Miss Sampson and she put a soft hand on me that thrilled me, while it made me feel like a villain. "I won't discharge you. I need you. Sally needs you. After all, it's none of my business what you do away from here. But I hoped I would be so happy to—to reclaim you from—Didn't you ever have a sister, Russ?"

I kept silent for fear that I would perjure myself anew. Yet the situation was delicious, and suddenly I conceived a wild idea.

"Miss Sampson," I began haltingly, but with brave front, "I've been wild in the past. But I've been tolerably straight here, trying to please you. Lately I have been going to the bad again. Not drunk, but leaning that way. Lord knows what I'll do soon if—if my trouble isn't cured."

"Russ! What trouble?"

"You know what's the matter with me," I went on hurriedly. "Anybody could see that."

Sally turned a flaming scarlet. Miss Sampson made it easier for me by reason of her quick glance of divination.

"I've fallen in love with Miss Sally. I'm crazy about her. Here I've got to see these fellows flirting with her. And it's killing me. I've—"

"If you are crazy about me, you don't have to tell!" cried Sally, red and white by turns.

"I want to stop your flirting one way or another. I've been in earnest. I wasn't flirting. I begged you to—to..."

"You never did," interrupted Sally furiously. That hint had been a spark.

"I couldn't have dreamed it," I protested, in a passion to be earnest, yet tingling with the fun of it. "That day when I—didn't I ask..."

"If my memory serves me correctly, you didn't ask anything," she replied, with anger and scorn now struggling with mirth.

"But, Sally, I meant to. You understood me? Say you didn't believe I could take that liberty without honorable intentions."

That was too much for Sally. She jumped at her horse, made the quickest kind of a mount, and was off like a flash.

"Stop me if you can," she called back over her shoulder, her face alight and saucy.

"Russ, go after her," said Miss Sampson. "In that mood she'll ride to Sanderson. My dear fellow, don't stare so. I understand many things now. Sally is a flirt. She would drive any man mad. Russ, I've grown in a short time to like you. If you'll be a man—give up drinking and gambling—maybe you'll have a chance with her. Hurry now—go after her."

I mounted and spurred my horse after Sally's. She was down on the level now, out in the open, and giving her mount his head. Even had I wanted to overhaul her at once the matter would have been difficult, well nigh impossible under five miles.

Sally had as fast a horse as there was on the range; she made no weight in the saddle, and she could ride. From time to time she looked back over her shoulder.

I gained enough to make her think I was trying to catch her. Sally loved a horse; she loved a race; she loved to win.

My good fortune had given me more than one ride alone with Sally. Miss Sampson enjoyed riding, too; but she was not a madcap, and when she accompanied us there was never any race.

When Sally got out alone with me she made me ride to keep her from disappearing somewhere on the horizon. This morning I wanted her to enjoy to the fullest her utter freedom and to feel that for once I could not catch her.

Perhaps my declaration to Miss Sampson had liberated my strongest emotions.

However that might be, the fact was that no ride before had ever been like this one—no sky so blue, no scene so open, free, and enchanting as that beautiful gray-green range, no wind so sweet. The breeze that rushed at me might have been laden with the perfume of Sally Langdon's hair.

I sailed along on what seemed a strange ride. Grazing horses pranced and whistled as I went by; jack-rabbits bounded away to hide in the longer clumps of grass; a prowling wolf trotted from his covert near a herd of cattle.

Far to the west rose the low, dark lines of bleak mountains. They were always mysterious to me, as if holding a secret I needed to know.

It was a strange ride because in the back of my head worked a haunting consciousness of the deadly nature of my business there on the frontier, a business in such contrast with this dreaming and dallying, this longing for what surely was futile.

Any moment I might be stripped of my disguise. Any moment I might have to be the Ranger.

Sally kept the lead across the wide plain, and mounted to the top of a ridge, where tired out, and satisfied with her victory, she awaited me. I was in no hurry to reach the summit of the long, slow-sloping ridge, and I let my horse walk.

Just how would Sally Langdon meet me now, after my regretted exhibition before her cousin? There was no use to conjecture, but I was not hopeful.

When I got there to find her in her sweetest mood, with some little difference never before noted—a touch of shyness—I concealed my surprise.

"Russ, I gave you a run that time," she said. "Ten miles and you never caught me!"

"But look at the start you had. I've had my troubles beating you with an even break."

Sally was susceptible to flattery in regard to her riding, a fact that I made subtle use of.

"But in a long race I was afraid you'd beat me. Russ, I've learned to ride out here. Back home I never had room to ride a horse. Just look. Miles and miles of level, of green. Little hills with black bunches of trees. Not a soul in sight. Even the town hidden in the green. All wild and lonely. Isn't it glorious, Russ?"

"Lately it's been getting to me," I replied soberly.

We both gazed out over the sea of gray-green, at the undulating waves of ground in the distance. On these rides with her I had learned to appreciate the beauty of the lonely reaches of plain.

But when I could look at her I seldom wasted time on scenery. Looking at her now I tried to get again that impression of a difference in her. It eluded me.

Just now with the rose in her brown cheeks, her hair flying, her eyes with grave instead of mocking light, she seemed only prettier than usual. I got down ostensibly to tighten the saddle girths on her horse. But I lingered over the task.

Presently, when she looked down at me, I received that subtle impression of change, and read it as her soft mood of dangerous sweetness that came so seldom, mingled with something deeper, more of character and womanliness than I had ever sensed in her.

"Russ, it wasn't nice to tell Diane that," she said.

"Nice! It was—oh, I'd like to swear!" I ejaculated. "But now I understand my miserable feeling. I was jealous, Sally, I'm sorry. I apologize."

She had drawn off her gloves, and one little hand, brown, shapely, rested upon her knee very near to me. I took it in mine. She let it stay, though she looked away from me, the color rich in her cheeks.

"I can forgive that," she murmured. "But the lie. Jealousy doesn't excuse a lie."

"You mean—what I intimated to your cousin," I said, trying to make her look at me. "That was the devil in me. Only it's true."

"How can it be true when you never asked—said a word—you hinted of?" she queried. "Diane believed what you said. I know she thinks me horrid."

"No she doesn't. As for what I said, or meant to say, which is the same thing, how'd you take my actions? I hope not the same as you take Wright's or the other fellow's."

Sally was silent, a little pale now, and I saw that I did not need to say any more about the other fellows. The change, the difference was now marked. It drove me to give in wholly to this earnest and passionate side of myself.

"Sally, I do love you. I don't know how you took my actions. Anyway, now I'll make them plain. I was beside myself with love and jealousy. Will you marry me?"

She did not answer. But the old willful Sally was not in evidence. Watching her face I gave her a slow and gentle pull, one she could easily resist if she cared to, and she slipped from her saddle into my arms.

Then there was one wildly sweet moment in which I had the blissful certainty that she kissed me of her own accord. She was abashed, yet yielding; she let herself go, yet seemed not utterly unstrung. Perhaps I was rough, held her too hard, for she cried out a little.

"Russ! Let me go. Help me—back."

I righted her in the saddle, although not entirely releasing her.

"But, Sally, you haven't told me anything," I remonstrated tenderly. "Do you love me?"

"I think so," she whispered.

"Sally, will you marry me?"

She disengaged herself then, sat erect and faced away from me, with her breast heaving.

"No, Russ," she presently said, once more calm.

"But Sally—if you love me—" I burst out, and then stopped, stilled by something in her face.

"I can't help—loving you, Russ," she said. "But to promise to marry you, that's different. Why, Russ, I know nothing about you, not even your last name. You're not a—a steady fellow. You drink, gamble, fight. You'll kill somebody yet. Then I'll *not* love you. Besides, I've always felt you're not just what you seemed. I can't trust you. There's something wrong about you."

I knew my face darkened, and perhaps hope and happiness died in it. Swiftly she placed a kind hand on my shoulder.

"Now, I've hurt you. Oh, I'm sorry. Your asking me makes such a difference. *They* are not in earnest. But, Russ, I had to tell you why I couldn't be engaged to you."

"I'm not good enough for you. I'd no right to ask you to marry me," I replied abjectly.

"Russ, don't think me proud," she faltered. "I wouldn't care who you were if I could only—only respect you. Some things about you are splendid, you're such a man, that's why I cared. But you gamble. You drink—and I *hate* that. You're dangerous they say, and I'd be, I *am* in constant dread you'll kill somebody. Remember, Russ, I'm no Texan."

This regret of Sally's, this faltering distress at giving me pain, was such sweet assurance that she did love me, better than she knew, that I was divided between extremes of emotion.

"Will you wait? Will you trust me a little? Will you give me a chance? After all, maybe I'm not so bad as I seem."

"Oh, if you weren't! Russ, are you asking me to trust you?"

"I beg you to—dearest. Trust me and wait."

"Wait? What for? Are you really on the square, Russ? Or are you what George calls you—a drunken cowboy, a gambler, sharp with the cards, a gun-fighter?"

My face grew cold as I felt the blood leave it. At that moment mention of George Wright fixed once for all my hate of him.

Bitter indeed was it that I dared not give him the lie. But what could I do? The character Wright gave me was scarcely worse than what I had chosen to represent. I had to acknowledge the justice of his claim, but nevertheless I hated him.

"Sally, I ask you to trust me in spite of my reputation."

"You ask me a great deal," she replied.

"Yes, it's too much. Let it be then only this—you'll wait. And while you wait, promise not to flirt with Wright and Waters."

"Russ, I'll not let George or any of them so much as dare touch me," she declared in girlish earnestness, her voice rising. "I'll promise if you'll promise me not to go into those saloons any more."

One word would have brought her into my arms for good and all. The better side of Sally Langdon showed then in her appeal. That appeal was as strong as the drawing power of her little face, all eloquent with its light, and eyes dark with tears, and lips wanting to smile.

My response should have been instant. How I yearned to give it and win the reward I imagined I saw on her tremulous lips! But I was bound. The grim, dark nature of my enterprise there in Linrock returned to stultify my eagerness, dispel my illusion, shatter my dream.

For one instant it flashed through my mind to tell Sally who I was, what my errand was, after the truth. But the secret was not mine to tell. And I kept my pledges.

The hopeful glow left Sally's face. Her disappointment seemed keen. Then a little scorn of certainty was the bitterest of all for me to bear.

"That's too much to promise all at once," I protested lamely, and I knew I would have done better to keep silence.

"Russ, a promise like that is nothing—if a man loves a girl," she retorted. "Don't make any more love to me, please, unless you want me to laugh at you. And don't feel such terrible trouble if you happen to see me flirting occasionally."

She ended with a little mocking laugh. That was the perverse side of her, the cat using her claws. I tried not to be angry, but failed.

"All right. I'll take my medicine," I replied bitterly. "I'll certainly never make love to you again. And I'll stand it if I happen to see Waters kiss you, or any other decent fellow. But look out how you let that damned backbiter Wright fool around you!"

I spoke to her as I had never spoken before, in quick, fierce meaning, with eyes holding hers.

She paled. But even my scarce-veiled hint did not chill her anger. Tossing her head she wheeled and rode away.

I followed at a little distance, and thus we traveled the ten miles back to the ranch. When we reached the corrals she dismounted and, turning her horse over to Dick, she went off toward the house without so much as a nod or good-by to me.

I went down to town for once in a mood to live up to what had been heretofore only a sham character.

But turning a corner into the main street I instantly forgot myself at the sight of a crowd congregated before the town hall. There was a babel of voices and an air of excitement that I immediately associated with Sampson, who as mayor of Linrock, once in a month of moons held court in this hall.

It took slipping and elbowing to get through the crowd. Once inside the door I saw that the crowd was mostly outside, and evidently not so desirous as I was to enter.

The first man I saw was Steele looming up; the next was Sampson chewing his mustache—the third, Wright, whose dark and sinister face told much. Something was up in Linrock. Steele had opened the hall.

There were other men in the hall, a dozen or more, and all seemed shouting excitedly in unison with the crowd outside. I did not try to hear what was said. I edged closer in, among the men to the front.

Sampson sat at a table up on a platform. Near him sat a thick-set grizzled man, with deep eyes; and this was Hanford Owens, county judge.

To the right stood a tall, angular, yellow-faced fellow with a drooping, sandy mustache. Conspicuous on his vest was a huge silver shield. This was Gorsech, one of Sampson's sheriffs.

There were four other men whom I knew, several whose faces were familiar, and half a dozen strangers, all dusty horsemen.

Steele stood apart from them, a little to one side, so that he faced them all. His hair was disheveled, and his shirt open at the neck. He looked cool and hard.

When I caught his eye I realized in an instant that the long deferred action, the beginning of our real fight was at hand.

Sampson pounded hard on the table to be heard. Mayor or not, he was unable at once to quell the excitement.

Gradually, however, it subsided and from the last few utterances before quiet was restored I gathered that Steele had intruded upon some kind of a meeting in the hall.

"Steele, what'd you break in here for?" demanded Sampson.

"Isn't this court? Aren't you the mayor of Linrock?" interrogated Steele. His voice was so clear and loud, almost piercing, that I saw at once that he wanted all those outside to hear.

"Yes," replied Sampson. Like flint he seemed, yet I felt his intense interest.

I had no doubt then that Steele intended to make him stand out before this crowd as the real mayor of Linrock or as a man whose office was a sham.

"I've arrested a criminal," said Steele. "Bud Snell. I charge him with assault on Jim Hoden and attempted robbery—if not murder. Snell had a shady past here, as the court will know if it keeps a record."

Then I saw Snell hunching down on a bench, a nerveless and shaken man if there ever was one. He had been a hanger-on round the gambling dens, the kind of sneak I never turned my back to.

Jim Hoden, the restaurant keeper, was present also, and on second glance I saw that he was pale. There was blood on his face. I knew Jim, liked him, had tried to make a friend of him.

I was not dead to the stinging interrogation in the concluding sentence of Steele's speech. Then I felt sure I had correctly judged Steele's motive. I began to warm to the situation.

"What's this I hear about you, Bud? Get up and speak for yourself," said Sampson, gruffly.

Snell got up, not without a furtive glance at Steele, and he had shuffled forward a few steps toward the mayor. He had an evil front, but not the boldness even of a rustler.

"It ain't so, Sampson," he began loudly. "I went in Hoden's place fer grub. Some feller I never seen before come in from the hall an' hit him an' wrastled him on the floor. Then this big Ranger grabbed me an' fetched me here. I didn't do nothin'. This Ranger's hankerin' to arrest somebody. Thet's my hunch, Sampson."

"What have you to say about this, Hoden?" sharply queried Sampson. "I call to your mind the fact that you once testified falsely in court, and got punished for it."

Why did my sharpened and experienced wits interpret a hint of threat or menace in Sampson's reminder? Hoden rose from the bench and with an unsteady hand reached down to support himself.

He was no longer young, and he seemed broken in health and spirit. He had been hurt somewhat about the head.

"I haven't much to say," he replied. "The Ranger dragged me here. I told him I didn't take my troubles to court. Besides, I can't swear it was Snell who hit me."

Sampson said something in an undertone to Judge Owens, and that worthy nodded his great, bushy head.

"Bud, you're discharged," said Sampson bluntly. "Now, the rest of you clear out of here."

He absolutely ignored the Ranger. That was his rebuff to Steele's advances, his slap in the face to an interfering Ranger Service.

If Sampson was crooked he certainly had magnificent nerve. I almost decided he was above suspicion. But his nonchalance, his air of finality, his authoritative assurance—these to my keen and practiced eyes were in significant contrast to a certain tenseness of line about his mouth and a slow paling of his olive skin.

He had crossed the path of Vaughn Steele; he had blocked the way of this Texas Ranger. If he had intelligence and remembered Steele's fame, which surely he had, then he had some appreciation of what he had undertaken.

In that momentary lull my scrutiny of Sampson gathered an impression of the man's intense curiosity.

Then Bud Snell, with a cough that broke the silence, shuffled a couple of steps toward the door.

"Hold on!" called Steele.

It was a bugle-call. It halted Snell as if it had been a bullet. He seemed to shrink.

"Sampson, I *saw* Snell attack Hoden," said Steele, his voice still ringing. "What has the court to say to that?"

The moment for open rupture between Ranger Service and Sampson's idea of law was at hand. Sampson showed not the slightest hesitation.

"The court has to say this: West of the Pecos we'll not aid or abet or accept any Ranger Service. Steele, we don't want you out here. Linrock doesn't need you."

"That's a lie, Sampson," retorted Steele. "I've a pocket full of letters from Linrock citizens, all begging for Ranger Service."

Sampson turned white. The veins corded at his temples. He appeared about to burst into rage. He was at a loss for a quick reply.

Steele shook a long arm at the mayor.

"I need your help. You refuse. Now, I'll work alone. This man Snell goes to Del Rio in irons."

George Wright rushed up to the table. The blood showed black and thick in his face; his utterance was incoherent, his uncontrollable outbreak of temper seemed out of all proportion to any cause he should reasonably have had for anger.

Sampson shoved him back with a curse and warning glare.

"Where's your warrant to arrest Snell?" shouted Sampson. "I won't give you one. You can't take him without a warrant."

"I don't need warrants to make arrests. Sampson, you're ignorant of the power of Texas Rangers."

"You'll take Snell without papers?" bellowed Sampson.

"He goes to Del Rio to jail," answered Steele.

"He won't. You'll pull none of your damned Ranger stunts out here. I'll block you, Steele."

That passionate reply of Sampson's appeared to be the signal Steele had been waiting for.

He had helped on the crisis. I believed I saw how he wanted to force Sampson's hand and show the town his stand.

Steele backed clear of everybody and like two swift flashes of light his guns leaped forth. He was transformed. My wish was fulfilled.

Here was Steele, the Ranger, in one of his lone lion stands. Not exactly alone either, for my hands itched for my guns!

"Men! I call on you all!" cried Steele, piercingly. "I call on you to witness the arrest of a criminal opposed by Sampson, mayor of Linrock. It will be recorded in the report sent to the Adjutant General at Austin. Sampson, I warn you—don't follow up your threat."

Sampson sat white with working jaw.

"Snell, come here," ordered Steele.

The man went as if drawn and appeared to slink out of line with the guns. Steele's cold gray glance held every eye in the hall.

"Take the handcuffs out of my pocket. This side. Go over to Gorsech with them. Gorsech, snap those irons on Snell's wrists. Now, Snell, back here to the right of me."

It was no wonder to me to see how instantly Steele was obeyed. He might have seen more danger in that moment than was manifest to me; on the other hand he might have wanted to drive home hard what he meant.

It was a critical moment for those who opposed him. There was death in the balance.

This Ranger, whose last resort was gun-play, had instantly taken the initiative, and his nerve chilled even me. Perhaps though, he read this crowd differently from me and saw that intimidation was his cue. I forgot I was not a spectator, but an ally.

"Sampson, you've shown your hand," said Steele, in the deep voice that carried so far and held those who heard. "Any honest citizen of Linrock can now see what's plain—yours is a damn poor hand!

"You're going to hear me call a spade a spade. Your office is a farce. In the two years you've been mayor you've never arrested one rustler. Strange, when Linrock's a nest for rustlers! You've never sent a prisoner to Del Rio, let alone to Austin. You have no jail.

"There have been nine murders since you took office, innumerable street fights and hold-ups. *Not one arrest!* But you have ordered arrests for trivial offenses, and have punished these out of all proportion.

"There have been law-suits in your court—suits over water rights, cattle deals, property lines. Strange how in these law-suits, you or Wright or other men close to you were always involved! Stranger how it seems the law was stretched to favor your interests!"

Steele paused in his cold, ringing speech. In the silence, both outside and inside the hall, could be heard the deep breathing of agitated men.

I would have liked to search for possible satisfaction on the faces of any present, but I was concerned only with Sampson. I did not need to fear that any man might draw on Steele.

Never had I seen a crowd so sold, so stiff, so held! Sampson was indeed a study. Yet did he betray anything but rage at this interloper?

"Sampson, here's plain talk for you and Linrock to digest," went on Steele. "I don't accuse you and your court of dishonesty. I say—*strange*! Law here has been a farce. The motive behind all this laxity isn't plain to me—yet. But I call your hand!"

Chapter 3

SOUNDING THE TIMBER

When Steele left the hall, pushing Snell before him, making a lane through the crowd, it was not any longer possible to watch everybody.

Yet now he seemed to ignore the men behind him. Any friend of Snell's among the vicious element might have pulled a gun. I wondered if Steele knew how I watched those men at his back—how fatal it would have been for any of them to make a significant move.

No—I decided that Steele trusted to the effect his boldness had created. It was this power to cow ordinary men that explained so many of his feats; just the same it was his keenness to read desperate men, his nerve to confront them, that made him great.

The crowd followed Steele and his captive down the middle of the main street and watched him secure a team and buckboard and drive off on the road to Sanderson.

Only then did that crowd appear to realize what had happened. Then my long-looked-for opportunity arrived. In the expression of silent men I found something which I had sought; from the hurried departure of others homeward I gathered import; on the husky, whispering lips of yet others I read words I needed to hear.

The other part of that crowd—to my surprise, the smaller part—was the roaring, threatening, complaining one.

Thus I segregated Linrock that was lawless from Linrock that wanted law, but for some reason not yet clear the latter did not dare to voice their choice.

How could Steele and I win them openly to our cause? If that could be done long before the year was up Linrock would be free of violence and Captain Neal's Ranger Service saved to the State.

I went from place to place, corner to corner, bar to bar, watching, listening, recording; and not until long after sunset did I go out to the ranch.

The excitement had preceded me and speculation was rife. Hurrying through my supper, to get away from questions and to go on with my spying, I went out to the front of the house.

The evening was warm; the doors were open; and in the twilight the only lamps that had been lit were in Sampson's big sitting room at the far end of the house. Neither Sampson nor Wright had come home to supper.

I would have given much to hear their talk right then, and certainly intended to try to hear it when they did come home.

When the buckboard drove up and they alighted I was well hidden in the bushes, so well screened that I could get but a fleeting glimpse of Sampson as he went in.

For all I could see, he appeared to be a calm and quiet man, intense beneath the surface, with an air of dignity under insult. My chance to observe Wright was lost.

They went into the house without speaking, and closed the door.

At the other end of the porch, close under a window, was an offset between step and wall, and there in the shadow I hid. If Sampson or Wright visited the girls that evening I wanted to hear what was said about Steele.

It seemed to me that it might be a good clue for me—the circumstance whether or not Diane Sampson was told the truth. So I waited there in the darkness with patience born of many hours of like duty.

Presently the small lamp was lit—I could tell the difference in light when the big one was burning—and I heard the swish of skirts.

"Something's happened, surely, Sally," I heard Miss Sampson say anxiously. "Papa just met me in the hall and didn't speak. He seemed pale, worried."

"Cousin George looked like a thundercloud," said Sally. "For once, he didn't try to kiss me. Something's happened. Well, Diane, this has been a bad day for me, too."

Plainly I heard Sally's sigh, and the little pathetic sound brought me vividly out of my sordid business of suspicion and speculation. So she was sorry.

"Bad for you, too?" replied Diane in amused surprise. "Oh, I see—I forgot. You and Russ had it out."

"Out? We fought like the very old deuce. I'll never speak to him again."

"So your little—affair with Russ is all over?"

"Yes." Here she sighed again.

"Well, Sally, it began swiftly and it's just as well short," said Diane earnestly. "We know nothing at all of Russ."

"Diane, after to-day I respect him in—in spite of things—even though he seems no good. I—I cared a lot, too."

"My dear, your loves are like the summer flowers. I thought maybe your flirting with Russ might amount to something. Yet he seems so different now from what he was at first. It's only occasionally I get the impression I had of him after that night he saved me from violence. He's strange. Perhaps it all comes of his infatuation for you. He is in love with you. I'm afraid of what may come of it."

"Diane, he'll do something dreadful to George, mark my words," whispered Sally. "He swore he would if George fooled around me any more."

"Oh, dear. Sally, what can we do? These are wild men. George makes life miserable for me. And he teases you unmer..."

"I don't call it teasing. George wants to spoon," declared Sally emphatically. "He'd run after any woman."

"A fine compliment to me, Cousin Sally," laughed Diane.

"I don't agree," replied Sally stubbornly. "It's so. He's spoony. And when he's been drinking and tries to kiss me, I hate him."

"Sally, you look as if you'd rather like Russ to do something dreadful to George," said Diane with a laugh that this time was only half mirth.

"Half of me would and half of me would not," returned Sally. "But all of me would if I weren't afraid of Russ. I've got a feeling—I don't know what— something will happen between George and Russ some day."

There were quick steps on the hall floor, steps I thought I recognized.

"Hello, girls!" sounded out Wright's voice, minus its usual gaiety. Then ensued a pause that made me bring to mind a picture of Wright's glum face.

"George, what's the matter?" asked Diane presently. "I never saw papa as he is to-night, nor you so—so worried. Tell me, what has happened?"

"Well, Diane, we had a jar to-day," replied Wright, with a blunt, expressive laugh.

"Jar?" echoed both the girls curiously.

"Jar? We had to submit to a damnable outrage," added Wright passionately, as if the sound of his voice augmented his feeling. "Listen, girls. I'll tell you all about it."

He coughed, clearing his throat in a way that betrayed he had been drinking.

I sunk deeper in the shadow of my covert, and stiffening my muscles for a protracted spell of rigidity, prepared to listen with all acuteness and intensity.

Just one word from this Wright, inadvertently uttered in a moment of passion, might be the word Steele needed for his clue.

"It happened at the town hall," began Wright rapidly. "Your father and Judge Owens and I were there in consultation with three ranchers from out of town. First we were disturbed by gunshots from somewhere, but not close at hand. Then we heard the loud voices outside.

"A crowd was coming down street. It stopped before the hall. Men came running in, yelling. We thought there was a fire. Then that Ranger, Steele, stalked in, dragging a fellow by the name of Snell. We couldn't tell what was wanted because of the uproar. Finally your father restored order.

"Steele had arrested Snell for alleged assault on a restaurant keeper named Hoden. It developed that Hoden didn't accuse anybody, didn't know who attacked him. Snell, being obviously innocent, was discharged. Then this— this gun fighting Ranger pulled his guns on the court and halted the proceedings."

When Wright paused I plainly heard his intake of breath. Far indeed was he from calm.

"Steele held everybody in that hall in fear of death, and he began shouting his insults. Law was a farce in Linrock. The court was a farce. There was no law. Your father's office as mayor should be impeached. He made arrests only for petty offenses. He was afraid of the rustlers, highwaymen, murderers. He was afraid or—he just let them alone. He used his office to cheat ranchers and cattlemen in law-suits.

"All of this Steele yelled for everyone to hear. A damnable outrage! Your father, Diane, insulted in his own court by a rowdy Ranger! Not only insulted, but threatened with death—two big guns thrust almost in his face!"

"Oh! How horrible!" cried Diane, in mingled distress and anger.

"Steele's a Ranger. The Ranger Service wants to rule western Texas," went on Wright. "These Rangers are all a low set, many of them worse than the outlaws they hunt. Some of them were outlaws and gun fighters before they became Rangers.

"This Steele is one of the worst of the lot. He's keen, intelligent, smooth, and that makes him more to be feared. For he is to be feared. He wanted to kill. He meant to kill. If your father had made the least move Steele would have shot him. He's a cold-nerved devil—the born gunman. My God, any instant I expected to see your father fall dead at my feet!"

"Oh, George! The—the unspeakable ruffian!" cried Diane, passionately.

"You see, Diane, this fellow Steele has failed here in Linrock. He's been here weeks and done nothing. He must have got desperate. He's infamous and he loves his name. He seeks notoriety. He made that play with Snell just for a chance to rant against your father. He tried to inflame all Linrock against him. That about law-suits was the worst! Damn him! He'll make us enemies."

"What do you care for the insinuations of such a man?" said Diane Sampson, her voice now deep and rich with feeling. "After a moment's thought no one will be influenced by them. Do not worry, George, tell papa not to worry. Surely after all these years he can't be injured in reputation by—by an adventurer."

"Yes, he can be injured," replied George quickly. "The frontier is a queer place. There are many bitter men here, men who have failed at ranching. And your father has been wonderfully successful. Steele has dropped some poison, and it'll spread."

Then followed a silence, during which, evidently, the worried Wright bestrode the floor.

"Cousin George, what became of Steele and his prisoner?" suddenly asked Sally.

How like her it was, with her inquisitive bent of mind and shifting points of view, to ask a question the answering of which would be gall and wormwood to Wright!

It amused while it thrilled me. Sally might be a flirt, but she was no fool.

"What became of them? Ha! Steele bluffed the whole town—at least all of it who had heard the mayor's order to discharge Snell," growled Wright. "He took Snell—rode off for Del Rio to jail him."

"George!" exclaimed Diane. "Then, after all, this Ranger was able to arrest Snell, the innocent man father discharged, and take him to jail?"

"Exactly. That's the toughest part...." Wright ended abruptly, and then broke out fiercely: "But, by God, he'll never come back!"

Wright's slow pacing quickened and he strode from the parlor, leaving behind him a silence eloquent of the effect of his sinister prediction.

"Sally, what did he mean?" asked Diane in a low voice.

"Steele will be killed," replied Sally, just as low-voiced.

"Killed! That magnificent fellow! Ah, I forgot. Sally, my wits are sadly mixed. I ought to be glad if somebody kills my father's defamer. But, oh, I can't be!

"This bloody frontier makes me sick. Papa doesn't want me to stay for good. And no wonder. Shall I go back? I hate to show a white feather.

"Do you know, Sally, I was—a little taken with this Texas Ranger. Miserably, I confess. He seemed so like in spirit to the grand stature of him. How can so splendid a man be so bloody, base at heart? It's hideous. How little we know of men! I had my dream about Vaughn Steele. I confess because it shames me—because I hate myself!"

Next morning I awakened with a feeling that I was more like my old self. In the experience of activity of body and mind, with a prospect that this was merely the forerunner of great events, I came round to my own again.

Sally was not forgotten; she had just become a sorrow. So perhaps my downfall as a lover was a precursor of better results as an officer.

I held in abeyance my last conclusion regarding Sampson and Wright, and only awaited Steele's return to have fixed in mind what these men were.

Wright's remark about Steele not returning did not worry me. I had heard many such dark sayings in reference to Rangers.

Rangers had a trick of coming back. I did not see any man or men on the present horizon of Linrock equal to the killing of Steele.

As Miss Sampson and Sally had no inclination to ride, I had even more freedom. I went down to the town and burst, cheerily whistling, into Jim Hoden's place.

Jim always made me welcome there, as much for my society as for the money I spent, and I never neglected being free with both. I bought a handful of cigars and shoved some of them in his pocket.

"How's tricks, Jim?" I asked cheerily.

"Reckon I'm feelin' as well as could be expected," replied Jim. His head was circled by a bandage that did not conceal the lump where he had been struck. Jim looked a little pale, but he was bright enough.

"That was a hell of a biff Snell gave you, the skunk," I remarked with the same cheery assurance.

"Russ, I ain't accusin' Snell," remonstrated Jim with eyes that made me thoughtful.

"Sure, I know you're too good a sport to send a fellow up. But Snell deserved what he got. I saw his face when he made his talk to Sampson's court. Snell lied. And I'll tell you what, Jim, if it'd been me instead of that Ranger, Bud Snell would have got settled."

Jim appeared to be agitated by my forcible intimation of friendship.

"Jim, that's between ourselves," I went on. "I'm no fool. And much as I blab when I'm hunky, it's all air. Maybe you've noticed that about me. In some parts of Texas it's policy to be close-mouthed. Policy and healthy. Between ourselves, as friends, I want you to know I lean some on Steele's side of the fence."

As I lighted a cigar I saw, out of the corner of my eye, how Hoden gave a quick start. I expected some kind of a startling idea to flash into his mind.

Presently I turned and frankly met his gaze. I had startled him out of his habitual set taciturnity, but even as I looked the light that might have been amaze and joy faded out of his face, leaving it the same old mask.

Still I had seen enough. Like a bloodhound, I had a scent. "Thet's funny, Russ, seein' as you drift with the gang Steele's bound to fight," remarked Hoden.

"Sure. I'm a sport. If I can't gamble with gentlemen I'll gamble with rustlers."

Again he gave a slight start, and this time he hid his eyes.

"Wal, Russ, I've heard you was slick," he said.

"You tumble, Jim. I'm a little better on the draw."

"On the draw? With cards, an' gun, too, eh?"

"Now, Jim, that last follows natural. I haven't had much chance to show how good I am on the draw with a gun. But that'll come soon."

"Reckon thet talk's a little air," said Hoden with his dry laugh. "Same as you leanin' a little on the Ranger's side of the fence."

"But, Jim, wasn't he game? What'd you think of that stand? Bluffed the whole gang! The way he called Sampson—why, it was great! The justice of that call doesn't bother me. It was Steele's nerve that got me. That'd warm any man's blood."

There was a little red in Hoden's pale cheeks and I saw him swallow hard. I had struck deep again.

"Say, don't you work for Sampson?" he queried.

"Me? I *guess* not. I'm Miss Sampson's man. He and Wright have tried to fire me many a time."

"Thet so?" he said curiously. "What for?"

"Too many silver trimmings on me, Jim. And I pack my gun low down."

"Wal, them two don't go much together out here," replied Hoden. "But I ain't seen thet anyone has shot off the trimmin's."

"Maybe it'll commence, Jim, as soon as I stop buying drinks. Talking about work—who'd you say Snell worked for?"

"I didn't say."

"Well, say so now, can't you? Jim, you're powerful peevish to-day. It's the bump on your head. Who does Snell work for?"

"When he works at all, which sure ain't often, he rides for Sampson."

"Humph! Seems to me, Jim, that Sampson's the whole circus round Linrock. I was some sore the other day to find I was losing good money at Sampson's faro game. Sure if I'd won I wouldn't have been sorry, eh? But I was surprised to hear some scully say Sampson owned the Hope So dive."

"I've heard he owned considerable property hereabouts," replied Jim constrainedly.

"Humph again! Why, Jim, you *know* it, only like every other scully you meet in this town, you're afraid to open your mug about Sampson. Get me straight, Jim Hoden. I don't care a damn for Colonel Mayor Sampson. And for cause I'd throw a gun on him just as quick as on any rustler in Pecos."

"Talk's cheap, my boy," replied Hoden, making light of my bluster, but the red was deep in his face.

"Sure, I know that," I said, calming down. "My temper gets up, Jim. Then it's not well known that Sampson owns the Hope So?"

"Reckon it's known in Pecos, all right. But Sampson's name isn't connected with the Hope So. Blandy runs the place."

"That Blandy—I've got no use for him. His faro game's crooked, or I'm locoed bronc. Not that we don't have lots of crooked faro dealers. A fellow can stand for them. But Blandy's mean, back handed, never looks you in the eyes. That Hope So place ought to be run by a good fellow like you, Hoden."

"Thanks, Russ," replied he, and I imagined his voice a little husky. "Didn't you ever hear *I* used to run it?"

"No. Did you?" I said quickly.

"I reckon. I built the place, made additions twice, owned it for eleven years."

"Well, I'll be doggoned!"

It was indeed my turn to be surprised, and with the surprise came glimmering.

"I'm sorry you're not there now, Jim. Did you sell out?"

"No. Just lost the place."

Hoden was bursting for relief now—to talk—to tell. Sympathy had made him soft. I did not need to ask another question.

"It was two years ago—two years last March," he went on. "I was in a big cattle deal with Sampson. We got the stock, an' my share, eighteen hundred head, was rustled off. I owed Sampson. He pressed me. It come to a lawsuit, an' I—was ruined."

It hurt me to look at Hoden. He was white, and tears rolled down his cheeks.

I saw the bitterness, the defeat, the agony of the man. He had failed to meet his obligation; nevertheless he had been swindled.

All that he suppressed, all that would have been passion had the man's spirit not been broken, lay bare for me to see. I had now the secret of his bitterness.

But the reason he did not openly accuse Sampson, the secret of his reticence and fear—these I thought best to try to learn at some later time, after I had consulted with Steele.

"Hard luck! Jim, it certainly was tough," I said. "But you're a good loser. And the wheel turns!

"Now, Jim, here's what I come particular to see you for. I need your advice. I've got a little money. Between you and me, as friends, I've been adding some to that roll all the time. But before I lose it I want to invest some. Buy some stock or buy an interest in some rancher's herd.

"What I want you to steer me on is a good, square rancher. Or maybe a couple of ranchers if there happen to be two honest ones in Pecos. Eh? No deals with ranchers who ride in the dark with rustlers! I've a hunch Linrock's full of them.

"Now, Jim, you've been here for years. So you must know a couple of men above suspicion."

"Thank God I do, Russ," he replied feelingly. "Frank Morton an' Si Zimmer, my friends an' neighbors all my prosperous days. An' friends still. You can gamble on Frank and Si. But Russ, if you want advice from me, don't invest money in stock now."

"Why?"

"Because any new feller buyin' stock in Pecos these days will be rustled quicker'n he can say Jack Robinson. The pioneers, the new cattlemen—these are easy pickin'. But the new fellers have to learn the ropes. They don't know anythin' or anybody. An' the old ranchers are wise an' sore. They'd fight if they...."

"What?" I put in as he paused. "If they knew who was rustling the stock?"

"Nope."

"If they had the nerve?"

"Not thet so much."

"What then? What'd make them fight?"

"A leader!"

I went out of Hoden's with that word ringing in my ears. A leader! In my mind's eye I saw a horde of dark faced, dusty-booted cattlemen riding grim and armed behind Vaughn Steele.

More thoughtful than usual, I walked on, passing some of my old haunts, and was about to turn in front of a feed and grain store when a hearty slap on my back disturbed my reflection.

"Howdy thar, cowboy," boomed a big voice.

It was Morton, the rancher whom Jim had mentioned, and whose acquaintance I had made. He was a man of great bulk, with a ruddy, merry face.

"Hello, Morton. Let's have a drink," I replied.

"Gotta rustle home," he said. "Young feller, I've a ranch to work."

"Sell it to me, Morton."

He laughed and said he wished he could. His buckboard stood at the rail, the horses stamping impatiently.

"Cards must be runnin' lucky," he went on, with another hearty laugh.

"Can't kick on the luck. But I'm afraid it will change. Morton, my friend Hoden gave me a hunch you'd be a good man to tie to. Now, I've a little money, and before I lose it I'd like to invest it in stock."

He smiled broadly, but for all his doubt of me he took definite interest.

"I'm not drunk, and I'm on the square," I said bluntly. "You've taken me for a no-good cow puncher without any brains. Wake up, Morton. If you never size up your neighbors any better than you have me—well, you won't get any richer."

It was sheer enjoyment for me to make my remarks to these men, pregnant with meaning. Morton showed his pleasure, his interest, but his faith held aloof.

"I've got some money. I had some. Then the cards have run lucky. Will you let me in on some kind of deal? Will you start me up as a stockman, with a little herd all my own?"

"Russ, this's durn strange, comin' from Sampson's cowboy," he said.

"I'm not in his outfit. My job's with Miss Sampson. She's fine, but the old man? Nit! He's been after me for weeks. I won't last long. That's one reason why I want to start up for myself."

"Hoden sent you to me, did he? Poor ol' Jim. Wal, Russ, to come out flat-footed, you'd be foolish to buy cattle now. I don't want to take your money an' see you lose out. Better go back across the Pecos where the rustlers ain't so strong. I haven't had more'n twenty-five-hundred head of stock for ten years. The rustlers let me hang on to a breedin' herd. Kind of them, ain't it?"

"Sort of kind. All I hear is rustlers." I replied with impatience. "You see, I haven't ever lived long in a rustler-run county. Who heads the gang anyway?"

Frank Morton looked at me with a curiously-amused smile.

"I hear lots about Jack Blome and Snecker. Everybody calls them out and out bad. Do they head this mysterious gang?"

"Russ, I opine Blome an' Snecker parade themselves off boss rustlers same as gun throwers. But thet's the love such men have for bein' thought hell. That's brains headin' the rustler gang hereabouts."

"Maybe Blome and Snecker are blinds. Savvy what I mean, Morton? Maybe there's more in the parade than just the fame of it."

Morton snapped his big jaw as if to shut in impulsive words.

"Look here, Morton. I'm not so young in years even if I am young west of the Pecos. I can figure ahead. It stands to reason, no matter how damn strong these rustlers are, how hidden their work, however involved with supposedly honest men—they can't last."

"They come with the pioneers an' they'll last as long as thar's a single steer left," he declared.

"Well, if you take that view of circumstances I just figure you as one of the rustlers!"

Morton looked as if he were about to brain me with the butt of his whip. His anger flashed by then as unworthy of him, and, something striking him as funny, he boomed out a laugh.

"It's not so funny," I went on. "If you're going to pretend a yellow streak, what else will I think?"

"Pretend?" he repeated.

"Sure. You can't fool me, Morton. I know men of nerve. And here in Pecos they're not any different from those in other places. I say if you show anything like a lack of sand it's all bluff.

"By nature you've got nerve. There are a lot of men round Linrock who're afraid of their shadows, afraid to be out after dark, afraid to open their mouths. But you're not one.

"So, I say, if you claim these rustlers will last, you're pretending lack of nerve just to help the popular idea along. For they can't last.

"Morton, I don't want to be a hard-riding cowboy all my days. Do you think I'd let fear of a gang of rustlers stop me from going in business with a rancher? Nit! What you need out here in Pecos is some new blood—a few youngsters like me to get you old guys started. Savvy what I mean?"

"Wal, I reckon I do," he replied, looking as if a storm had blown over him.

I gauged the hold the rustler gang had on Linrock by the difficult job it was to stir this really courageous old cattleman. He had grown up with the evil. To him it must have been a necessary one, the same as dry seasons and cyclones.

"Russ, I'll look you up the next time I come to town," he said soberly.

We parted, and I, more than content with the meeting, retraced my steps down street to the Hope So saloon.

Here I entered, bent on tasks as sincere as the ones just finished, but displeasing, because I had to mix with a low, profane set, to cultivate them, to drink occasionally despite my deftness at emptying glasses on the floor, to gamble with them and strangers, always playing the part of a flush and flashy cowboy, half drunk, ready to laugh or fight.

On the night of the fifth day after Steele's departure, I went, as was my habit, to the rendezvous we maintained at the pile of rocks out in the open.

The night was clear, bright starlight, without any moon, and for this latter fact safer to be abroad. Often from my covert I had seen dark figures skulking in and out of Linrock.

It would have been interesting to hold up these mysterious travelers; so far, however, this had not been our game. I had enough to keep my own tracks hidden, and my own comings and goings.

I liked to be out in the night, with the darkness close down to the earth, and the feeling of a limitless open all around. Not only did I listen for Steele's soft step, but for any sound—the yelp of coyote or mourn of wolf, the creak of wind in the dead brush, the distant clatter of hoofs, a woman's singing voice faint from the town.

This time, just when I was about to give up for that evening, Steele came looming like a black giant long before I heard his soft step. It was good to feel his grip, even if it hurt, because after five days I had begun to worry.

"Well, old boy, how's tricks?" he asked easily.

"Well, old man, did you land that son of a gun in jail?"

"You bet I did. And he'll stay there for a while. Del Rio rather liked the idea, Russ. All right there. I side-stepped Sanderson on the way back. But over here at the little village—Sampson they call it—I was held up. Couldn't help it, because there wasn't any road around."

"Held up?" I queried.

"That's it, the buckboard was held up. I got into the brush in time to save my bacon. They began to shoot too soon."

"Did you get any of them?"

"Didn't stay to see," he chuckled. "Had to hoof it to Linrock, and it's a good long walk."

"Been to your 'dobe yet to-night?"

"I slipped in at the back. Russ, it bothered me some to make sure no one was laying for me in the dark."

"You'll have to get a safer place. Why not take to the open every night?"

"Russ, that's well enough on a trail. But I need grub, and I've got to have a few comforts. I'll risk the 'dobe yet a little."

Then I narrated all that I had seen and done and heard during his absence, holding back one thing. What I did tell him sobered him at once, brought the quiet, somber mood, the thoughtful air.

"So that's all. Well, it's enough."

"All pertaining to our job, Vaughn," I replied. "The rest is sentiment, perhaps. I had a pretty bad case of moons over the little Langdon girl. But we quarreled. And it's ended now. Just as well, too, because if she'd...."

"Russ, did you honestly care for her? The real thing, I mean?"

"I—I'm afraid so. I'm sort of hurt inside. But, hell! There's one thing sure, a love affair might have hindered me, made me soft. I'm glad it's over."

He said no more, but his big hand pressing on my knee told me of his sympathy, another indication that there was nothing wanting in this Ranger.

"The other thing concerns you," I went on, somehow reluctant now to tell this. "You remember how I heard Wright making you out vile to Miss Sampson? Swore you'd never come back? Well, after he had gone, when Sally said he'd meant you'd be killed, Miss Sampson felt bad about it. She said she ought to be glad if someone killed you, but she couldn't be. She called you a bloody ruffian, yet she didn't want you shot.

"She said some things about the difference between your hideous character and your splendid stature. Called you a magnificent fellow—that was it. Well, then she choked up and confessed something to Sally in shame and disgrace."

"Shame—disgrace?" echoed Steele, greatly interested. "What?"

"She confessed she had been taken with you—had her little dream about you. And she hated herself for it."

Never, I thought, would I forget Vaughn Steele's eyes. It did not matter that it was dark; I saw the fixed gleam, then the leaping, shadowy light.

"Did she say that?" His voice was not quite steady. "Wonderful! Even if it only lasted a minute! She might—we might—If it wasn't for this hellish job! Russ, has it dawned on you yet, what I've got to do to Diane Sampson?"

"Yes," I replied. "Vaughn, you haven't gone sweet on her?"

What else could I make of that terrible thing in his eyes? He did not reply to that at all. I thought my arm would break in his clutch.

"You said you knew what I've got to do to Diane Sampson," he repeated hoarsely.

"Yes, you've got to ruin her happiness, if not her life."

"Why? Speak out, Russ. All this comes like a blow. There for a little I hoped you had worked out things differently from me. No hope. Ruin her life! Why?"

I could explain this strange agitation in Steele in no other way except that realization had brought keen suffering as incomprehensible as it was painful. I could not tell if it came from suddenly divined love for Diane Sampson equally with a poignant conviction that his fate was to wreck her. But I did see that he needed to speak out the brutal truth.

"Steele, old man, you'll ruin Diane Sampson, because, as arrest looks improbable to me, you'll have to kill her father."

"My God! Why, why? Say it!"

"Because Sampson is the leader of the Linrock gang of rustlers."

That night before we parted we had gone rather deeply into the plan of action for the immediate future.

First I gave Steele my earnest counsel and then as stiff an argument as I knew how to put up, all anent the absolute necessity of his eternal vigilance. If he got shot in a fair encounter with his enemies—well, that was a Ranger's risk and no disgrace. But to be massacred in bed, knifed, in the dark, shot in the back, ambushed in any manner—not one of these miserable ends must be the last record of Vaughn Steele.

He promised me in a way that made me wonder if he would ever sleep again or turn his back on anyone—made me wonder too, at the menace in his voice. Steele seemed likely to be torn two ways, and already there was a hint of future desperation.

It was agreed that I make cautious advances to Hoden and Morton, and when I could satisfy myself of their trustworthiness reveal my identity to them. Through this I was to cultivate Zimmer, and then other ranchers whom we should decide could be let into the secret.

It was not only imperative that we learn through them clues by which we might eventually fix guilt on the rustler gang, but also just as imperative that we develop a band of deputies to help us when the fight began.

Steele, now that he was back in Linrock, would have the center of the stage, with all eyes upon him. We agreed, moreover, that the bolder the front now the better the chance of ultimate success. The more nerve he showed the less danger of being ambushed, the less peril in facing vicious men.

But we needed a jail. Prisoners had to be corraled after arrest, or the work would be useless, almost a farce, and there was no possibility of repeating trips to Del Rio.

We could not use an adobe house for a jail, because that could be easily cut out of or torn down.

Finally I remembered an old stone house near the end of the main street; it had one window and one door, and had been long in disuse. Steele would rent it, hire men to guard and feed his prisoners; and if these prisoners bribed or fought their way to freedom, that would not injure the great principle for which he stood.

Both Steele and I simultaneously, from different angles of reasoning, had arrived at a conviction of Sampson's guilt. It was not so strong as realization; rather a divination.

Long experience in detecting, in feeling the hidden guilt of men, had sharpened our senses for that particular thing. Steele acknowledged a few mistakes in his day; but I, allowing for the same strength of conviction, had never made a single mistake.

But conviction was one thing and proof vastly another. Furthermore, when proof was secured, then came the crowning task—that of taking desperate men in a wild country they dominated.

Verily, Steele and I had our work cut out for us. However, we were prepared to go at it with infinite patience and implacable resolve. Steele and I differed only in the driving incentive; of course, outside of that one binding vow to save the Ranger Service.

He had a strange passion, almost an obsession, to represent the law of Texas, and by so doing render something of safety and happiness to the honest pioneers.

Beside Steele I knew I shrunk to a shadow. I was not exactly a heathen, and certainly I wanted to help harassed people, especially women and children; but mainly with me it was the zest, the thrill, the hazard, the matching of wits—in a word, the adventure of the game.

Next morning I rode with the young ladies. In the light of Sally's persistently flagrant advances, to which I was apparently blind, I saw that my hard-won victory over self was likely to be short-lived.

That possibility made me outwardly like ice. I was an attentive, careful, reliable, and respectful attendant, seeing to the safety of my charges; but the one-time gay and debonair cowboy was a thing of the past.

Sally, womanlike, had been a little—a very little—repentant; she had showed it, my indifference had piqued her; she had made advances and then my coldness had roused her spirit. She was the kind of girl to value most what she had lost, and to throw consequences to the winds in winning it back.

When I divined this I saw my revenge. To be sure, when I thought of it I had no reason to want revenge. She had been most gracious to me.

But there was the catty thing she had said about being kissed again by her admirers. Then, in all seriousness, sentiment aside, I dared not make up with her.

So the cold and indifferent part I played was imperative.

We halted out on the ridge and dismounted for the usual little rest. Mine I took in the shade of a scrubby mesquite. The girls strolled away out of sight. It was a drowsy day, and I nearly fell asleep.

Something aroused me—a patter of footsteps or a rustle of skirts. Then a soft thud behind me gave me at once a start and a thrill. First I saw Sally's little brown hands on my shoulders. Then her head, with hair all shiny and flying and fragrant, came round over my shoulder, softly smoothing my cheek, until her sweet, saucy, heated face was right under my eyes.

"Russ, don't you love me any more?" she whispered.

Chapter 4

STEELE BREAKS UP THE PARTY

That night, I saw Steele at our meeting place, and we compared notes and pondered details of our problem.

Steele had rented the stone house to be used as a jail. While the blacksmith was putting up a door and window calculated to withstand many onslaughts, all the idlers and strangers in town went to see the sight. Manifestly it was an occasion for Linrock. When Steele let it be known that he wanted to hire a jailer and a guard this caustically humorous element offered itself *en masse*. The men made a joke out of it.

When Steele and I were about to separate I remembered a party that was to be given by Miss Sampson, and I told him about it. He shook his head sadly, almost doubtfully.

Was it possible that Sampson could be a deep eyed, cunning scoundrel, the true leader of the cattle rustlers, yet keep that beautiful and innocent girl out on the frontier and let her give parties to sons and daughters of a community he had robbed? To any but remorseless Rangers the idea was incredible.

Thursday evening came in spite of what the girls must have regarded as an interminably dragging day.

It was easy to differentiate their attitudes toward this party. Sally wanted to look beautiful, to excell all the young ladies who were to attend, to attach to her train all the young men, and have them fighting to dance with her. Miss Sampson had an earnest desire to open her father's house to the people of Linrock, to show that a daughter had come into his long cheerless home, to make the evening one of pleasure and entertainment.

I happened to be present in the parlor, was carrying in some flowers for final decoration, when Miss Sampson learned that her father had just ridden off with three horsemen whom Dick, who brought the news, had not recognized.

In her keen disappointment she scarcely heard Dick's concluding remark about the hurry of the colonel. My sharp ears, however, took this in and it was thought-provoking. Sampson was known to ride off at all hours, yet this incident seemed unusual.

At eight o'clock the house and porch and patio were ablaze with lights. Every lantern and lamp on the place, together with all that could be bought and borrowed, had been brought into requisition.

The cowboys arrived first, all dressed in their best, clean shaven, red faced, bright eyed, eager for the fun to commence. Then the young people from town, and a good sprinkling of older people, came in a steady stream.

Miss Sampson received them graciously, excused her father's absence, and bade them be at home.

The music, or the discordance that went by that name, was furnished by two cowboys with banjos and an antediluvian gentleman with a fiddle. Nevertheless, it was music that could be danced to, and there was no lack of enthusiasm.

I went from porch to parlor and thence to patio, watching and amused. The lights and the decorations of flowers, the bright dresses and the flashy scarfs of the cowboys furnished a gay enough scene to a man of lonesome and stern life like mine. During the dance there was a steady, continuous shuffling tramp of boots, and during the interval following a steady, low hum of merry talk and laughter.

My wandering from place to place, apart from my usual careful observation, was an unobtrusive but, to me, a sneaking pursuit of Sally Langdon.

She had on a white dress I had never seen with a low neck and short sleeves, and she looked so sweet, so dainty, so altogether desirable, that I groaned a hundred times in my jealousy. Because, manifestly, Sally did not intend to run any risk of my not seeing her in her glory, no matter where my eyes looked.

A couple of times in promenading I passed her on the arm of some proud cowboy or gallant young buck from town, and on these occasions she favored her escort with a languishing glance that probably did as much damage to him as to me.

Presently she caught me red-handed in my careless, sauntering pursuit of her, and then, whether by intent or from indifference, she apparently deigned me no more notice. But, quick to feel a difference in her, I marked that from that moment her gaiety gradually merged into coquettishness, and soon into flirtation.

Then, just to see how far she would go, perhaps desperately hoping she would make me hate her, I followed her shamelessly from patio to parlor, porch to court, even to the waltz.

To her credit, she always weakened when some young fellow got her in a corner and tried to push the flirting to extremes. Young Waters was the only one lucky enough to kiss her, and there was more of strength in his conquest of her than any decent fellow could be proud of.

When George Wright sought Sally out there was added to my jealousy a real anxiety. I had brushed against Wright more than once that evening. He was not drunk, yet under the influence of liquor.

Sally, however, evidently did not discover that, because, knowing her abhorrence of drink, I believed she would not have walked out with him had she known. Anyway, I followed them, close in the shadow.

Wright was unusually gay. I saw him put his arm around her without remonstrance. When the music recommenced they went back to the house. Wright danced with Sally, not ungracefully for a man who rode a horse as much as he. After the dance he waved aside Sally's many partners, not so gaily as would have been consistent with good feeling, and led her away. I followed. They ended up that walk at the extreme corner of the patio, where, under gaily colored lights, a little arbor had been made among the flowers and vines.

Sally seemed to have lost something of her vivacity. They had not been out of my sight for a moment before Sally cried out. It was a cry of impatience or remonstrance, rather than alarm, but I decided that it would serve me an excuse.

I dashed back, leaped to the door of the arbor, my hand on my gun.

Wright was holding Sally. When he heard me he let her go. Then she uttered a cry that was one of alarm. Her face blanched; her eyes grew strained. One hand went to her breast. She thought I meant to kill Wright.

"Excuse me," I burst out frankly, turning to Wright. I never saw a hyena, but he looked like one. "I heard a squeal. Thought a girl was hurt, or something. Miss Sampson gave me orders to watch out for accidents, fire, anything. So excuse me, Wright."

As I stepped back, to my amazement, Sally, excusing herself to the scowling Wright, hurriedly joined me.

"Oh, it's our dance, Russ!"

She took my arm and we walked through the patio.

"I'm afraid of him, Russ," she whispered. "You frightened me worse though. You didn't mean to—to—"

"I made a bluff. Saw he'd been drinking, so I kept near you."

"You return good for evil," she replied, squeezing my arm. "Russ, let me tell you—whenever anything frightens me since we got here I think of you. If you're only near I feel safe."

We paused at the door leading into the big parlor. Couples were passing. Here I could scarcely distinguish the last words she said. She stood before me, eyes downcast, face flushed, as sweet and pretty a lass as man could want to see, and with her hand she twisted round and round a silver button on my buckskin vest.

"Dance with me, the rest of this," she said. "George shooed away my partner. I'm glad for the chance. Dance with me, Russ—not gallantly or dutifully because I ask you, but because you *want* to. Else not at all."

There was a limit to my endurance. There would hardly be another evening like this, at least, for me, in that country. I capitulated with what grace I could express.

We went into the parlor, and as we joined the dancers, despite all that confusion I heard her whisper: "I've been a little beast to you."

That dance seemingly lasted only a moment—a moment while she was all airy grace, radiant, and alluring, floating close to me, with our hands clasped. Then it appeared the music had ceased, the couples were finding seats, and Sally and I were accosted by Miss Sampson.

She said we made a graceful couple in the dance. And Sally said she did not have to reach up a mile to me—I was not so awfully tall.

And I, tongue-tied for once, said nothing.

Wright had returned and was now standing, cigarette between lips, in the door leading out to the patio. At the same moment that I heard a heavy tramp of boots, from the porch side I saw Wright's face change remarkably, expressing amaze, consternation, then fear.

I wheeled in time to see Vaughn Steele bend his head to enter the door on that side. The dancers fell back.

At sight of him I was again the Ranger, his ally. Steele was pale, yet heated. He panted. He wore no hat. He had his coat turned up and with left hand he held the lapels together.

In a quick ensuing silence Miss Sampson rose, white as her dress. The young women present stared in astonishment and their partners showed excitement.

"Miss Sampson, I came to search your house!" panted Steele, courteously, yet with authority.

I disengaged myself from Sally, who was clinging to my hands, and I stepped forward out of the corner. Steele had been running. Why did he hold his coat like that? I sensed action, and the cold thrill animated me.

Miss Sampson's astonishment was succeeded by anger difficult to control.

"In the absence of my father I am mistress here. I will not permit you to search my house."

"Then I regret to say I must do so without your permission," he said sternly.

"Do not dare!" she flashed. She stood erect, her bosom swelling, her eyes magnificently black with passion. "How dare you intrude here? Have you not insulted us enough? To search my house to-night—to break up my party—oh, it's worse than outrage! Why on earth do you want to search here? Ah, for the same reason you dragged a poor innocent man into my father's court! Sir, I forbid you to take another step into this house."

Steele's face was bloodless now, and I wondered if it had to do with her scathing scorn or something that he hid with his hand closing his coat that way.

"Miss Sampson, I don't need warrants to search houses," he said. "But this time I'll respect your command. It would be too bad to spoil your party. Let me add, perhaps you do me a little wrong. God knows I hope so. I was shot by a rustler. He fled. I chased him here. He has taken refuge here—in your father's house. He's hidden somewhere."

Steele spread wide his coat lapels. He wore a light shirt, the color of which in places was white. The rest was all a bloody mass from which dark red drops fell to the floor.

"Oh!" cried Miss Sampson.

Scorn and passion vanished in the horror, the pity, of a woman who imagined she saw a man mortally wounded. It was a hard sight for a woman's eyes, that crimson, heaving breast.

"Surely I didn't see that," went on Steele, closing his coat. "You used unforgettable words, Miss Sampson. From you they hurt. For I stand alone. My fight is to make Linrock safer, cleaner, a better home for women and children. Some day you will remember what you said."

How splendid he looked, how strong against odds. How simple a dignity fitted his words. Why, a woman far blinder than Diane Sampson could have seen that here stood a man.

Steele bowed, turned on his heel, and strode out to vanish in the dark.

Then while she stood bewildered, still shocked, I elected to do some rapid thinking.

How seriously was Steele injured? An instant's thought was enough to tell me that if he had sustained any more than a flesh wound he would not have chased his assailant, not with so much at stake in the future.

Then I concerned myself with a cold grip of desire to get near the rustler who had wounded Steele. As I started forward, however, Miss Sampson defeated me. Sally once more clung to my hands, and directly we were surrounded by an excited circle.

It took a moment or two to calm them.

"Then there's a rustler—here—hiding?" repeated Miss Sampson.

"Miss Sampson, I'll find him. I'll rout him out," I said.

"Yes, yes, find him, Russ, but don't use violence," she replied. "Send him away—no, give him over to—"

"Nothing of the kind," interrupted George Wright, loud-voiced. "Cousin, go on with your dance. I'll take a couple of cowboys. I'll find this—this rustler, if there's one here. But I think it's only another bluff of Steele's."

This from Wright angered me deeply, and I strode right for the door.

"Where are you going?" he demanded.

"I've Miss Sampson's orders. She wants me to find this hidden man. She trusts me not to allow any violence."

"Didn't I say I'd see to that?" he snarled.

"Wright, I don't care what you say," I retorted. "But I'm thinking you might not want me to find this rustler."

Wright turned black in the face. Verily, if he had worn a gun he would have pulled it on me. As it was, Miss Sampson's interference probably prevented more words, if no worse.

"Don't quarrel," she said. "George, you go with Russ. Please hurry. I'll be nervous till the rustler's found or you're sure there's not one."

We started with several cowboys to ransack the house. We went through the rooms, searching, calling out, flashing our lanterns in dark places.

It struck me forcibly that Wright did all the calling. He hurried, too, tried to keep in the lead. I wondered if he knew his voice would be recognized by the hiding man.

Be that as it might, it was I who peered into a dark corner, and then with a cocked gun leveled I said: "Come out!"

He came forth into the flare of lanterns, a tall, slim, dark-faced youth, wearing dark sombrero, blouse and trousers. I collared him before any of the others could move, and I held the gun close enough to make him shrink.

But he did not impress me as being frightened just then; nevertheless, he had a clammy face, the pallid look of a man who had just gotten over a shock. He peered into my face, then into that of the cowboy next to me, then into Wright's and if ever in my life I beheld relief I saw it then.

That was all I needed to know, but I meant to find out more if I could.

"Who're you?" I asked quietly.

He gazed rather arrogantly down at me. It always irritated me to be looked down at that way.

"Say, don't be gay with me or you'll get it good," I yelled, prodding him in the side with the cocked gun. "Who are you? Quick!"

"Bo Snecker," he said.

"Any relation to Bill Snecker?"

"His son."

"What'd you hide here for?"

He appeared to grow sullen.

"Reckoned I'd be as safe in Sampson's as anywheres."

"Ahuh! You're taking a long chance," I replied, and he never knew, or any of the others, just how long a chance that was.

Sight of Steele's bloody breast remained with me, and I had something sinister to combat. This was no time for me to reveal myself or to show unusual feeling or interest for Steele.

As Steele had abandoned his search, I had nothing to do now but let the others decide what disposition was to be made of Snecker.

"Wright, what'll you do with him?" I queried, as if uncertain, now the capture was made. I let Snecker go and sheathed my weapon.

That seemed a signal for him to come to life. I guessed he had not much fancied the wide and somewhat variable sweep of that cocked gun.

"I'll see to that," replied Wright gruffly, and he pushed Snecker in front of him into the hall. I followed them out into the court at the back of the house.

As I had very little further curiosity I did not wait to see where they went, but hurried back to relieve Miss Sampson and Sally.

I found them as I had left them—Sally quiet, pale, Miss Sampson nervous and distressed. I soon calmed their fears of any further trouble or possible disturbance. Miss Sampson then became curious and wanted to know who the rustler was.

"How strange he should come here," she said several times.

"Probably he'd run this way or thought he had a better chance to hide where there was dancing and confusion," I replied glibly.

I wondered how much longer I would find myself keen to shunt her mind from any channel leading to suspicion.

"Would papa have arrested him?" she asked.

"Colonel Sampson might have made it hot for him," I replied frankly, feeling that if what I said had a double meaning it still was no lie.

"Oh, I forgot—the Ranger!" she exclaimed suddenly. "That awful sight—the whole front of him bloody! Russ, how could he stand up under such a wound? Do you think it'll kill him?"

"That's hard to say. A man like Steele can stand a lot."

"Russ, please go find him! See how it is with him!" she said, almost pleadingly.

I started, glad of the chance and hurried down toward the town.

There was a light in the little adobe house where he lived, and proceeding cautiously, so as to be sure no one saw me, I went close and whistled low in a way he would recognize. Then he opened the door and I went in.

"Hello, son!" he said. "You needn't have worried. Sling a blanket over that window so no one can see in."

He had his shirt off and had been in the act of bandaging a wound that the bullet had cut in his shoulder.

"Let me tie that up," I said, taking the strips of linen. "Ahuh! Shot you from behind, didn't he?"

"How else, you locoed lady-charmer? It's a wonder I didn't have to tell you that."

"Tell me about it."

Steele related a circumstance differing little from other attempts at his life, and concluded by saying that Snecker was a good runner if he was not a good shot.

I finished the bandaging and stood off, admiring Steele's magnificent shoulders. I noted, too, on the fine white skin more than one scar made by bullets. I got an impression that his strength and vitality were like his spirit—unconquerable!

"So you knew it was Bill Snecker's son?" I asked when I had told him about finding the rustler.

"Sure. Jim Hoden pointed him out to me yesterday. Both the Sneckers are in town. From now on we're going to be busy, Russ."

"It can't come too soon for me," I replied. "Shall I chuck my job? Come out from behind these cowboy togs?"

"Not yet. We need proof, Russ. We've got to be able to prove things. Hang on at the ranch yet awhile."

"This Bo Snecker was scared stiff till he recognized Wright. Isn't that proof?"

"No, that's nothing. We've got to catch Sampson and Wright red-handed."

"I don't like the idea of you trailing along alone," I protested. "Remember what Neal told me. I'm to kick. It's time for me to hang round with a couple of guns. You'll never use one."

"The hell I won't," he retorted, with a dark glance of passion. I was surprised that my remark had angered him. "You fellows are all wrong. I know *when* to throw a gun. You ought to remember that Rangers have a bad name for wanting to shoot. And I'm afraid it's deserved."

"Did you shoot at Snecker?" I queried.

"I could have got him in the back. But that wouldn't do. I shot three times at his legs—tried to let him down. I'd have made him tell everything he knew, but he ran. He was too fast for me."

"Shooting at his legs! No wonder he ran. He savvied your game all right. It's funny, Vaughn, how these rustlers and gunmen don't mind being killed. But to cripple them, rope them, jail them—that's hell to them! Well, I'm to go on, up at the ranch, falling further in love with that sweet kid instead of coming out straight to face things with you?"

Steele had to laugh, yet he was more thoughtful of my insistence.

"Russ, you think you have patience, but you don't know what patience is. I won't be hurried on this job. But I'll tell you what: I'll hang under cover most of the time when you're not close to me. See? That can be managed. I'll watch for you when you come in town. We'll go in the same places. And in case I get busy you can stand by and trail along after me. That satisfy you?"

"Fine!" I said, both delighted and relieved. "Well, I'll have to rustle back now to tell Miss Sampson you're all right."

Steele had about finished pulling on a clean shirt, exercising care not to disarrange the bandages; and he stopped short to turn squarely and look at me with hungry eyes.

"Russ, did she—show sympathy?"

"She was all broken up about it. Thought you were going to die."

"Did she send you?"

"Sure. And she said hurry," I replied.

I was not a little gleeful over the apparent possibility of Steele being in the same boat with me.

"Do you think she would have cared if—if I had been shot up bad?"

The great giant of a Ranger asked this like a boy, hesitatingly, with color in his face.

"Care! Vaughn, you're as thickheaded as you say I'm locoed. Diane Sampson has fallen in love with you! That's all. Love at first sight! She doesn't realize it. But I know."

There he stood as if another bullet had struck him, this time straight through the heart. Perhaps one had—and I repented a little of my overconfident declaration.

Still, I would not go back on it. I believed it.

"Russ, for God's sake! What a terrible thing to say!" he ejaculated hoarsely.

"No. It's not terrible to *say* it—only the fact is terrible," I went on. I may be wrong. But I swear I'm right. When you opened your coat, showed that bloody breast—well, I'll never forget her eyes.

"She had been furious. She showed passion—hate. Then all in a second something wonderful, beautiful broke through. Pity, fear, agonized thought of your death! If that's not love, if—if she did not betray love, then I never saw it. She thinks she hates you. But she loves you."

"Get out of here," he ordered thickly.

I went, not forgetting to peep out at the door and to listen a moment, then I hurried into the open, up toward the ranch.

The stars were very big and bright, so calm, so cold, that it somehow hurt me to look at them. Not like men's lives, surely!

What had fate done to Vaughn Steele and to me? I had a moment of bitterness, an emotion rare with me.

Most Rangers put love behind them when they entered the Service and seldom found it after that. But love had certainly met me on the way, and I now had confirmation of my fear that Vaughn was hard hit.

Then the wildness, the adventurer in me stirred to the wonder of it all. It was in me to exult even in the face of fate. Steele and I, while balancing our lives on the hair-trigger of a gun, had certainly fallen into a tangled web of circumstances not calculated in the role of Rangers.

I went back to the ranch with regret, remorse, sorrow knocking at my heart, but notwithstanding that, tingling alive to the devilish excitement of the game.

I knew not what it was that prompted me to sow the same seed in Diane Sampson's breast that I had sown in Steele's; probably it was just a propensity for sheer mischief, probably a certainty of the truth and a strange foreshadowing of a coming event.

If Diane Sampson loved, through her this event might be less tragic. Somehow love might save us all.

That was the shadowy portent flitting in the dark maze of my mind.

At the ranch dancing had been resumed. There might never have been any interruption of the gaiety. I found Miss Sampson on the lookout for me and she searched my face with eyes that silenced my one last qualm of conscience.

"Let's go out in the patio," I suggested. "I don't want any one to hear what I say."

Outside in the starlight she looked white and very beautiful. I felt her tremble. Perhaps my gravity presaged the worst. So it did in one way—poor Vaughn!

"I went down to Steele's 'dobe, the little place where he lives." I began, weighing my words. "He let me in—was surprised. He had been shot high in the shoulder, not a dangerous wound. I bandaged it for him. He was grateful—said he had no friends."

"Poor fellow! Oh, I'm glad it—it isn't bad," said Miss Sampson. Something glistened in her eyes.

"He looked strange, sort of forlorn. I think your words—what you said hurt him more than the bullet. I'm sure of that, Miss Sampson."

"Oh, I saw that myself! I was furious. But I—I meant what I said."

"You wronged Steele. I happen to know. I know his record along the Rio Grande. It's scarcely my place, Miss Sampson, to tell you what you'll find out for yourself, sooner or later."

"What shall I find out?" she demanded.

"I've said enough."

"No. You mean my father and cousin George are misinformed or wrong about Steele? I've feared it this last hour. It was his look. That pierced me. Oh, I'd hate to be unjust. You say I wronged him, Russ? Then you take sides with him against my father?"

"Yes," I replied very low.

She was keenly hurt and seemed, despite an effort, to shrink from me.

"It's only natural you should fight for your father," I went on. "Perhaps you don't understand. He has ruled here for long. He's been—well, let's say, easy with the evil-doers. But times are changing. He opposed the Ranger idea, which is also natural, I suppose. Still, he's wrong about Steele, terribly wrong, and it means trouble."

"Oh, I don't know what to believe!"

"It might be well for you to think things out for yourself."

"Russ, I feel as though I couldn't. I can't make head or tail of life out here. My father seems so strange. Though, of course, I've only seen him twice a year since I was a little girl. He has two sides to him. When I come upon that strange side, the one I never knew, he's like a man I never saw.

"I want to be a good and loving daughter. I want to help him fight his battles. But he doesn't—he doesn't *satisfy* me. He's grown impatient and wants me to go back to Louisiana. That gives me a feeling of mystery. Oh, it's *all* mystery!"

"True, you're right," I replied, my heart aching for her. "It's all mystery—and trouble for you, too. Perhaps you'd do well to go home."

"Russ, you suggest I leave here—leave my father?" she asked.

"I advise it. You struck a—a rather troublesome time. Later you might return if—"

"Never. I came to stay, and I'll stay," she declared, and there her temper spoke.

"Miss Sampson," I began again, after taking a long, deep breath, "I ought to tell you one thing more about Steele."

"Well, go on."

"Doesn't he strike you now as being the farthest removed from a ranting, brutal Ranger?"

"I confess he was at least a gentleman."

"Rangers don't allow anything to interfere with the discharge of their duty. He was courteous after you defamed him. He respected your wish. He did not break up the dance.

"This may not strike you particularly. But let me explain that Steele was chasing an outlaw who had shot him. Under ordinary circumstances he would have searched your house. He would have been like a lion. He would have torn the place down around our ears to get that rustler.

"But his action was so different from what I had expected, it amazed me. Just now, when I was with him, I learned, I guessed, what stayed his hand. I believe you ought to know."

"Know what?" she asked. How starry and magnetic her eyes! A woman's divining intuition made them wonderful with swift-varying emotion.

They drew me on to the fatal plunge. What was I doing to her—to Vaughn? Something bound my throat, making speech difficult.

"He's fallen in love with you," I hurried on in a husky voice. "Love at first sight! Terrible! Hopeless! I saw it—felt it. I can't explain how I know, but I do know.

"That's what stayed his hand here. And that's why I'm on his side. He's alone. He has a terrible task here without any handicaps. Every man is against him. If he fails, you might be the force that weakened him. So you ought to be kinder in your thought of him. Wait before you judge him further.

"If he isn't killed, time will prove him noble instead of vile. If he is killed, which is more than likely, you'll feel the happier for a generous doubt in favor of the man who loved you."

Like one stricken blind, she stood an instant; then, with her hands at her breast, she walked straight across the patio into the dark, open door of her room.

Chapter 5

CLEANING OUT LINROCK

Not much sleep visited me that night. In the morning, the young ladies not stirring and no prospects of duty for me, I rode down to town.

Sight of the wide street, lined by its hitching posts and saddled horses, the square buildings with their ugly signs, unfinished yet old, the lounging, dust-gray men at every corner—these awoke in me a significance that had gone into oblivion overnight.

That last talk with Miss Sampson had unnerved me, wrought strangely upon me. And afterward, waking and dozing, I had dreamed, lived in a warm, golden place where there were music and flowers and Sally's spritelike form leading me on after two tall, beautiful lovers, Diane and Vaughn, walking hand in hand.

Fine employment of mind for a Ranger whose single glance down a quiet street pictured it with darkgarbed men in grim action, guns spouting red, horses plunging!

In front of Hoden's restaurant I dismounted and threw my bridle. Jim was unmistakably glad to see me.

"Where've you been? Morton was in an' powerful set on seein' you. I steered him from goin' up to Sampson's. What kind of a game was you givin' Frank?"

"Jim, I just wanted to see if he was a safe rancher to make a stock deal for me."

"He says you told him he didn't have no yellow streak an' that he was a rustler. Frank can't git over them two hunches. When he sees you he's goin' to swear he's no rustler, but he *has* got a yellow streak, unless..."

This little, broken-down Texan had eyes like flint striking fire.

"Unless?" I queried sharply.

Jim breathed a deep breath and looked around the room before his gaze fixed again on mine.

"Wal," he replied, speaking low, "Me and Frank allows you've picked the right men. It was me that sent them letters to the Ranger captain at Austin. Now who in hell are you?"

It was my turn to draw a deep breath.

I had taken six weeks to strike fire from a Texan whom I instinctively felt had been prey to the power that shadowed Linrock. There was no one in the room except us, no one passing, nor near.

Reaching into the inside pocket of my buckskin vest, I turned the lining out. A star-shaped, bright, silver object flashed as I shoved it, pocket and all, under Jim's hard eyes.

He could not help but read; United States Deputy Marshall.

"By golly," he whispered, cracking the table with his fist. "Russ, you sure rung true to me. But never as a cowboy!"

"Jim, the woods is full of us!"

Heavy footsteps sounded on the walk. Presently Steele's bulk darkened the door.

"Hello," I greeted. "Steele, shake hands with Jim Hoden."

"Hello," replied Steele slowly. "Say, I reckon I know Hoden."

"Nit. Not this one. He's the old Hoden. He used to own the Hope So saloon. It was on the square when he ran it. Maybe he'll get it back pretty soon. Hope so!"

I laughed at my execrable pun. Steele leaned against the counter, his gray glance studying the man I had so oddly introduced.

Hoden in one flash associated the Ranger with me—a relation he had not dreamed of. Then, whether from shock or hope or fear I know not, he appeared about to faint.

"Hoden, do you know who's boss of this secret gang of rustlers hereabouts?" asked Steele bluntly.

It was characteristic of him to come sharp to the point. His voice, something deep, easy, cool about him, seemed to steady Hoden.

"No," replied Hoden.

"Does anybody know?" went on Steele.

"Wal, I reckon there's not one honest native of Pecos who *knows*."

"But you have your suspicions?"

"We have."

"You can keep your suspicions to yourself. But you can give me your idea about this crowd that hangs round the saloons, the regulars."

"Jest a bad lot," replied Hoden, with the quick assurance of knowledge. "Most of them have been here years. Others have drifted in. Some of them work odd times. They rustle a few steer, steal, rob, anythin' for a little money to drink an' gamble. Jest a bad lot!

"But the strangers as are always comin' an' goin'—strangers that never git acquainted—some of them are likely to be *the* rustlers. Bill an' Bo Snecker are in town now. Bill's a known cattle-thief. Bo's no good, the makin' of a gun-fighter. He heads thet way.

"They might be rustlers. But the boy, he's hardly careful enough for this gang. Then there's Jack Blome. He comes to town often. He lives up in the hills. He always has three or four strangers with him. Blome's the fancy gun fighter. He shot a gambler here last fall. Then he was in a fight in Sanderson lately. Got two cowboys then.

"Blome's killed a dozen Pecos men. He's a rustler, too, but I reckon he's not the brains of thet secret outfit, if he's in it at all."

Steele appeared pleased with Hoden's idea. Probably it coincided with the one he had arrived at himself.

"Now, I'm puzzled over this," said Steele. "Why do men, apparently honest men, seem to be so close-mouthed here? Is that a fact or only my impression?"

"It's sure a fact," replied Hoden darkly. "Men have lost cattle an' property in Linrock—lost them honestly or otherwise, as hasn't been proved. An' in some cases when they talked—hinted a little—they was found dead. Apparently held up an' robbed. But dead. Dead men don't talk. Thet's why we're close-mouthed."

Steele's face wore a dark, somber sternness.

Rustling cattle was not intolerable. Western Texas had gone on prospering, growing in spite of the horde of rustlers ranging its vast stretches; but this cold, secret, murderous hold on a little struggling community was something too strange, too terrible for men to stand long.

It had waited for a leader like Steele, and now it could not last. Hoden's revived spirit showed that.

The ranger was about to speak again when the clatter of hoofs interrupted him. Horses halted out in front.

A motion of Steele's hand caused me to dive through a curtained door back of Hoden's counter. I turned to peep out and was in time to see George Wright enter with the red-headed cowboy called Brick.

That was the first time I had ever seen Wright come into Hoden's. He called for tobacco.

If his visit surprised Jim he did not show any evidence. But Wright showed astonishment as he saw the Ranger, and then a dark glint flitted from the eyes that shifted from Steele to Hoden and back again.

Steele leaned easily against the counter, and he said good morning pleasantly. Wright deigned no reply, although he bent a curious and hard scrutiny upon Steele. In fact, Wright evinced nothing that would lead one to think he had any respect for Steele as a man or as a Ranger.

"Steele, that was the second break of yours last night," he said finally. "If you come fooling round the ranch again there'll be hell!"

It seemed strange that a man who had lived west of the Pecos for ten years could not see in Steele something which forbade that kind of talk.

It certainly was not nerve Wright showed; men of courage were seldom intolerant; and with the matchless nerve that characterized Steele or the great gunmen of the day there went a cool, unobtrusive manner, a speech brief, almost gentle, certainly courteous. Wright was a hot-headed Louisianian of French extraction; a man evidently who had never been crossed in anything, and who was strong, brutal, passionate, which qualities, in the face of a situation like this, made him simply a fool!

The way Steele looked at Wright was joy to me. I hated this smooth, dark-skinned Southerner. But, of course, an ordinary affront like Wright's only earned silence from Steele.

"I'm thinking you used your Ranger bluff just to get near Diane Sampson," Wright sneered. "Mind you, if you come up there again there'll be hell!"

"You're damn right there'll be hell!" retorted Steele, a kind of high ring in his voice. I saw thick, dark red creep into his face.

Had Wright's incomprehensible mention of Diane Sampson been an instinct of love—of jealousy? Verily, it had pierced into the depths of the Ranger, probably as no other thrust could have.

"Diane Sampson wouldn't stoop to know a dirty blood-tracker like you," said Wright hotly. His was not a deliberate intention to rouse Steele; the man was simply rancorous. "I'll call you right, you cheap bluffer! You four-flush! You damned interfering conceited Ranger!"

Long before Wright ended his tirade Steele's face had lost the tinge of color, so foreign to it in moments like this; and the cool shade, the steady eyes like ice on fire, the ruthless lips had warned me, if they had not Wright.

"Wright, I'll not take offense, because you seem to be championing your beautiful cousin," replied Steele in slow speech, biting. "But let me return your compliment. You're a fine Southerner! Why, you're only a cheap four-flush—damned bull-headed—*rustler!*"

Steele hissed the last word. Then for him—for me—for Hoden—there was the truth in Wright's working passion-blackened face.

Wright jerked, moved, meant to draw. But how slow! Steele lunged forward. His long arm swept up.

And Wright staggered backward, knocking table and chairs, to fall hard, in a half-sitting posture, against the wall.

"Don't draw!" warned Steele.

"Wright, get away from your gun!" yelled the cowboy Brick.

But Wright was crazed by fury. He tugged at his hip, his face corded with purple welts, malignant, murderous, while he got to his feet.

I was about to leap through the door when Steele shot. Wright's gun went ringing to the floor.

Like a beast in pain Wright screamed. Frantically he waved a limp arm, flinging blood over the white table-cloths. Steele had crippled him.

"Here, you cowboy," ordered Steele; "take him out, quick!"

Brick saw the need of expediency, if Wright did not realize it, and he pulled the raving man out of the place. He hurried Wright down the street, leaving the horses behind.

Steele calmly sheathed his gun.

"Well, I guess that opens the ball," he said as I came out.

Hoden seemed fascinated by the spots of blood on the table-cloths. It was horrible to see him rubbing his hands there like a ghoul!

"I tell you what, fellows," said Steele, "we've just had a few pleasant moments with the man who has made it healthy to keep close-mouthed in Linrock."

Hoden lifted his shaking hands.

"What'd you wing him for?" he wailed. "He was drawin' on you. Shootin' arms off men like him won't do out here."

I was inclined to agree with Hoden.

"That bull-headed fool will roar and butt himself with all his gang right into our hands. He's just the man I've needed to meet. Besides, shooting him would have been murder for me!"

"Murder!" exclaimed Hoden.

"He was a fool, and slow at that. Under such circumstances could I kill him when I didn't have to?"

"Sure it'd been the trick." declared Jim positively. "I'm not allowin' for whether he's really a rustler or not. It just won't do, because these fellers out here ain't goin' to be afraid of you."

"See here, Hoden. If a man's going to be afraid of me at all, that trick will make him more afraid of me. I know it. It works out. When Wright cools down he'll remember, he'll begin to think, he'll realize that I could more easily have killed him than risk a snapshot at his arm. I'll bet you he goes pale to the gills next time he even sees me."

"That may be true, Steele. But if Wright's the man you think he is he'll begin that secret underground bizness. It's been tolerable healthy these last six months. You can gamble on this. If thet secret work does commence you'll have more reason to suspect Wright. I won't feel very safe from now on.

"I heard you call him rustler. He knows thet. Why, Wright won't sleep at night now. He an' Sampson have always been after me."

"Hoden, what are your eyes for?" demanded Steele. "Watch out. And now here. See your friend Morton. Tell him this game grows hot. Together you approach four or five men you know well and can absolutely trust.

"Hello, there's somebody coming. You meet Russ and me to-night, out in the open a quarter of a mile, straight from the end of this street. You'll find a pile of stones. Meet us there to-night at ten o'clock."

The next few days, for the several hours each day that I was in town, I had Steele in sight all the time or knew that he was safe under cover.

Nothing happened. His presence in the saloons or any place where men congregated was marked by a certain uneasy watchfulness on the part of almost everybody, and some amusement on the part of a few.

It was natural to suppose that the lawless element would rise up in a mass and slay Steele on sight. But this sort of thing never happened. It was not so much that these enemies of the law awaited his next move, but just a slowness peculiar to the frontier.

The ranger was in their midst. He was interesting, if formidable. He would have been welcomed at card tables, at the bars, to play and drink with the men who knew they were under suspicion.

There was a rude kind of good humor even in their open hostility.

Besides, one Ranger, or a company of Rangers could not have held the undivided attention of these men from their games and drinks and quarrels except by some decided move. Excitement, greed, appetite were rife in them.

I marked, however, a striking exception to the usual run of strangers I had been in the habit of seeing. The Sneckers had gone or were under cover. Again I caught a vague rumor of the coming of Jack Blome, yet he never seemed to arrive.

Moreover, the goings-on among the habitues of the resorts and the cowboys who came in to drink and gamble were unusually mild in comparison with former conduct.

This lull, however, did not deceive Steele and me. It could not last. The wonder was that it had lasted so long.

There was, of course, no post office in Linrock. A stage arrived twice a week from Sanderson, if it did not get held up on the way, and the driver usually had letters, which he turned over to the elderly keeper of a little store.

This man's name was Jones, and everybody liked him. On the evenings the stage arrived there was always a crowd at his store, which fact was a source of no little revenue to him.

One night, so we ascertained, after the crowd had dispersed, two thugs entered his store, beat the old man and robbed him. He made no complaint; however, when Steele called him he rather reluctantly gave not only descriptions of his assailants, but their names.

Steele straightaway went in search of the men and came across them in Lerett's place. I was around when it happened.

Steele strode up to a table which was surrounded by seven or eight men and he tapped Sim Bass on the shoulder.

"Get up, I want you," he said.

Bass looked up only to see who had accosted him.

"The hell you say!" he replied impudently.

Steele's big hand shifted to the fellow's collar. One jerk, seemingly no effort at all, sent Bass sliding, chair and all, to crash into the bar and fall in a heap. He lay there, wondering what had struck him.

"Miller, I want you. Get up," said Steele.

Miller complied with alacrity. A sharp kick put more life and understanding into Bass.

Then Steele searched these men right before the eyes of their comrades, took what money and weapons they had, and marched them out, followed by a crowd that gathered more and more to it as they went down the street. Steele took his prisoners into Jones' store, had them identified; returned the money they had stolen, and then, pushing the two through the gaping crowd, he marched them down to his stone jail and locked them up.

Obviously the serious side of this incident was entirely lost upon the highly entertained audience. Many and loud were the coarse jokes cracked at the expense of Bass and Miller and after the rude door had closed upon them similar remarks were addressed to Steele's jailer and guard, who in truth, were just as disreputable looking as their prisoners.

Then the crowd returned to their pastimes, leaving their erstwhile comrades to taste the sweets of prison life.

When I got a chance I asked Steele if he could rely on his hired hands, and with a twinkle in his eye which surprised me as much as his reply, he said Miller and Bass would have flown the coop before morning.

He was right. When I reached the lower end of town next morning, the same old crowd, enlarged by other curious men and youths, had come to pay their respects to the new institution.

Jailer and guard were on hand, loud in their proclamations and explanations. Naturally they had fallen asleep, as all other hard working citizens had, and while they slept the prisoners made a hole somewhere and escaped.

Steele examined the hole, and then engaged a stripling of a youth to see if he could crawl through. The youngster essayed the job, stuck in the middle, and was with difficulty extricated.

Whereupon the crowd evinced its delight.

Steele, without more ado, shoved his jailer and guard inside his jail, deliberately closed, barred and chained the iron bolted door, and put the key in his pocket. Then he remained there all day without giving heed to his prisoners' threats.

Toward evening, having gone without drink infinitely longer than was customary, they made appeals, to which Steele was deaf.

He left the jail, however, just before dark, and when we met he told me to be on hand to help him watch that night. We went around the outskirts of town, carrying two heavy double-barreled shotguns Steele had gotten somewhere and taking up a position behind bushes in the lot adjoining the jail; we awaited developments.

Steele was not above paying back these fellows.

All the early part of the evening, gangs of half a dozen men or more came down the street and had their last treat at the expense of the jail guard and jailer. These prisoners yelled for drink—not water but drink, and the more they yelled the more merriment was loosed upon the night air.

About ten o'clock the last gang left, to the despair of the hungry and thirsty prisoners.

Steele and I had hugely enjoyed the fun, and thought the best part of the joke for us was yet to come. The moon had arisen, and though somewhat hazed by clouds, had lightened the night. We were hidden about sixty paces from the jail, a little above it, and we had a fine command of the door.

About eleven o'clock, when all was still, we heard soft steps back of the jail, and soon two dark forms stole round in front. They laid down something that gave forth a metallic clink, like a crowbar. We heard whisperings and then, low, coarse laughs.

Then the rescuers, who undoubtedly were Miller and Bass, set to work to open the door. Softly they worked at first, but as that door had been put there to stay, and they were not fond of hard work, they began to swear and make noises.

Steele whispered to me to wait until the door had been opened, and then when all four presented a good target, to fire both barrels. We could easily have slipped down and captured the rescuers, but that was not Steele's game.

A trick met by a trick; cunning matching craft would be the surest of all ways to command respect.

Four times the workers had to rest, and once they were so enraged at the insistence of the prisoners, who wanted to delay proceedings to send one of them after a bottle, that they swore they would go away and cut the job altogether.

But they were prevailed upon to stay and attack the stout door once more. Finally it yielded, with enough noise to have awakened sleepers a block distant, and forth into the moonlight came rescuers and rescued with low, satisfied grunts of laughter.

Just then Steele and I each discharged both barrels, and the reports blended as one in a tremendous boom.

That little compact bunch disintegrated like quicksilver. Two stumbled over; the others leaped out, and all yelled in pain and terror. Then the fallen ones scrambled up and began to hobble and limp and jerk along after their comrades.

Before the four of them got out of sight they had ceased their yells, but were moving slowly, hanging on to one another in a way that satisfied us they would be lame for many a day.

Next morning at breakfast Dick regaled me with an elaborate story about how the Ranger had turned the tables on the jokers. Evidently in a night the whole town knew it.

Probably a desperate stand of Steele's even to the extreme of killing men, could not have educated these crude natives so quickly into the realization that the Ranger was not to be fooled with.

That morning I went for a ride with the girls, and both had heard something and wanted to know everything. I had become a news-carrier, and Miss Sampson never thought of questioning me in regard to my fund of information.

She showed more than curiosity. The account I gave of the jail affair amused her and made Sally laugh heartily.

Diane questioned me also about a rumor that had come to her concerning George Wright.

He had wounded himself with a gun, it seemed, and though not seriously injured, was not able to go about. He had not been up to the ranch for days.

"I asked papa about him," said, Diane, "and papa laughed like—well, like a regular hyena. I was dumbfounded. Papa's so queer. He looked thunder-clouds at me.

"When I insisted, for I wanted to know, he ripped out: 'Yes, the damn fool got himself shot, and I'm sorry it's not worse.'

"Now, Russ, what do you make of my dad? Cheerful and kind, isn't he?"

I laughed with Sally, but I disclaimed any knowledge of George's accident. I hated the thought of Wright, let alone anything concerning the fatal certainty that sooner or later these cousins of his were to suffer through him.

Sally did not make these rides easy for me, for she was sweeter than anything that has a name. Since the evening of the dance I had tried to avoid her. Either she was sincerely sorry for her tantrum or she was bent upon utterly destroying my peace.

I took good care we were never alone, for in that case, if she ever got into my arms again I would find the ground slipping from under me.

Despite, however, the wear and constant strain of resisting Sally, I enjoyed the ride. There was a charm about being with these girls.

Then perhaps Miss Sampson's growing unconscious curiosity in regard to Steele was no little satisfaction to me.

I pretended a reluctance to speak of the Ranger, but when I did it was to drop a subtle word or briefly tell of an action that suggested such.

I never again hinted the thing that had been such a shock to her. What was in her mind I could not guess; her curiosity, perhaps the greater part, was due to a generous nature not entirely satisfied with itself. She probably had not abandoned her father's estimate of the Ranger but absolute assurance that this was just did not abide with her. For the rest she was like any other girl, a worshipper of the lion in a man, a weaver of romance, ignorant of her own heart.

Not the least talked of and speculated upon of all the details of the jail incident was the part played by Storekeeper Jones, who had informed upon his assailants. Steele and I both awaited results of this significant fact.

When would the town wake up, not only to a little nerve, but to the usefulness of a Ranger?

Three days afterward Steele told me a woman accosted him on the street. She seemed a poor, hardworking person, plain spoken and honest.

Her husband did not drink enough to complain of, but he liked to gamble and he had been fleeced by a crooked game in Jack Martin's saloon. Other wives could make the same complaints. It was God's blessing for such women that Ranger Steele had come to Linrock.

Of course, he could not get back the lost money, but would it be possible to close Martin's place, or at least break up the crooked game?

Steele had asked this woman, whose name was Price, how much her husband had lost, and, being told, he assured her that if he found evidence of cheating, not only would he get back the money, but also he would shut up Martin's place.

Steele instructed me to go that night to the saloon in question and get in the game. I complied, and, in order not to be overcarefully sized up by the dealer, I pretended to be well under the influence of liquor.

By nine o'clock, when Steele strolled in, I had the game well studied, and a more flagrantly crooked one I had never sat in. It was barefaced robbery.

Steele and I had agreed upon a sign from me, because he was not so adept in the intricacies of gambling as I was. I was not in a hurry, however, for there was a little frecklefaced cattleman in the game, and he had been losing, too. He had sold a bunch of stock that day and had considerable money, which evidently he was to be deprived of before he got started for Del Rio.

Steele stood at our backs, and I could feel his presence. He thrilled me. He had some kind of effect on the others, especially the dealer, who was honest enough while the Ranger looked on.

When, however, Steele shifted his attention to other tables and players our dealer reverted to his crooked work. I was about to make a disturbance, when the little cattleman, leaning over, fire in his eye and gun in hand, made it for me.

Evidently he was a keener and nervier gambler than he had been taken for. There might have been gun-play right then if Steele had not interfered.

"Hold on!" he yelled, leaping for our table. "Put up your gun!"

"Who are you?" demanded the cattleman, never moving. "Better keep out of this."

"I'm Steele. Put up your gun."

"You're thet Ranger, hey?" replied the other. "All right! But just a minute. I want this dealer to sit quiet. I've been robbed. And I want my money back."

Certainly the dealer and everyone else round the table sat quiet while the cattleman coolly held his gun leveled.

"Crooked game?" asked Steele, bending over the table. "Show me."

It did not take the aggrieved gambler more than a moment to prove his assertion. Steele, however, desired corroboration from others beside the cattleman, and one by one he questioned them.

To my surprise, one of the players admitted his conviction that the game was not straight.

"What do you say?" demanded Steele of me.

"Worse'n a hold-up, Mr. Ranger," I burst out. "Let me show you."

Deftly I made the dealer's guilt plain to all, and then I seconded the cattleman's angry claim for lost money. The players from other tables gathered round, curious, muttering.

And just then Martin strolled in. His appearance was not prepossessing.

"What's this holler?" he asked, and halted as he saw the cattleman's gun still in line with the dealer.

"Martin, you know what it's for," replied Steele. "Take your dealer and dig— unless you want to see me clean out your place."

Sullen and fierce, Martin stood looking from Steele to the cattleman and then the dealer. Some men in the crowd muttered, and that was a signal for Steele to shove the circle apart and get out, back to the wall.

The cattleman rose slowly in the center, pulling another gun, and he certainly looked business to me.

"Wal, Ranger, I reckon I'll hang round an' see you ain't bothered none," he said. "Friend," he went on, indicating me with a slight wave of one extended gun, "jest rustle the money in sight. We'll square up after the show."

I reached out and swept the considerable sum toward me, and, pocketing it, I too rose, ready for what might come.

"You-all give me elbow room!" yelled Steele at Martin and his cowed contingent.

Steele looked around, evidently for some kind of implement, and, espying a heavy ax in a corner, he grasped it, and, sweeping it to and fro as if it had been a buggy-whip, he advanced on the faro layout. The crowd fell back, edging toward the door.

One crashing blow wrecked the dealer's box and table, sending them splintering among the tumbled chairs. Then the giant Ranger began to spread further ruin about him.

Martin's place was rough and bare, of the most primitive order, and like a thousand other dens of its kind, consisted of a large room with adobe walls, a rude bar of boards, piles of kegs in a corner, a stove, and a few tables with chairs.

Steele required only one blow for each article he struck, and he demolished it. He stove in the head of each keg.

When the dark liquor gurgled out, Martin cursed, and the crowd followed suit. That was a loss!

The little cattleman, holding the men covered, backed them out of the room, Martin needing a plain, stern word to put him out entirely. I went out, too, for I did not want to miss any moves on the part of that gang.

Close behind me came the cattleman, the kind of cool, nervy Texan I liked. He had Martin well judged, too, for there was no evidence of any bold resistance.

But there were shouts and loud acclamations; and these, with the crashing blows of Steele's ax, brought a curious and growing addition to the crowd.

Soon sodden thuds from inside the saloon and red dust pouring out the door told that Steele was attacking the walls of Martin's place. Those adobe bricks when old and crumbly were easily demolished.

Steele made short work of the back wall, and then he smashed out half of the front of the building. That seemed to satisfy him.

When he stepped out of the dust he was wet with sweat, dirty, and disheveled, hot with his exertion—a man whose great stature and muscular development expressed a wonderful physical strength and energy. And his somber face, with the big gray eyes, like open furnaces, expressed a passion equal to his strength.

Perhaps only then did wild and lawless Linrock grasp the real significance of this Ranger.

Steele threw the ax at Martin's feet.

"Martin, don't reopen here," he said curtly. "Don't start another place in Linrock. If you do—jail at Austin for years."

Martin, livid and scowling, yet seemingly dazed with what had occurred, slunk away, accompanied by his cronies. Steele took the money I had appropriated, returned to me what I had lost, did likewise with the cattleman, and then, taking out the sum named by Mrs. Price, he divided the balance with the other players who had been in the game.

Then he stalked off through the crowd as if he knew that men who slunk from facing him would not have nerve enough to attack him even from behind.

"Wal, damn me!" ejaculated the little cattleman in mingled admiration and satisfaction. "So thet's that Texas Ranger, Steele, hey? Never seen him before. All Texas, thet Ranger!"

I lingered downtown as much to enjoy the sensation as to gain the different points of view.

No doubt about the sensation! In one hour every male resident of Linrock and almost every female had viewed the wreck of Martin's place. A fire could not have created half the excitement.

And in that excitement both men and women gave vent to speech they might not have voiced at a calmer moment. The women, at least, were not afraid to talk, and I made mental note of the things they said.

"Did he do it all alone?"

"Thank God a *man's* come to Linrock."

"Good for Molly Price!"

"Oh, it'll make bad times for Linrock."

It almost seemed that all the women were glad, and this was in itself a vindication of the Ranger's idea of law.

The men, however—Blandy, proprietor of the Hope So, and others of his ilk, together with the whole brood of idle gaming loungers, and in fact even storekeepers, ranchers, cowboys—all shook their heads sullenly or doubtfully.

Striking indeed now was the absence of any joking. Steele had showed his hand, and, as one gambler said: "It's a hard hand to call."

The truth was, this Ranger Service was hateful to the free-and-easy Texan who lived by anything except hard and honest work, and it was damnably hateful to the lawless class. Steele's authority, now obvious to all, was unlimited; it could go as far as he had power to carry it.

From present indications that power might be considerable. The work of native sheriffs and constables in western Texas had been a farce, an utter failure. If an honest native of a community undertook to be a sheriff he became immediately a target for rowdy cowboys and other vicious elements.

Many a town south and west of San Antonio owed its peace and prosperity to Rangers, and only to them. They had killed or driven out the criminals. They interpreted the law for themselves, and it was only such an attitude toward law—the stern, uncompromising, implacable extermination of the lawless—that was going to do for all Texas what it had done for part.

Steele was the driving wedge that had begun to split Linrock—split the honest from dominance by the dishonest. To be sure, Steele might be killed at any moment, and that contingency was voiced in the growl of one sullen man who said: "Wot the hell are we up against? Ain't somebody goin' to plug this Ranger?"

It was then that the thing for which Steele stood, the Ranger Service—to help, to save, to defend, to punish, with such somber menace of death as seemed embodied in his cold attitude toward resistance—took hold of Linrock and sunk deep into both black and honest hearts.

It was what was behind Steele that seemed to make him more than an officer—a man.

I could feel how he began to loom up, the embodiment of a powerful force— the Ranger Service—the fame of which, long known to this lawless Pecos gang, but scouted as a vague and distant thing, now became an actuality, a Ranger in the flesh, whose surprising attributes included both the law and the enforcement of it.

When I reached the ranch the excitement had preceded me. Miss Sampson and Sally, both talking at once, acquainted me with the fact that they had been in a store on the main street a block or more from Martin's place.

They had seen the crowd, heard the uproar; and, as they had been hurriedly started toward home by their attendant Dick, they had encountered Steele stalking by.

"He looked grand!" exclaimed Sally.

Then I told the girls the whole story in detail.

"Russ, is it true, just as you tell it?" inquired Diane earnestly.

"Absolutely. I know Mrs. Price went to Steele with her trouble. I was in Martin's place when he entered. Also I was playing in the crooked game. And I saw him wreck Martin's place. Also, I heard him forbid Martin to start another place in Linrock."

"Then he does do splendid things," she said softly, as if affirming to herself.

I walked on then, having gotten a glimpse of Colonel Sampson in the background. Before I reached the corrals Sally came running after me, quite flushed and excited.

"Russ, my uncle wants to see you," she said. "He's in a bad temper. Don't lose yours, please."

She actually took my hand. What a child she was, in all ways except that fatal propensity to flirt. Her statement startled me out of any further thought of her. Why did Sampson want to see me? He never noticed me. I dreaded facing him—not from fear, but because I must see more and more of the signs of guilt in Diane's father.

He awaited me on the porch. As usual, he wore riding garb, but evidently he had not been out so far this day. He looked worn. There was a furtive shadow in his eyes. The haughty, imperious temper, despite Sally's conviction, seemed to be in abeyance.

"Russ, what's this I hear about Martin's saloon being cleaned out?" he asked. "Dick can't give particulars."

Briefly and concisely I told the colonel exactly what had happened. He chewed his cigar, then spat it out with an unintelligible exclamation.

"Martin's no worse than others," he said. "Blandy leans to crooked faro. I've tried to stop that, anyway. If Steele can, more power to him!"

Sampson turned on his heel then and left me with a queer feeling of surprise and pity.

He had surprised me before, but he had never roused the least sympathy. It was probably that Sampson was indeed powerless, no matter what his position.

I had known men before who had become involved in crime, yet were too manly to sanction a crookedness they could not help.

Miss Sampson had been standing in her door. I could tell she had heard; she looked agitated. I knew she had been talking to her father.

"Russ, he hates the Ranger," she said. "That's what I fear. It'll bring trouble on us. Besides, like everybody here, he's biased. He can't see anything good in Steele. Yet he says: 'More power to him!' I'm mystified, and, oh, I'm between two fires!"

Steele's next noteworthy achievement was as new to me as it was strange to Linrock. I heard a good deal about it from my acquaintances, some little from Steele, and the concluding incident I saw and heard myself.

Andy Vey was a broken-down rustler whose activity had ceased and who spent his time hanging on at the places frequented by younger and better men of his kind. As he was a parasite, he was often thrown out of the dens.

Moreover, it was an open secret that he had been a rustler, and the men with whom he associated had not yet, to most of Linrock, become known as such.

One night Vey had been badly beaten in some back room of a saloon and carried out into a vacant lot and left there. He lay there all that night and all the next day. Probably he would have died there had not Steele happened along.

The Ranger gathered up the crippled rustler, took him home, attended to his wounds, nursed him, and in fact spent days in the little adobe house with him.

During this time I saw Steele twice, at night out in our rendezvous. He had little to communicate, but was eager to hear when I had seen Jim Hoden, Morton, Wright, Sampson, and all I could tell about them, and the significance of things in town.

Andy Vey recovered, and it was my good fortune to be in the Hope So when he came in and addressed a crowd of gamesters there.

"Fellers," he said, "I'm biddin' good-by to them as was once my friends. I'm leavin' Linrock. An' I'm askin' some of you to take thet good-by an' a partin' word to them as did me dirt.

"I ain't a-goin' to say if I'd crossed the trail of this Ranger years ago thet I'd of turned round an' gone straight. But mebbe I would—mebbe. There's a hell of a lot a man doesn't know till too late. I'm old now, ready fer the bone pile, an' it doesn't matter. But I've got a head on me yet, an' I want to give a hunch to thet gang who done me. An' that hunch wants to go around an' up to the big guns of Pecos.

"This Texas Star Ranger was the feller who took me in. I'd of died like a poisoned coyote but fer him. An' he talked to me. He gave me money to git out of Pecos. Mebbe everybody'll think he helped me because he wanted me to squeal. To squeal who's who round these rustler diggin's. Wal, he never asked me. Mebbe he seen I wasn't a squealer. But I'm thinkin' he wouldn't ask a feller thet nohow.

"An' here's my hunch. Steele has spotted the outfit. Thet ain't so much, mebbe. But I've been with him, an' I'm old figgerin' men. Jest as sure as God made little apples he's a goin' to put thet outfit through—or he's a-goin' to kill them!"

Chapter 6

ENTER JACK BLOME

Strange that the narrating of this incident made Diane Sampson unhappy.

When I told her she exhibited one flash of gladness, such as any woman might have shown for a noble deed and then she became thoughtful, almost gloomy, sad. I could not understand her complex emotions. Perhaps she contrasted Steele with her father; perhaps she wanted to believe in Steele and dared not; perhaps she had all at once seen the Ranger in his true light, and to her undoing.

She bade me take Sally for a ride and sought her room. I had my misgivings when I saw Sally come out in that trim cowgirl suit and look at me as if to say this day would be my Waterloo.

But she rode hard and long ahead of me before she put any machinations into effect. The first one found me with a respectful demeanor but an internal conflict.

"Russ, tighten my cinch," she said when I caught up with her.

Dismounting, I drew the cinch up another hole and fastened it.

"My boot's unlaced, too," she added, slipping a shapely foot out of the stirrup.

To be sure, it was very much unlaced. I had to take off my gloves to lace it up, and I did it heroically, with bent head and outward calm, when all the time I was mad to snatch the girl out of the saddle and hold her tight or run off with her or do some other fool thing.

"Russ, I believe Diane's in love with Steele," she said soberly, with the sweet confidence she sometimes manifested in me.

"Small wonder. It's in the air," I replied.

She regarded me doubtfully.

"It was," she retorted demurely.

"The fickleness of women is no new thing to me. I didn't expect Waters to last long."

"Certainly not when there are nicer fellows around. One, anyway, when he cares."

A little brown hand slid out of its glove and dropped to my shoulder.

"Make up. You've been hateful lately. Make up with me."

It was not so much what she said as the sweet tone of her voice and the nearness of her that made a tumult within me. I felt the blood tingle to my face.

"Why should I make up with you?" I queried in self defense. "You are only flirting. You won't—you can't ever be anything to me, really."

Sally bent over me and I had not the nerve to look up.

"Never mind things—really," she replied. "The future's far off. Let it alone. We're together. I—I like you, Russ. And I've got to be—to be loved. There. I never confessed that to any other man. You've been hateful when we might have had such fun. The rides in the sun, in the open with the wind in our faces. The walks at night in the moonlight. Russ, haven't you missed something?"

The sweetness and seductiveness of her, the little luring devil of her, irresistible as they were, were no more irresistible than the naturalness, the truth of her.

I trembled even before I looked up into her flushed face and arch eyes; and after that I knew if I could not frighten her out of this daring mood I would have to yield despite my conviction that she only trifled. As my manhood, as well as duty to Steele, forced me to be unyielding, all that was left seemed to be to frighten her.

The instant this was decided a wave of emotion—love, regret, bitterness, anger—surged over me, making me shake. I felt the skin on my face tighten and chill. I grasped her with strength that might have need to hold a plunging, unruly horse. I hurt her. I held her as in a vise.

And the action, the feel of her, her suddenly uttered cry wrought against all pretense, hurt me as my brutality hurt her, and then I spoke what was hard, passionate truth.

"Girl, you're playing with fire!" I cried out hoarsely. "I love you—love you as I'd want my sister loved. I asked you to marry me. That was proof, if it was foolish. Even if you were on the square, which you're not, we couldn't ever be anything to each other. Understand? There's a reason, besides your being above me. I can't stand it. Stop playing with me or I'll—I'll..."

Whatever I meant to say was not spoken, for Sally turned deathly white, probably from my grasp and my looks as well as my threat.

I let go of her, and stepping back to my horse choked down my emotion.

"Russ!" she faltered, and there was womanliness and regret trembling with the fear in her voice. "I—I am on the square."

That had touched the real heart of the girl.

"If you are, then play the game square," I replied darkly.

"I will, Russ, I promise. I'll never tease or coax you again. If I do, then I'll deserve what you—what I get. But, Russ, don't think me a—a four-flush."

All the long ride home we did not exchange another word. The traveling gait of Sally's horse was a lope, that of mine a trot; and therefore, to my relief, she was always out in front.

As we neared the ranch, however, Sally slowed down until I caught up with her; and side by side we rode the remainder of the way. At the corrals, while I unsaddled, she lingered.

"Russ, you didn't tell me if you agreed with me about Diane," she said finally.

"Maybe you're right. I hope she's fallen in love with Steele. Lord knows I hope so," I blurted out.

I bit my tongue. There was no use in trying to be as shrewd with women as I was with men. I made no reply.

"Misery loves company. Maybe that's why," she added. "You told me Steele lost his head over Diane at first sight. Well, we all have company. Good night, Russ."

That night I told Steele about the singular effect the story of his treatment of Vey had upon Miss Sampson. He could not conceal his feelings. I read him like an open book.

If she was unhappy because he did something really good, then she was unhappy because she was realizing she had wronged him.

Steele never asked questions, but the hungry look in his eyes was enough to make even a truthful fellow exaggerate things.

I told him how Diane was dressed, how her face changed with each emotion, how her eyes burned and softened and shadowed, how her voice had been deep and full when she admitted her father hated him, how much she must have meant when she said she was between two fires. I divined how he felt and I tried to satisfy in some little measure his craving for news of her.

When I had exhausted my fund and stretched my imagination I was rewarded by being told that I was a regular old woman for gossip.

Much taken back by this remarkable statement I could but gape at my comrade. Irritation had followed shortly upon his curiosity and pleasure, and then the old sane mind reasserted itself, the old stern look, a little sad now, replaced the glow, the strange eagerness of youth on his face.

"Son, I beg your pardon," he said, with his hand on my shoulder. "We're Rangers, but we can't help being human. To speak right out, it seems two sweet and lovable girls have come, unfortunately for us all, across the dark trail we're on. Let us find what solace we can in the hope that somehow, God only knows how, in doing our duty as Rangers we may yet be doing right by these two innocent girls. I ask you, as my friend, please do not speak again to me of—Miss Sampson."

I left him and went up the quiet trail with the thick shadows all around me and the cold stars overhead; and I was sober in thought, sick at heart for him as much as for myself, and I tortured my mind in fruitless conjecture as to what the end of this strange and fateful adventure would be.

I discovered that less and less the old wild spirit abided with me and I become conscious of a dull, deep-seated ache in my breast, a pang in the bone.

From that day there was a change in Diane Sampson. She became feverishly active. She wanted to ride, to see for herself what was going on in Linrock, to learn of that wild Pecos county life at first hand.

She made such demands on my time now that I scarcely ever found an hour to be with or near Steele until after dark. However, as he was playing a waiting game on the rustlers, keeping out of the resorts for the present, I had not great cause for worry. Hoden was slowly gathering men together, a band of trustworthy ones, and until this organization was complete and ready, Steele thought better to go slow.

It was of little use for me to remonstrate with Miss Sampson when she refused to obey a distracted and angry father. I began to feel sorry for Sampson. He was an unscrupulous man, but he loved this daughter who belonged to another and better and past side of his life.

I heard him appeal to her to go back to Louisiana; to let him take her home, giving as urgent reason the probability of trouble for him. She could not help, could only handicap him.

She agreed to go, provided he sold his property, took the best of his horses and went with her back to the old home to live there the rest of their lives. He replied with considerable feeling that he wished he could go, but it was impossible. Then that settled the matter for her, she averred.

Failing to persuade her to leave Linrock, he told her to keep to the ranch. Naturally, in spite of his anger, Miss Sampson refused to obey; and she frankly told him that it was the free, unfettered life of the country, the riding here and there that appealed so much to her.

Sampson came to me a little later and his worn face showed traces of internal storm.

"Russ, for a while there I wanted to get rid of you," he said. "I've changed. Diane always was a spoiled kid. Now she's a woman. Something's fired her blood. Maybe it's this damned wild country. Anyway, she's got the bit between her teeth. She'll run till she's run herself out.

"Now, it seems the safety of Diane, and Sally, too, has fallen into your hands. The girls won't have one of my cowboys near them. Lately they've got shy of George, too. Between you and me I want to tell you that conditions here in Pecos are worse than they've seemed since you-all reached the ranch. But bad work will break out again—it's coming soon.

"I can't stop it. The town will be full of the hardest gang in western Texas. My daughter and Sally would not be safe if left alone to go anywhere. With you, perhaps, they'll be safe. Can I rely on you?"

"Yes, Sampson, you sure can," I replied. "I'm on pretty good terms with most everybody in town. I think I can say none of the tough set who hang out down there would ever made any move while I'm with the girls. But I'll be pretty careful to avoid them, and particularly strange fellows who may come riding in.

"And if any of them do meet us and start trouble, I'm going for my gun, that's all. There won't be any talk."

"Good! I'll back you," Sampson replied. "Understand, Russ, I didn't want you here, but I always had you sized up as a pretty hard nut, a man not to be trifled with. You've got a bad name. Diane insists the name's not deserved. She'd trust you with herself under any circumstances. And the kid, Sally, she'd be fond of you if it wasn't for the drink. Have you been drunk a good deal? Straight now, between you and me."

"Not once," I replied.

"George's a liar then. He's had it in for you since that day at Sanderson. Look out you two don't clash. He's got a temper, and when he's drinking he's a devil. Keep out of his way."

"I've stood a good deal from Wright, and guess I can stand more."

"All right, Russ," he continued, as if relieved. "Chuck the drink and cards for a while and keep an eye on the girls. When my affairs straighten out maybe I'll make you a proposition."

Sampson left me material for thought. Perhaps it was not only the presence of a Ranger in town that gave him concern, nor the wilfulness of his daughter. There must be internal strife in the rustler gang with which we had associated him.

Perhaps a menace of publicity, rather than risk, was the cause of the wearing strain on him. I began to get a closer insight into Sampson, and in the absence of any conclusive evidence of his personal baseness I felt pity for him.

In the beginning he had opposed me just because I did not happen to be a cowboy he had selected. This latest interview with me, amounting in some instances to confidence, proved absolutely that he had not the slightest suspicion that I was otherwise than the cowboy I pretended to be.

Another interesting deduction was that he appeared to be out of patience with Wright. In fact, I imagined I sensed something of fear and distrust in this spoken attitude toward his relative. Not improbably here was the internal strife between Sampson and Wright, and there flashed into my mind, absolutely without reason, an idea that the clash was over Diane Sampson.

I scouted this intuitive idea as absurd; but, just the same, it refused to be dismissed.

As I turned my back on the coarse and exciting life in the saloons and gambling hells, and spent all my time except when sleeping, out in the windy open under blue sky and starry heaven, my spirit had an uplift.

I was glad to be free of that job. It was bad enough to have to go into these dens to arrest men, let alone living with them, almost being one.

Diane Sampson noted a change in me, attributed it to the absence of the influence of drink, and she was glad. Sally made no attempt to conceal her happiness; and to my dismay, she utterly failed to keep her promise not to tease or tempt me further.

She was adorable, distracting.

We rode every day and almost all day. We took our dinner and went clear to the foothills to return as the sun set. We visited outlying ranches, water-holes, old adobe houses famous in one way or another as scenes of past fights of rustlers and ranchers.

We rode to the little village of Sampson, and half-way to Sanderson, and all over the country.

There was no satisfying Miss Sampson with rides, new places, new faces, new adventures. And every time we rode out she insisted on first riding through Linrock; and every time we rode home she insisted on going back that way.

We visited all the stores, the blacksmith, the wagon shop, the feed and grain houses—everywhere that she could find excuse for visiting. I had to point out to her all the infamous dens in town, and all the lawless and lounging men we met.

She insisted upon being shown the inside of the Hope So, to the extreme confusion of that bewildered resort.

I pretended to be blind to this restless curiosity. Sally understood the cause, too, and it divided her between a sweet gravity and a naughty humor.

The last, however, she never evinced in sight or hearing of Diane.

It seemed that we were indeed fated to cross the path of Vaughn Steele. We saw him working round his adobe house; then we saw him on horseback. Once we met him face to face in a store.

He gazed steadily into Diane Sampson's eyes and went his way without any sign of recognition. There was red in her face when he passed and white when he had gone.

That day she rode as I had never seen her, risking her life, unmindful of her horse.

Another day we met Steele down in the valley, where, inquiry discovered to us, he had gone to the home of an old cattleman who lived alone and was ill.

Last and perhaps most significant of all these meetings was the one when we were walking tired horses home through the main street of Linrock and came upon Steele just in time to see him in action.

It happened at a corner where the usual slouchy, shirt-sleeved loungers were congregated. They were in high glee over the predicament of one ruffian who had purchased or been given a poor, emaciated little burro that was on his last legs. The burro evidently did not want to go with its new owner, who pulled on a halter and then viciously swung the end of the rope to make welts on the worn and scarred back.

If there was one thing that Diane Sampson could not bear it was to see an animal in pain. She passionately loved horses, and hated the sight of a spur or whip.

When we saw the man beating the little burro she cried out to me:

"Make the brute stop!"

I might have made a move had I not on the instant seen Steele heaving into sight round the corner.

Just then the fellow, whom I now recognized to be a despicable character named Andrews, began to bestow heavy and brutal kicks upon the body of the little burro. These kicks sounded deep, hollow, almost like the boom of a drum.

The burro uttered the strangest sound I ever heard issue from any beast and it dropped in its tracks with jerking legs that told any horseman what had happened. Steele saw the last swings of Andrews' heavy boot. He yelled. It was a sharp yell that would have made anyone start. But it came too late, for the burro had dropped.

Steele knocked over several of the jeering men to get to Andrews. He kicked the fellow's feet from under him, sending him hard to the ground.

Then Steele picked up the end of the halter and began to swing it powerfully. Resounding smacks mingled with hoarse bellows of fury and pain. Andrews flopped here and there, trying to arise, but every time the heavy knotted halter beat him down.

Presently Steele stopped. Andrews rose right in front of the Ranger, and there, like the madman he was, he went for his gun.

But it scarcely leaped from its holster when Steele's swift hand intercepted it. Steele clutched Andrews' arm.

Then came a wrench, a cracking of bones, a scream of agony.

The gun dropped into the dust; and in a moment of wrestling fury Andrews, broken, beaten down, just able to moan, lay beside it.

Steele, so cool and dark for a man who had acted with such passionate swiftness, faced the others as if to dare them to move. They neither moved nor spoke, and then he strode away.

Miss Sampson did not speak a word while we were riding the rest of the way home, but she was strangely white of face and dark of eye. Sally could not speak fast enough to say all she felt.

And I, of course, had my measure of feelings. One of them was that as sure as the sun rose and set it was written that Diane Sampson was to love Vaughn Steele.

I could not read her mind, but I had a mind of my own.

How could any woman, seeing this maligned and menaced Ranger, whose life was in danger every moment he spent on the streets, in the light of his action on behalf of a poor little beast, help but wonder and brood over the magnificent height he might reach if he had love—passion—a woman for his inspiration?

It was the day after this incident that, as Sally, Diane, and I were riding homeward on the road from Sampson, I caught sight of a group of dark horses and riders swiftly catching up with us.

We were on the main road, in plain sight of town and passing by ranches; nevertheless, I did not like the looks of the horsemen and grew uneasy. Still, I scarcely thought it needful to race our horses just to reach town a little ahead of these strangers.

Accordingly, they soon caught up with us.

They were five in number, all dark-faced except one, dark-clad and superbly mounted on dark bays and blacks. They had no pack animals and, for that matter, carried no packs at all.

Four of them, at a swinging canter, passed us, and the fifth pulled his horse to suit our pace and fell in between Sally and me.

"Good day," he said pleasantly to me. "Don't mind my ridin' in with you-all, I hope?"

Considering his pleasant approach, I could not but be civil.

He was a singularly handsome fellow, at a quick glance, under forty years, with curly, blond hair, almost gold, a skin very fair for that country, and the keenest, clearest, boldest blue eyes I had ever seen in a man.

"You're Russ, I reckon," he said. "Some of my men have seen you ridin' round with Sampson's girls. I'm Jack Blome."

He did not speak that name with any flaunt or flourish. He merely stated it.

Blome, the rustler! I grew tight all over.

Still, manifestly there was nothing for me to do but return his pleasantry. I really felt less uneasiness after he had made himself known to me. And without any awkwardness, I introduced him to the girls.

He took off his sombrero and made gallant bows to both.

Miss Sampson had heard of him and his record, and she could not help a paleness, a shrinking, which, however, he did not appear to notice. Sally had been dying to meet a real rustler, and here he was, a very prince of rascals.

But I gathered that she would require a little time before she could be natural. Blome seemed to have more of an eye for Sally than for Diane. "Do you like Pecos?" he asked Sally.

"Out here? Oh, yes, indeed!" she replied.

"Like ridin'?"

"I love horses."

Like almost every man who made Sally's acquaintance, he hit upon the subject best calculated to make her interesting to free-riding, outdoor Western men.

That he loved a thoroughbred horse himself was plain. He spoke naturally to Sally with interest, just as I had upon first meeting her, and he might not have been Jack Blome, for all the indication he gave of the fact in his talk.

But the look of the man was different. He was a desperado, one of the dashing, reckless kind—more famous along the Pecos and Rio Grande than more really desperate men. His attire proclaimed a vanity seldom seen in any Westerner except of that unusual brand, yet it was neither gaudy or showy.

One had to be close to Blome to see the silk, the velvet, the gold, the fine leather. When I envied a man's spurs then they were indeed worth coveting.

Blome had a short rifle and a gun in saddle-sheaths. My sharp eye, running over him, caught a row of notches on the bone handle of the big Colt he packed.

It was then that the marshal, the Ranger in me, went hot under the collar. The custom that desperadoes and gun-fighters had of cutting a notch on their guns for every man killed was one of which the mere mention made my gorge rise.

At the edge of town Blome doffed his sombrero again, said "*Adios,*" and rode on ahead of us. And it was then I was hard put to it to keep track of the queries, exclamations, and other wild talk of two very much excited young ladies; I wanted to think; I *needed* to think.

"Wasn't he lovely? Oh, I could adore him!" rapturously uttered Miss Sally Langdon several times, to my ultimate disgust.

Also, after Blome had ridden out of sight, Miss Sampson lost the evident effect of his sinister presence, and she joined Miss Langdon in paying the rustler compliments, too. Perhaps my irritation was an indication of the quick and subtle shifting of my mind to harsher thought.

"Jack Blome!" I broke in upon their adulations. "Rustler and gunman. Did you see the notches on his gun? Every notch for a man he's killed! For weeks reports have come to Linrock that soon as he could get round to it he'd ride down and rid the community of that bothersome fellow, that Texas Ranger! He's come to kill Vaughn Steele!"

Chapter 7

DIANE AND VAUGHN

Then as gloom descended on me with my uttered thought, my heart smote me at Sally's broken: "Oh, Russ! No! No!" Diane Sampson bent dark, shocked eyes upon the hill and ranch in front of her; but they were sightless, they looked into space and eternity, and in them I read the truth suddenly and cruelly revealed to her—she loved Steele!

I found it impossible to leave Miss Sampson with the impression I had given. My own mood fitted a kind of ruthless pleasure in seeing her suffer through love as I had intimation I was to suffer.

But now, when my strange desire that she should love Steele had its fulfilment, and my fiendish subtleties to that end had been crowned with success, I was confounded in pity and the enormity of my crime. For it had been a crime to make, or help to make, this noble and beautiful woman love a Ranger, the enemy of her father, and surely the author of her coming misery. I felt shocked at my work. I tried to hang an excuse on my old motive that through her love we might all be saved. When it was too late, however, I found that this motive was wrong and perhaps without warrant.

We rode home in silence. Miss Sampson, contrary to her usual custom of riding to the corrals or the porch, dismounted at a path leading in among the trees and flowers. "I want to rest, to think before I go in," she said.

Sally accompanied me to the corrals. As our horses stopped at the gate I turned to find confirmation of my fears in Sally's wet eyes.

"Russ," she said, "it's worse than we thought."

"Worse? I should say so," I replied.

"It'll about kill her. She never cared that way for any man. When the Sampson women love, they love."

"Well, you're lucky to be a Langdon," I retorted bitterly.

"I'm Sampson enough to be unhappy," she flashed back at me, "and I'm Langdon enough to have some sense. You haven't any sense or kindness, either. Why'd you want to blurt out that Jack Blome was here to kill Steele?"

"I'm ashamed, Sally," I returned, with hanging head. "I've been a brute. I've wanted her to love Steele. I thought I had a reason, but now it seems silly. Just now I wanted to see how much she did care.

"Sally, the other day you said misery loved company. That's the trouble. I'm sore—bitter. I'm like a sick coyote that snaps at everything. I've wanted you to go into the very depths of despair. But I couldn't send you. So I took out my spite on poor Miss Sampson. It was a damn unmanly thing for me to do."

"Oh, it's not so bad as all that. But you might have been less abrupt. Russ, you seem to take an—an awful tragic view of your—your own case."

"Tragic? Hah!" I cried like the villain in the play. "What other way could I look at it? I tell you I love you so I can't sleep or do anything."

"That's not tragic. When you've no chance, *then* that's tragic."

Sally, as swiftly as she had blushed, could change into that deadly sweet mood. She did both now. She seemed warm, softened, agitated. How could this be anything but sincere? I felt myself slipping; so I laughed harshly.

"Chance! I've no chance on earth."

"Try!" she whispered.

But I caught myself in time. Then the shock of bitter renunciation made it easy for me to simulate anger.

"You promised not to—not to—" I began, choking. My voice was hoarse and it broke, matters surely far removed from pretense.

I had seen Sally Langdon in varying degrees of emotion, but never as she appeared now. She was pale and she trembled a little. If it was not fright, then I could not tell what it was. But there were contrition and earnestness about her, too.

"Russ, I know. I promised not to—to tease—to tempt you anymore," she faltered. "I've broken it. I'm ashamed. I haven't played the game square. But I couldn't—I can't help myself. I've got sense enough not to engage myself to you, but I can't keep from loving you. I can't let you alone. There—if you want it on the square! What's more, I'll go on as I have done unless you keep away from me. I don't care what I deserve—what you do—I will—I will!"

She had begun falteringly and she ended passionately.

Somehow I kept my head, even though my heart pounded like a hammer and the blood drummed in my ears. It was the thought of Steele that saved me. But I felt cold at the narrow margin. I had reached a point, I feared, where a kiss, one touch from this bewildering creature of fire and change and sweetness would make me put her before Steele and my duty.

"Sally, if you dare break your promise again, you'll wish you never had been born," I said with all the fierceness at my command.

"I wish that now. And you can't bluff me, Mr. Gambler. I may have no hand to play, but you can't make me lay it down," she replied.

Something told me Sally Langdon was finding herself; that presently I could not frighten her, and then—then I would be doomed.

"Why, if I got drunk, I might do anything," I said cool and hard now. "Cut off your beautiful chestnut hair for bracelets for my arms."

Sally laughed, but she was still white. She was indeed finding herself. "If you ever get drunk again you can't kiss me any more. And if you don't—you can."

I felt myself shake and, with all of the iron will I could assert, I hid from her the sweetness of this thing that was my weakness and her strength.

"I might lasso you from my horse, drag you through the cactus," I added with the implacability of an Apache.

"Russ!" she cried. Something in this last ridiculous threat had found a vital mark. "After all, maybe those awful stories Joe Harper told about you were true."

"They sure were," I declared with great relief. "And now to forget ourselves. I'm more than sorry I distressed Miss Sampson; more than sorry because what I said wasn't on the square. Blome, no doubt, has come to Linrock after Steele. His intention is to kill him. I said that—let Miss Sampson think it all meant fatality to the Ranger. But, Sally, I don't believe that Blome can kill Steele any more than—than you can."

"Why?" she asked; and she seemed eager, glad.

"Because he's not man enough. That's all, without details. You need not worry; and I wish you'd go tell Miss Sampson—"

"Go yourself," interrupted Sally. "I think she's afraid of my eyes. But she won't fear you'd guess her secret.

"Go to her, Russ. Find some excuse to tell her. Say you thought it over, believed she'd be distressed about what might never happen. Go—and afterward pray for your sins, you queer, good-natured, love-meddling cowboy-devil, you!"

For once I had no retort ready for Sally. I hurried off as quickly as I could walk in chaps and spurs.

I found Miss Sampson sitting on a bench in the shade of a tree. Her pallor and quiet composure told of the conquering and passing of the storm. Always she had a smile for me, and now it smote me, for I in a sense, had betrayed her.

"Miss Sampson," I began, awkwardly yet swiftly, "I—I got to thinking it over, and the idea struck me, maybe you felt bad about this gun-fighter Blome coming down here to kill Steele. At first I imagined you felt sick just because there might be blood spilled. Then I thought you've showed interest in Steele—naturally his kind of Ranger work is bound to appeal to women—you might be sorry it couldn't go on, you might care."

"Russ, don't beat about the bush," she said interrupting my floundering. "You know I care."

How wonderful her eyes were then—great dark, sad gulfs with the soul of a woman at the bottom! Almost I loved her myself; I did love her truth, the woman in her that scorned any subterfuge.

Instantly she inspired me to command over myself. "Listen," I said. "Jack Blome has come here to meet Steele. There will be a fight. But Blome can't kill Steele."

"How is that? Why can't he? You said this Blome was a killer of men. You spoke of notches on his gun. I've heard my father and my cousin, too, speak of Blome's record. He must be a terrible ruffian. If his intent is evil, why will he fail in it?"

"Because, Miss Sampson, when it comes to the last word, Steele will be on the lookout and Blome won't be quick enough on the draw to kill him. That's all."

"Quick enough on the draw? I understand, but I want to know more."

"I doubt if there's a man on the frontier to-day quick enough to kill Steele in an even break. That means a fair fight. This Blome is conceited. He'll make the meeting fair enough. It'll come off about like this, Miss Sampson.

"Blome will send out his bluff—he'll begin to blow—to look for Steele. But Steele will avoid him as long as possible—perhaps altogether, though that's improbable. If they do meet, then Blome must force the issue. It's interesting to figure on that. Steele affects men strangely. It's all very well for this Blome to rant about himself and to hunt Steele up. But the test'll come when he faces the Ranger. He never saw Steele. He doesn't know what he's up against. He knows Steele's reputation, but I don't mean that. I mean Steele in the flesh, his nerve, the something that's in his eyes.

"Now, when it comes to handling a gun the man doesn't breathe who has anything on Steele. There was an outlaw, Duane, who might have killed Steele, had they ever met. I'll tell you Duane's story some day. A girl saved him, made a Ranger of him, then got him to go far away from Texas."

"That was wise. Indeed, I'd like to hear the story," she replied. "Then, after all, Russ, in this dreadful part of Texas life, when man faces man, it's all in the quickness of hand?"

"Absolutely. It's the draw. And Steele's a wonder. See here. Look at this."

I stepped back and drew my gun.

"I didn't see how you did that," she said curiously. "Try it again."

I complied, and still she was not quick enough of eye to see my draw. Then I did it slowly, explaining to her the action of hand and then of finger. She seemed fascinated, as a woman might have been by the striking power of a rattlesnake.

"So men's lives depend on that! How horrible for me to be interested—to ask about it—to watch you! But I'm out here on the frontier now, caught somehow in its wildness, and I feel a relief, a gladness to know Vaughn Steele has the skill you claim. Thank you, Russ."

She seemed about to dismiss me then, for she rose and half turned away. Then she hesitated. She had one hand at her breast, the other on the bench. "Have you been with him—talked to him lately?" she asked, and a faint rose tint came into her cheeks. But her eyes were steady, dark, and deep, and peered through and far beyond me.

"Yes, I've met him a few times, around places."

"Did he ever speak of—of me?"

"Once or twice, and then as if he couldn't help it."

"What did he say?"

"Well, the last time he seemed hungry to hear something about you. He didn't exactly ask, but, all the same, he was begging. So I told him."

"What?"

"Oh, how you were dressed, how you looked, what you said, what you did—all about you. Don't be offended with me, Miss Sampson. It was real charity. I talk too much. It's my weakness. Please don't be offended."

She never heard my apology or my entreaty. There was a kind of glory in her eyes. Looking at her, I found a dimness hazing my sight, and when I rubbed it away it came back.

"Then—what did he say?" This was whispered, almost shyly, and I could scarcely believe the proud Miss Sampson stood before me.

"Why, he flew into a fury, called me an—" Hastily I caught myself. "Well, he said if I wanted to talk to him any more not to speak of you. He was sure unreasonable."

"Russ—you think—you told me once—he—you think he still—" She was not facing me at all now. She had her head bent. Both hands were at her breast, and I saw it heave. Her cheek was white as a flower, her neck darkly, richly red with mounting blood.

I understood. And I pitied her and hated myself and marveled at this thing, love. It made another woman out of Diane Sampson. I could scarcely comprehend that she was asking me, almost beseechingly, for further assurance of Steele's love. I knew nothing of women, but this seemed strange. Then a thought sent the blood chilling back to my heart. Had Diane Sampson guessed the guilt of her father? Was it more for his sake than for her own that she hoped—for surely she hoped—that Steele loved her?

Here was more mystery, more food for reflection. Only a powerful motive or a self-leveling love could have made a woman of Diane Sampson's pride ask such a question. Whatever her reason, I determined to assure her, once and forever, what I knew to be true. Accordingly, I told her in unforgettable words, with my own regard for her and love for Sally filling my voice with emotion, how I could see that Steele loved her, how madly he was destined to love her, how terribly hard that was going to make his work in Linrock.

There was a stillness about her then, a light on her face, which brought to my mind thought of Sally when I had asked her to marry me.

"Russ, I beg you—bring us together," said Miss Sampson. "Bring about a meeting. You are my friend." Then she went swiftly away through the flowers, leaving me there, thrilled to my soul at her betrayal of herself, ready to die in her service, yet cursing the fatal day Vaughn Steele had chosen me for his comrade in this tragic game.

That evening in the girls' sitting-room, where they invited me, I was led into a discourse upon the gun-fighters, outlaws, desperadoes, and bad men of the frontier. Miss Sampson and Sally had been, before their arrival in Texas, as ignorant of such characters as any girls in the North or East. They were now peculiarly interested, fascinated, and at the same time repelled.

Miss Sampson must have placed the Rangers in one of those classes, somewhat as Governor Smith had, and her father, too. Sally thought she was in love with a cowboy whom she had been led to believe had as bad a record as any. They were certainly a most persuasive and appreciative audience. So as it was in regard to horses, if I knew any subject well, it was this one of dangerous and bad men. Texas, and the whole developing Southwest, was full of such characters. It was a very difficult thing to distinguish between fighters who were bad men and fighters who were good men. However, it was no difficult thing for one of my calling to tell the difference between a real bad man and the imitation "four-flush."

Then I told the girls the story of Buck Duane, famous outlaw and Ranger. And I narrated the histories of Murrell, most terrible of blood-spillers ever known to Texas; of Hardin, whose long career of crime ended in the main street in Huntsville when he faced Buck Duane; of Sandobal, the Mexican terror; of Cheseldine, Bland, Alloway, and other outlaws of the Rio Grande; of King Fisher and Thompson and Sterrett, all still living and still busy adding notches to their guns.

I ended my little talk by telling the story of Amos Clark, a criminal of a higher type than most bad men, yet infinitely more dangerous because of that. He was a Southerner of good family. After the war he went to Dimmick County and there developed and prospered with the country. He became the most influential citizen of his town and the richest in that section. He held offices. He was energetic in his opposition to rustlers and outlaws. He was held in high esteem by his countrymen. But this Amos Clark was the leader of a band of rustlers, highwaymen, and murderers.

Captain Neal and some of his Rangers ferreted out Clark's relation to this lawless gang, and in the end caught him red-handed. He was arrested and eventually hanged. His case was unusual, and it furnished an example of what was possible in that wild country. Clark had a son who was honest and a wife whom he dearly loved, both of whom had been utterly ignorant of the other and wicked side of life. I told this last story deliberately, yet with some misgivings. I wanted to see—I convinced myself it was needful for me to see—if Miss Sampson had any suspicion of her father. To look into her face then was no easy task. But when I did I experienced a shock, though not exactly the kind I had prepared myself for.

She knew something; maybe she knew actually more than Steele or I; still, if it were a crime, she had a marvelous control over her true feelings.

Jack Blome and his men had been in Linrock for several days; old Snecker and his son Bo had reappeared, and other hard-looking customers, new to me if not to Linrock. These helped to create a charged and waiting atmosphere. The saloons did unusual business and were never closed. Respectable citizens of the town were awakened in the early dawn by rowdies carousing in the streets.

Steele kept pretty closely under cover. He did not entertain the opinion, nor did I, that the first time he walked down the street he would be a target for Blome and his gang. Things seldom happened that way, and when they did happen so it was more accident than design. Blome was setting the stage for his little drama.

Meanwhile Steele was not idle. He told me he had met Jim Hoden, Morton and Zimmer, and that these men had approached others of like character; a secret club had been formed and all the members were ready for action.

Steele also told me that he had spent hours at night watching the house where George Wright stayed when he was not up at Sampson's. Wright had almost recovered from the injury to his arm, but he still remained most of the time indoors. At night he was visited, or at least his house was, by strange men who were swift, stealthy, mysterious—all men who formerly would not have been friends or neighbors.

Steele had not been able to recognize any of these night visitors, and he did not think the time was ripe for a bold holding up of one of them.

Jim Hoden had forcibly declared and stated that some deviltry was afoot, something vastly different from Blome's open intention of meeting the Ranger.

Hoden was right. Not twenty-four hours after his last talk with Steele, in which he advised quick action, he was found behind the little room of his restaurant, with a bullet hole in his breast, dead. No one could be found who had heard a shot.

It had been deliberate murder, for behind the bar had been left a piece of paper rudely scrawled with a pencil:

"All friends of Ranger Steele look for the same."

Later that day I met Steele at Hoden's and was with him when he looked at the body and the written message which spoke so tersely of the enmity toward him. We left there together, and I hoped Steele would let me stay with him from that moment.

"Russ, it's all in the dark," he said. "I feel Wright's hand in this."

I agreed. "I remember his face at Hoden's that day you winged him. Because Jim swore you were wrong not to kill instead of wing him. You were wrong."

"No, Russ, I never let feeling run wild with my head. We can't prove a thing on Wright."

"Come on; let's hunt him up. I'll bet I can accuse him and make him show his hand. Come on!"

That Steele found me hard to resist was all the satisfaction I got for the anger and desire to avenge Jim Hoden that consumed me.

"Son, you'll have your belly full of trouble soon enough," replied Steele. "Hold yourself in. Wait. Try to keep your eye on Sampson at night. See if anyone visits him. Spy on him. I'll watch Wright."

"Don't you think you'd do well to keep out of town, especially when you sleep?"

"Sure. I've got blankets out in the brush, and I go there every night late and leave before daylight. But I keep a light burning in the 'dobe house and make it look as if I were there."

"Good. That worried me. Now, what's this murder of Jim Hoden going to do to Morton, Zimmer, and their crowd?"

"Russ, they've all got blood in their eyes. This'll make them see red. I've only to say the word and we'll have all the backing we need."

"Have you run into Blome?"

"Once. I was across the street. He came out of the Hope So with some of his gang. They lined up and watched me. But I went right on."

"He's here looking for trouble, Steele."

"Yes; and he'd have found it before this if I just knew his relation to Sampson and Wright."

"Do you think Blome a dangerous man to meet?"

"Hardly. He's a genuine bad man, but for all that he's not much to be feared. If he were quietly keeping away from trouble, then that'd be different. Blome will probably die in his boots, thinking he's the worst man and the quickest one on the draw in the West."

That was conclusive enough for me. The little shadow of worry that had haunted me in spite of my confidence vanished entirely.

"Russ, for the present help me do something for Jim Hoden's family," went on Steele. "His wife's in bad shape. She's not a strong woman. There are a lot of kids, and you know Jim Hoden was poor. She told me her neighbors would keep shy of her now. They'd be afraid. Oh, it's tough! But we can put Jim away decently and help his family."

Several days after this talk with Steele I took Miss Sampson and Sally out to see Jim Hoden's wife and children. I knew Steele would be there that afternoon, but I did not mention this fact to Miss Sampson. We rode down to the little adobe house which belonged to Mrs. Hoden's people, and where Steele and I had moved her and the children after Jim Hoden's funeral. The house was small, but comfortable, and the yard green and shady.

If this poor wife and mother had not been utterly forsaken by neighbors and friends it certainly appeared so, for to my knowledge no one besides Steele and me visited her. Miss Sampson had packed a big basket full of good things to eat, and I carried this in front of me on the pommel as we rode. We hitched our horses to the fence and went round to the back of the house. There was a little porch with a stone flooring, and here several children were playing.

The door stood open. At my knock Mrs. Hoden bade me come in. Evidently Steele was not there, so I went in with the girls.

"Mrs. Hoden, I've brought Miss Sampson and her cousin to see you," I said cheerfully.

The little room was not very light, there being only one window and the door; but Mrs. Hoden could be seen plainly enough as she lay, hollow-cheeked and haggard, on a bed. Once she had evidently been a woman of some comeliness. The ravages of trouble and grief were there to read in her worn face; it had not, however, any of the hard and bitter lines that had characterized her husband's.

I wondered, considering that Sampson had ruined Hoden, how Mrs. Hoden was going to regard the daughter of an enemy.

"So you're Roger Sampson's girl?" queried the woman, with her bright black eyes fixed on her visitor.

"Yes," replied Miss Sampson, simply. "This is my cousin, Sally Langdon. We've come to nurse you, take care of the children, help you in any way you'll let us."

There was a long silence.

"Well, you look a little like Sampson," finally said Mrs. Hoden, "but you're not at all like him. You must take after your mother. Miss Sampson, I don't know if I can—if I *ought* to accept anything from you. Your father ruined my husband."

"Yes, I know," replied the girl sadly. "That's all the more reason you should let me help you. Pray don't refuse. It will—mean so much to me."

If this poor, stricken woman had any resentment it speedily melted in the warmth and sweetness of Miss Sampson's manner. My idea was that the impression of Diane Sampson's beauty was always swiftly succeeded by that of her generosity and nobility. At any rate, she had started well with Mrs. Hoden, and no sooner had she begun to talk to the children than both they and the mother were won.

The opening of that big basket was an event. Poor, starved little beggars! I went out on the porch to get away from them. My feelings seemed too easily aroused. Hard indeed would it have gone with Jim Hoden's slayer if I could have laid my eyes on him then. However, Miss Sampson and Sally, after the nature of tender and practical girls, did not appear to take the sad situation to heart. The havoc had already been wrought in that household. The needs now were cheerfulness, kindness, help, action, and these the girls furnished with a spirit that did me good.

"Mrs. Hoden, who dressed this baby?" presently asked Miss Sampson. I peeped in to see a dilapidated youngster on her knees. That sight, if any other was needed, completed my full and splendid estimate of Diane Sampson.

"Mr. Steele," replied Mrs. Hoden.

"Mr. Steele!" exclaimed Miss Sampson.

"Yes; he's taken care of us all since—since—" Mrs. Hoden choked.

"Oh, so you've had no help but his," replied Miss Sampson hastily. "No women? Too bad! I'll send someone, Mrs. Hoden, and I'll come myself."

"It'll be good of you," went on the older woman. "You see, Jim had few friends—that is, right in town. And they've been afraid to help us—afraid they'd get what poor Jim—"

"That's awful!" burst out Miss Sampson passionately. "A brave lot of friends! Mrs. Hoden, don't you worry any more. We'll take care of you. Here, Sally help me. Whatever is the matter with baby's dress?" Manifestly Miss Sampson had some difficulty in subduing her emotion.

"Why, it's on hind side before," declared Sally. "I guess Mr. Steele hasn't dressed many babies."

"He did the best he could," said Mrs. Hoden. "Lord only knows what would have become of us! He brought your cowboy, Russ, who's been very good too."

"Mr. Steele, then is—is something more than a Ranger?" queried Miss Sampson, with a little break in her voice.

"He's more than I can tell," replied Mrs. Hoden. "He buried Jim. He paid our debts. He fetched us here. He bought food for us. He cooked for us and fed us. He washed and dressed the baby. He sat with me the first two nights after Jim's death, when I thought I'd die myself.

"He's so kind, so gentle, so patient. He has kept me up just by being near. Sometimes I'd wake from a doze an', seeing him there, I'd know how false were all these tales Jim heard about him and believed at first. Why, he plays with the children just—just like any good man might. When he has the baby up I just can't believe he's a bloody gunman, as they say.

"He's good, but he isn't happy. He has such sad eyes. He looks far off sometimes when the children climb round him. They love him. I think he must have loved some woman. His life is sad. Nobody need tell me—he sees the good in things. Once he said somebody had to be a Ranger. Well, I say, thank God for a Ranger like him!"

After that there was a long silence in the little room, broken only by the cooing of the baby. I did not dare to peep in at Miss Sampson then.

Somehow I expected Steele to arrive at that moment, and his step did not surprise me. He came round the corner as he always turned any corner, quick, alert, with his hand down. If I had been an enemy waiting there with a gun I would have needed to hurry. Steele was instinctively and habitually on the defense.

"Hello, son! How are Mrs. Hoden and the youngster to-day?" he asked.

"Hello yourself! Why, they're doing fine! I brought the girls down—"

Then in the semishadow of the room, across Mrs. Hoden's bed, Diane Sampson and Steele faced each other.

That was a moment! Having seen her face then I would not have missed sight of it for anything I could name; never so long as memory remained with me would I forget. She did not speak. Sally, however, bowed and spoke to the Ranger. Steele, after the first start, showed no unusual feeling. He greeted both girls pleasantly.

"Russ, that was thoughtful of you," he said. "It was womankind needed here. I could do so little—Mrs. Hoden, you look better to-day. I'm glad. And here's baby, all clean and white. Baby, what a time I had trying to puzzle out the way your clothes went on! Well, Mrs. Hoden, didn't I tell you friends would come? So will the brighter side."

"Yes; I've more faith than I had," replied Mrs. Hoden. "Roger Sampson's daughter has come to me. There for a while after Jim's death I thought I'd sink. We have nothing. How could I ever take care of my little ones? But I'm gaining courage."

"Mrs. Hoden, do not distress yourself any more," said Miss Sampson. "I shall see you are well cared for. I promise you."

"Miss Sampson, that's fine!" exclaimed Steele, with a ring in his voice. "It's what I'd have hoped—expected of you..."

It must have been sweet praise to her, for the whiteness of her face burned in a beautiful blush.

"And it's good of you, too, Miss Langdon, to come," added Steele. "Let me thank you both. I'm glad I have you girls as allies in part of my lonely task here. More than glad, for the sake of this good woman and the little ones. But both of you be careful. Don't stir without Russ. There's risk. And now I'll be going. Good-by. Mrs. Hoden, I'll drop in again to-night. Good-by!"

Steele backed to the door, and I slipped out before him.

"Mr. Steele—wait!" called Miss Sampson as he stepped out. He uttered a little sound like a hiss or a gasp or an intake of breath, I did not know what; and then the incomprehensible fellow bestowed a kick upon me that I thought about broke my leg. But I understood and gamely endured the pain. Then we were looking at Diane Sampson. She was white and wonderful. She stepped out of the door, close to Steele. She did not see me; she cared nothing for my presence. All the world would not have mattered to her then.

"I have wronged you!" she said impulsively.

Looking on, I seemed to see or feel some slow, mighty force gathering in Steele to meet this ordeal. Then he appeared as always—yet, to me, how different!

"Miss Sampson, how can you say that?" he returned.

"I believed what my father and George Wright said about you—that bloody, despicable record! Now I do *not* believe. I see—I wronged you."

"You make me very glad when you tell me this. It was hard to have you think so ill of me. But, Miss Sampson, please don't speak of wronging me. I am a Ranger, and much said of me is true. My duty is hard on others—sometimes on those who are innocent, alas! But God knows that duty is hard, too, on me."

"I did wrong you. In thought—in word. I ordered you from my home as if you were indeed what they called you. But I was deceived. I see my error. If you entered my home again I would think it an honor. I—"

"Please—please don't, Miss Sampson," interrupted poor Steele. I could see the gray beneath his bronze and something that was like gold deep in his eyes.

"But, sir, my conscience flays me," she went on. There was no other sound like her voice. If I was all distraught with emotion, what must Steele have been? "I make amends. Will you take my hand? Will you forgive me?" She gave it royally, while the other was there pressing at her breast.

Steele took the proffered hand and held it, and did not release it. What else could he have done? But he could not speak. Then it seemed to dawn upon Steele there was more behind this white, sweet, noble intensity of her than just making amends for a fancied or real wrong. For myself, I thought the man did not live on earth who could have resisted her then. And there was resistance; I felt it; she must have felt it. It was poor Steele's hard fate to fight the charm and eloquence and sweetness of this woman when, for some reason unknown to him, and only guessed at by me, she was burning with all the fire and passion of her soul.

"Mr. Steele, I honor you for your goodness to this unfortunate woman," she said, and now her speech came swiftly. "When she was all alone and helpless you were her friend. It was the deed of a man. But Mrs. Hoden isn't the only unfortunate woman in the world. I, too, am unfortunate. Ah, how I may soon need a friend!

"Vaughn Steele, the man whom I need most to be my friend—want most to lean upon—is the one whose duty is to stab me to the heart, to ruin me. You! Will you be my friend? If you knew Diane Sampson you would know she would never ask you to be false to your duty. Be true to us both! I'm so alone—no one but Sally loves me. I'll need a friend soon—soon.

"Oh, I know—I know what you'll find out sooner or later. I know *now*! I want to help you. Let us save life, if not honor. Must I stand alone—all alone? Will you—will you be—"

Her voice failed. She was swaying toward Steele. I expected to see his arms spread wide and enfold her in their embrace.

"Diane Sampson, I love you!" whispered Steele hoarsely, white now to his lips. "I must be true to my duty. But if I can't be true to you, then by God, I want no more of life!" He kissed her hand and rushed away.

She stood a moment as if blindly watching the place where he had vanished, and then as a sister might have turned to a brother, she reached for me.

Chapter 8

THE EAVESDROPPER

We silently rode home in the gathering dusk. Miss Sampson dismounted at the porch, but Sally went on with me to the corrals. I felt heavy and somber, as if a catastrophe was near at hand.

"Help me down," said Sally. Her voice was low and tremulous.

"Sally, did you hear what Miss Sampson said to Steele?" I asked.

"A little, here and there. I heard Steele tell her he loved her. Isn't this a terrible mix?"

"It sure is. Did you hear—do you understand why she appealed to Steele, asked him to be her friend?"

"Did she? No, I didn't hear that. I heard her say she had wronged him. Then I tried not to hear any more. Tell me."

"No Sally; it's not my secret. I wish I could do something—help them somehow. Yes, it's sure a terrible mix. I don't care so much about myself."

"Nor me," Sally retorted.

"You! Oh, you're only a shallow spoiled child! You'd cease to love anything the moment you won it. And I—well, I'm no good, you say. But their love! My God, what a tragedy! You've no idea, Sally. They've hardly spoken to each other, yet are ready to be overwhelmed."

Sally sat so still and silent that I thought I had angered or offended her. But I did not care much, one way or another. Her coquettish fancy for me and my own trouble had sunk into insignificance. I did not look up at her, though she was so close I could feel her little, restless foot touching me. The horses in the corrals were trooping up to the bars. Dusk had about given place to night, although in the west a broad flare of golden sky showed bright behind dark mountains.

"So I say you're no good?" asked Sally after a long silence. Then her voice and the way her hand stole to my shoulder should have been warning for me. But it was not, or I did not care.

"Yes, you said that, didn't you?" I replied absently.

"I can change my mind, can't I? Maybe you're only wild and reckless when you drink. Mrs. Hoden said such nice things about you. They made me feel so good."

I had no reply for that and still did not look up at her. I heard her swing herself around in the saddle. "Lift me down," she said.

Perhaps at any other time I would have remarked that this request was rather unusual, considering the fact that she was very light and sure of action, extremely proud of it, and likely to be insulted by an offer of assistance. But my spirit was dead. I reached for her hands, but they eluded mine, slipped up my arms as she came sliding out of the saddle, and then her face was very close to mine. "Russ!" she whispered. It was torment, wistfulness, uncertainty, and yet tenderness all in one little whisper. It caught me off guard or indifferent to consequences. So I kissed her, without passion, with all regret and sadness. She uttered a little cry that might have been mingled exultation and remorse for her victory and her broken faith. Certainly the instant I kissed her she remembered the latter. She trembled against me, and leaving unsaid something she had meant to say, she slipped out of my arms and ran. She assuredly was frightened, and I thought it just as well that she was.

Presently she disappeared in the darkness and then the swift little clinks of her spurs ceased. I laughed somewhat ruefully and hoped she would be satisfied. Then I put away the horses and went in for my supper.

After supper I noisily bustled around my room, and soon stole out for my usual evening's spying. The night was dark, without starlight, and the stiff wind rustled the leaves and tore through the vines on the old house. The fact that I had seen and heard so little during my constant vigilance did not make me careless or the task monotonous. I had so much to think about that sometimes I sat in one place for hours and never knew where the time went.

This night, the very first thing, I heard Wright's well-known footsteps, and I saw Sampson's door open, flashing a broad bar of light into the darkness. Wright crossed the threshold, the door closed, and all was dark again outside. Not a ray of light escaped from the window. This was the first visit of Wright for a considerable stretch of time. Little doubt there was that his talk with Sampson would be interesting to me.

I tiptoed to the door and listened, but I could hear only a murmur of voices. Besides, that position was too risky. I went round the corner of the house. Some time before I had made a discovery that I imagined would be valuable to me. This side of the big adobe house was of much older construction than the back and larger part. There was a narrow passage about a foot wide between the old and new walls, and this ran from the outside through to the patio. I had discovered the entrance by accident, as it was concealed by vines and shrubbery. I crawled in there, upon an opportune occasion, with the intention of boring a small hole through the adobe bricks. But it was not necessary to do that, for the wall was cracked; and in one place I could see into Sampson's room. This passage now afforded me my opportunity, and I decided to avail myself of it in spite of the very great danger. Crawling on my hands and knees very stealthily, I got under the shrubbery to the entrance of the passage. In the blackness a faint streak of light showed the location of the crack in the wall.

I had to slip in sidewise. It was a tight squeeze, but I entered without the slightest sound. If my position were to be betrayed it would not be from noise. As I progressed the passage grew a very little wider in that direction, and this fact gave rise to the thought that in case of a necessary and hurried exit I would do best by working toward the patio. It seemed a good deal of time was consumed in reaching my vantage-point. When I did get there the crack was a foot over my head. If I had only been tall like Steele! There was nothing to do but find toe-holes in the crumbling walls, and by bracing knees on one side, back against the other, hold myself up to the crack.

Once with my eye there I did not care what risk I ran. Sampson appeared disturbed; he sat stroking his mustache; his brow was clouded. Wright's face seemed darker, more sullen, yet lighted by some indomitable resolve.

"We'll settle both deals to-night," Wright was saying. "That's what I came for. That's why I've asked Snecker and Blome to be here."

"But suppose I don't choose to talk here?" protested Sampson impatiently. "I never before made my house a place to—"

"We've waited long enough. This place's as good as any. You've lost your nerve since that Ranger hit the town. First, now, will you give Diane to me?"

"George, you talk like a spoiled boy. Give Diane to you! Why, she's a woman and I'm finding out that she's got a mind of her own. I told you I was willing for her to marry you. I tried to persuade her. But Diane hasn't any use for you now. She liked you at first; but now she doesn't. So what can I do?"

"You can make her marry me," replied Wright.

"Make that girl do what she doesn't want to? It couldn't be done, even if I tried. And I don't believe I'll try. I haven't the highest opinion of you as a prospective son-in-law, George. But if Diane loved you I would consent. We'd all go away together before this damned miserable business is out. Then she'd never know. And maybe you might be more like you used to be before the West ruined you. But as matters stand you fight your own game with her; and I'll tell you now, you'll lose."

"What'd you want to let her come out here for?" demanded Wright hotly. "It was a dead mistake. I've lost my head over her. I'll have her or die. Don't you think if she was my wife I'd soon pull myself together? Since she came we've none of us been right. And the gang has put up a holler. No, Sampson, we've got to settle things to-night."

"Well, we can settle what Diane's concerned in right now," replied Sampson, rising. "Come on; we'll go ask her. See where you stand."

They went out, leaving the door open. I dropped down to rest myself and to wait. I would have liked to hear Miss Sampson's answer to him. But I could guess what it would be. Wright appeared to be all I had thought of him, and I believed I was going to find out presently that he was worse. Just then I wanted Steele as never before. Still, he was too big to worm his way into this place.

The men seemed to be absent a good while, though that feeling might have been occasioned by my interest and anxiety. Finally I heard heavy steps. Wright came in alone. He was leaden-faced, humiliated. Then something abject in him gave place to rage. He strode the room; he cursed.

Sampson returned, now appreciably calmer. I could not but decide that he felt relief at the evident rejection of Wright's proposal. "Don't fume about it, George," he said. "You see I can't help it. We're pretty wild out here, but I can't rope my daughter and give her to you as I would an unruly steer."

"Sampson, I can *make* her marry me," declared Wright thickly.

"How?"

"You know the hold I got on you—the deal that made you boss of this rustler gang?"

"It isn't likely I'd forget," replied Sampson grimly.

"I can go to Diane—tell her that—make her believe I'd tell it broadcast, tell this Ranger Steele, unless she'd marry me!" Wright spoke breathlessly, with haggard face and shadowed eyes. He had no shame. He was simply in the grip of passion. Sampson gazed with dark, controlled fury at his relative. In that look I saw a strong, unscrupulous man fallen into evil ways, but still a man. It betrayed Wright to be the wild and passionate weakling.

I seemed to see also how, during all the years of association, this strong man had upheld the weak one. But that time had gone forever, both in intent on Sampson's part and in possibility. Wright, like the great majority of evil and unrestrained men on the border, had reached a point where influence was futile. Reason had degenerated. He saw only himself.

"But, George, Diane's the one person on earth who must never know I'm a rustler, a thief, a red-handed ruler of the worst gang on the border," replied Sampson impressively.

George bowed his head at that, as if the significance had just occurred to him. But he was not long at a loss. "She's going to find it out sooner or later. I tell you she knows now there's something wrong out here. She's got eyes. And that meddling cowboy of hers is smarter than you give him credit for. They're always together. You'll regret the day Russ ever straddled a horse on this ranch. Mark what I say."

"Diane's changed, I know; but she hasn't any idea yet that her daddy's a boss rustler. Diane's concerned about what she calls my duty as mayor. Also I think she's not satisfied with my explanations in regard to certain property."

Wright halted in his restless walk and leaned against the stone mantelpiece. He squared himself as if this was his last stand. He looked desperate, but on the moment showed an absence of his usual nervous excitement. "Sampson, that may well be true," he said. "No doubt all you say is true. But it doesn't help me. I want the girl. If I don't get her I reckon we'll all go to hell!" He might have meant anything, probably meant the worst. He certainly had something more in mind.

Sampson gave a slight start, barely perceptible like the twitch of an awakening tiger. He sat there, head down, stroking his mustache. Almost I saw his thought. I had long experience in reading men under stress of such emotion. I had no means to vindicate my judgment, but my conviction was that Sampson right then and there decided that the thing to do was to kill Wright. For my part, I wondered that he had not come to such a conclusion before. Not improbably the advent of his daughter had put Sampson in conflict with himself.

Suddenly he threw off a somber cast of countenance and began to talk. He talked swiftly, persuasively, yet I imagined he was talking to smooth Wright's passion for the moment. Wright no more caught the fateful significance of a line crossed, a limit reached, a decree decided, than if he had not been present. He was obsessed with himself.

How, I wondered, had a man of his mind ever lived so long and gone so far among the exacting conditions of Pecos County? The answer was perhaps, that Sampson had guided him, upheld him, protected him. The coming of Diane Sampson had been the entering wedge of dissension.

"You're too impatient," concluded Sampson. "You'll ruin any chance of happiness if you rush Diane. She might be won. If you told her who I am she'd hate you forever. She might marry you to save me, but she'd hate you.

"That isn't the way. Wait. Play for time. Be different with her. Cut out your drinking. She despises that. Let's plan to sell out here, stock, ranch, property, and leave the country. Then you'd have a show with her."

"I told you we've got to stick," growled Wright. "The gang won't stand for our going. It can't be done unless you want to sacrifice everything."

"You mean double-cross the men? Go without their knowing? Leave them here to face whatever comes?"

"I mean just that."

"I'm bad enough, but not that bad," returned Sampson. "If I can't get the gang to let me off I'll stay and face the music. All the same, Wright, did it ever strike you that most of our deals the last few years have been yours?"

"Yes. If I hadn't rung them in, there wouldn't have been any. You've had cold feet, Owens says, especially since this Ranger Steele has been here."

"Well, call it cold feet if you like. But I call it sense. We reached our limit long ago. We began by rustling a few cattle at a time when rustling was laughed at. But as our greed grew so did our boldness. Then came the gang, the regular trips, and one thing and another till, before we knew it—before *I* knew it, we had shady deals, hold-ups, and murders on our record. Then we had to go on. Too late to turn back!"

"I reckon we've all said that. None of the gang wants to quit. They all think, and I think, we can't be touched. We may be blamed, but nothing can be proved. We're too strong."

"There's where you're dead wrong," rejoined Sampson, emphatically. "I imagined that once, not long ago. I was bull-headed. Who would ever connect Roger Sampson with a rustler gang? I've changed my mind. I've begun to think. I've reasoned out things. We're crooked and we can't last. It's the nature of life, even in wild Pecos, for conditions to grow better. The wise deal for us would be to divide equally and leave the country, all of us."

"But you and I have all the stock—all the gain," protested Wright.

"I'll split mine."

"I won't—that settles that," added Wright instantly.

Sampson spread wide his hands as if it was useless to try to convince this man. Talking had not increased his calmness, and he now showed more than impatience. A dull glint gleamed deep in his eyes. "Your stock and property will last a long time—do you lots of good when Steele—"

"Bah!" hoarsely croaked Wright. The Ranger's name was a match applied to powder. "Haven't I told you he'd be dead soon same as Hoden is?"

"Yes, you mentioned the supposition," replied Sampson sarcastically. "I inquired, too just how that very desired event was to be brought about."

"Blome's here to kill Steele."

"Bah!" retorted Sampson in turn. "Blome can't kill this Ranger. He can't face him with a ghost of a show—he'll never get a chance at Steele's back. The man don't live on this border who's quick and smart enough to kill Steele."

"I'd like to know why?" demanded Wright sullenly.

"You ought to know. You've seen the Ranger pull a gun."

"Who told you?" queried Wright, his face working.

"Oh, I guessed it, if that'll do you."

"If Jack doesn't kill this damned Ranger I will," replied Wright, pounding the table.

Sampson laughed contemptuously. "George, don't make so much noise. And don't be a fool. You've been on the border for ten years. You've packed a gun and you've used it. You've been with Blome and Snecker when they killed their men. You've been present at many fights. But you never saw a man like Steele. You haven't got sense enough to see him right if you had a chance. Neither has Blome. The only way to get rid of Steele is for the gang to draw on him, all at once. And even then he's going to drop some of them."

"Sampson, you say that like a man who wouldn't care much if Steele did drop some of them," declared Wright, and now he was sarcastic.

"To tell you the truth I wouldn't," returned the other bluntly. "I'm pretty sick of this mess."

Wright cursed in amaze. His emotions were out of all proportion to his intelligence. He was not at all quick-witted. I had never seen a vainer or more arrogant man. "Sampson, I don't like your talk," he said.

"If you don't like the way I talk you know what you can do," replied Sampson quickly. He stood up then, cool and quiet, with flash of eyes and set of lips that told me he was dangerous.

"Well, after all, that's neither here nor there," went on Wright, unconsciously cowed by the other. "The thing is, do I get the girl?"

"Not by any means, except her consent."

"You'll not make her marry me?"

"No. No," replied Sampson, his voice still cold, low-pitched.

"All right. Then I'll make her."

Evidently Sampson understood the man before him so well that he wasted no more words. I knew what Wright never dreamed of, and that was that Sampson had a gun somewhere within reach and meant to use it.

Then heavy footsteps sounded outside, tramping upon the porch. I might have been mistaken, but I believed those footsteps saved Wright's life.

"There they are," said Wright, and he opened the door. Five masked men entered. About two of them I could not recognize anything familiar. I thought one had old Snecker's burly shoulders and another Bo Snecker's stripling shape. I did recognize Blome in spite of his mask, because his fair skin and hair, his garb and air of distinction made plain his identity. They all wore coats, hiding any weapons. The big man with burly shoulders shook hands with Sampson and the others stood back.

The atmosphere of that room had changed. Wright might have been a nonentity for all he counted. Sampson was another man—a stranger to me. If he had entertained a hope of freeing himself from his band, of getting away to a safer country, he abandoned it at the very sight of these men. There was power here and he was bound.

The big man spoke in low, hoarse whispers, and at this all the others gathered round him, close to the table. There were evidently some signs of membership not plain to me. Then all the heads were bent over the table. Low voices spoke, queried, answered, argued. By straining my ears I caught a word here and there. They were planning. I did not attempt to get at the meaning of the few words and phrases I distinguished, but held them in mind so to piece all together afterward. Before the plotters finished conferring I had an involuntary flashed knowledge of much and my whirling, excited mind made reception difficult.

When these rustlers finished whispering I was in a cold sweat. Steele was to be killed as soon as possible by Blome, or by the gang going to Steele's house at night. Morton had been seen with the Ranger. He was to meet the same fate as Hoden, dealt by Bo Snecker, who evidently worked in the dark like a ferret. Any other person known to be communing with Steele, or interested in him, or suspected of either, was to be silenced. Then the town was to suffer a short deadly spell of violence, directed anywhere, for the purpose of intimidating those people who had begun to be restless under the influence of the Ranger. After that, big herds of stock were to be rustled off the ranches to the north and driven to El Paso.

Then the big man, who evidently was the leader of the present convention, got up to depart. He went as swiftly as he had come, and was followed by the slender fellow. As far as it was possible for me to be sure, I identified these two as Snecker and his son. The others, however, remained. Blome removed his mask, which action was duplicated by the two rustlers who had stayed with him. They were both young, bronzed, hard of countenance, not unlike cowboys. Evidently this was now a social call on Sampson. He set out cigars and liquors for his guests, and a general conversation ensued, differing little from what might have been indulged in by neighborly ranchers. There was not a word spoken that would have caused suspicion.

Blome was genial, gay, and he talked the most. Wright alone seemed uncommunicative and unsociable. He smoked fiercely and drank continually. All at once he straightened up as if listening. "What's that?" he called suddenly.

The talking and laughter ceased. My own strained ears were pervaded by a slight rustling sound.

"Must be a rat," replied Sampson in relief. Strange how any sudden or unknown thing weighed upon him.

The rustling became a rattle.

"Sounds like a rattlesnake to me," said Blome.

Sampson got up from the table and peered round the room. Just at that instant I felt an almost inappreciable movement of the adobe wall which supported me. I could scarcely credit my senses. But the rattle inside Sampson's room was mingling with little dull thuds of falling dirt. The adobe wall, merely dried mud was crumbling. I distinctly felt a tremor pass through it. Then the blood gushed with sickening coldness back to my heart and seemingly clogged it.

"What in the hell!" exclaimed Sampson.

"I smell dust," said Blome sharply.

That was the signal for me to drop down from my perch, yet despite my care I made a noise.

"Did you hear a step?" queried Sampson.

Then a section of the wall fell inward with a crash. I began to squeeze my body through the narrow passage toward the patio.

"Hear him!" yelled Wright. "This side."

"No, he's going that way," yelled someone else. The tramp of heavy boots lent me the strength and speed of desperation. I was not shirking a fight, but to be cornered like a trapped coyote was another matter. I almost tore my clothes off in that passage. The dust nearly stifled me.

When I burst into the patio it was not one single instant too soon. But one deep gash of breath revived me, and I was up, gun in hand, running for the outlet into the court. Thumping footsteps turned me back. While there was a chance to get away I did not want to meet odds in a fight. I thought I heard some one running into the patio from the other end. I stole along, and coming to a door, without any idea of where it might lead, I softly pushed it open a little way and slipped in.

Chapter 9

IN FLAGRANTE DELICTO

A low cry greeted me. The room was light. I saw Sally Langdon sitting on her bed in her dressing gown. Shaking my gun at her with a fierce warning gesture to be silent, I turned to close the door. It was a heavy door, without bolt or bar, and when I had shut it I felt safe only for the moment. Then I gazed around the room. There was one window with blind closely drawn. I listened and seemed to hear footsteps retreating, dying away. Then I turned to Sally. She had slipped off the bed to her knees and was holding out trembling hands as if both to supplicate mercy and to ward me off. She was as white as the pillow on her bed. She was terribly frightened. Again with warning hand commanding silence I stepped softly forward, meaning to reassure her.

"Russ! Russ!" she whispered wildly, and I thought she was going to faint. When I got close and looked into her eyes I understood the strange dark expression in them. She was terrified because she believed I meant to kill her, or do worse, probably worse. She had believed many a hard story about me and had cared for me in spite of them. I remembered, then, that she had broken her promise, she had tempted me, led me to kiss her, made a fool out of me. I remembered, also how I had threatened her. This intrusion of mine was the wild cowboy's vengeance.

I verily believed she thought I was drunk. I must have looked pretty hard and fierce, bursting into her room with that big gun in hand. My first action then was to lay the gun on her bureau.

"You poor kid!" I whispered, taking her hands and trying to raise her. But she stayed on her knees and clung to me.

"Russ! It was vile of me," she whispered. "I know it. I deserve anything—anything! But I am only a kid. Russ, I didn't break my word—I didn't make you kiss me just for, vanity's sake. I swear I didn't. I wanted you to. For I care, Russ, I can't help it. Please forgive me. Please let me off this time. Don't—don't—"

"Will you shut up!" I interrupted, half beside myself. And I used force in another way than speech. I shook her and sat her on the bed. "You little fool, I didn't come in here to kill you or do some other awful thing, as you think. For God's sake, Sally, what do you take me for?"

"Russ, you swore you'd do something terrible if I tempted you anymore," she faltered. The way she searched my face with doubtful, fearful eyes hurt me.

"Listen," and with the word I seemed to be pervaded by peace. "I didn't know this was your room. I came in here to get away—to save my life. I was pursued. I was spying on Sampson and his men. They heard me, but did not see me. They don't know who was listening. They're after me now. I'm Special United States Deputy Marshal Sittell—Russell Archibald Sittell. I'm a Ranger. I'm here as secret aid to Steele."

Sally's eyes changed from blank gulfs to dilating, shadowing, quickening windows of thought. "Russ-ell Archi-bald Sittell," she echoed. "Ranger! Secret aid to Steele!"

"Yes."

"Then you're no cowboy?"

"No."

"Only a make-believe one?"

"Yes."

"And the drinking, the gambling, the association with those low men—that was all put on?"

"Part of the game, Sally. I'm not a drinking man. And I sure hate those places I had to go in, and all that pertains to them."

"Oh, so *that's* it! I knew there was something. How glad—how glad I am!" Then Sally threw her arms around my neck, and without reserve or restraint began to kiss me and love me. It must have been a moment of sheer gladness to feel that I was not disreputable, a moment when something deep and womanly in her was vindicated. Assuredly she was entirely different from what she had ever been before.

There was a little space of time, a sweet confusion of senses, when I could not but meet her half-way in tenderness. Quite as suddenly, then she began to cry. I whispered in her ear, cautioning her to be careful, that my life was at stake; and after that she cried silently, with one of her arms round my neck, her head on my breast, and her hand clasping mine. So I held her for what seemed a long time. Indistinct voices came to me and footsteps seemingly a long way off. I heard the wind in the rose-bush outside. Some one walked down the stony court. Then a shrill neigh of a horse pierced the silence. A rider was mounting out there for some reason. With my life at stake I grasped all the sweetness of that situation. Sally stirred in my arms, raised a red, tear-stained yet happy face, and tried to smile. "It isn't any time to cry," she whispered. "But I had to. You can't understand what it made me feel to learn you're no drunkard, no desperado, but a *man*—a man like that Ranger!" Very sweetly and seriously she kissed me again. "Russ, if I didn't honestly and truly love you before, I do now."

Then she stood up and faced me with the fire and intelligence of a woman in her eyes. "Tell me now. You were spying on my uncle?"

Briefly I told her what had happened before I entered her room, not omitting a terse word as to the character of the men I had watched.

"My God! So it's Uncle Roger! I knew something was very wrong here—with him, with the place, the people. And right off I hated George Wright. Russ, does Diane know?"

"She knows something. I haven't any idea how much."

"This explains her appeal to Steele. Oh, it'll kill her! You don't know how proud, how good Diane is. Oh, it'll kill her!"

"Sally, she's no baby. She's got sand, that girl—"

The sound of soft steps somewhere near distracted my attention, reminded me of my peril, and now, what counted more with me, made clear the probability of being discovered in Sally's room. "I'll have to get out of here," I whispered.

"Wait," she replied, detaining me. "Didn't you say they were hunting for you?"

"They sure are," I returned grimly.

"Oh! Then you mustn't go. They might shoot you before you got away. Stay. If we hear them you can hide under my bed. I'll turn out the light. I'll meet them at the door. You can trust me. Stay, Russ. Wait till all quiets down, if we have to wait till morning. Then you can slip out."

"Sally, I oughtn't to stay. I don't want to—I won't," I replied perplexed and stubborn.

"But you must. It's the only safe way. They won't come here."

"Suppose they should? It's an even chance Sampson'll search every room and corner in this old house. If they found me here I couldn't start a fight. You might be hurt. Then—the fact of my being here—" I did not finish what I meant, but instead made a step toward the door.

Sally was on me like a little whirlwind, white of face and dark of eye, with a resoluteness I could not have deemed her capable of. She was as strong and supple as a panther, too. But she need not have been either resolute or strong, for the clasp of her arms, the feel of her warm breast as she pressed me back were enough to make me weak as water. My knees buckled as I touched the chair, and I was glad to sit down. My face was wet with perspiration and a kind of cold ripple shot over me. I imagined I was losing my nerve then. Proof beyond doubt that Sally loved me was so sweet, so overwhelming a thing, that I could not resist, even to save her disgrace.

"Russ, the fact of your being here is the very thing to save you—if they come," Sally whispered softly. "What do I care what they think?" She put her arms round my neck. I gave up then and held her as if she indeed were my only hope. A noise, a stealthy sound, a step, froze that embrace into stone.

"Up yet, Sally?" came Sampson's clear voice, too strained, too eager to be natural.

"No. I'm in bed, reading. Good night, Uncle," instantly replied Sally, so calmly and naturally that I marveled at the difference between man and woman. Perhaps that was the difference between love and hate.

"Are you alone?" went on Sampson's penetrating voice, colder now.

"Yes," replied Sally.

The door swung inward with a swift scrape and jar. Sampson half entered, haggard, flaming-eyed. His leveled gun did not have to move an inch to cover me. Behind him I saw Wright and indistinctly, another man.

"Well!" gasped Sampson. He showed amazement. "Hands up, Russ!"

I put up my hands quickly, but all the time I was calculating what chance I had to leap for my gun or dash out the light. I was trapped. And fury, like the hot teeth of a wolf, bit into me. That leveled gun, the menace in Sampson's puzzled eyes, Wright's dark and hateful face, these loosened the spirit of fight in me. If Sally had not been there I would have made some desperate move.

Sampson barred Wright from entering, which action showed control as well as distrust.

"You lied!" said Sampson to Sally. He was hard as flint, yet doubtful and curious, too.

"Certainly I lied," snapped Sally in reply. She was cool, almost flippant. I awakened to the knowledge that she was to be reckoned with in this situation. Suddenly she stepped squarely between Sampson and me.

"Move aside," ordered Sampson sternly.

"I won't! What do I care for your old gun? You shan't shoot Russ or do anything else to him. It's my fault he's here in my room. I coaxed him to come."

"You little hussy!" exclaimed Sampson, and he lowered the gun.

If I ever before had occasion to glory in Sally I had it then. She betrayed not the slightest fear. She looked as if she could fight like a little tigress. She was white, composed, defiant.

"How long has Russ been in here?" demanded Sampson.

"All evening. I left Diane at eight o'clock. Russ came right after that."

"But you'd undressed for bed!" ejaculated the angry and perplexed uncle.

"Yes." That simple answer was so noncommittal, so above subterfuge, so innocent, and yet so confounding in its provocation of thought that Sampson just stared his astonishment. But I started as if I had been struck.

"See here Sampson—" I began, passionately.

Like a flash Sally whirled into my arms and one hand crossed my lips. "It's my fault. I will take the blame," she cried, and now the agony of fear in her voice quieted me. I realized I would be wise to be silent. "Uncle," began Sally, turning her head, yet still clinging to me, "I've tormented Russ into loving me. I've flirted with him—teased him—tempted him. We love each other now. We're engaged. Please—please don't—" She began to falter and I felt her weight sag a little against me.

"Well, let go of him," said Sampson. "I won't hurt him. Sally, how long has this affair been going on?"

"For weeks—I don't know how long."

"Does Diane know?"

"She knows we love each other, but not that we met—did this—" Light swift steps, the rustle of silk interrupted Sampson, and made my heart sink like lead.

"Is that you, George?" came Miss Sampson's deep voice, nervous, hurried. "What's all this commotion? I hear—"

"Diane, go on back," ordered Sampson.

Just then Miss Sampson's beautiful agitated face appeared beside Wright. He failed to prevent her from seeing all of us.

"Papa! Sally!" she exclaimed, in consternation. Then she swept into the room. "What has happened?"

Sampson, like the devil he was, laughed when it was too late. He had good impulses, but they never interfered with his sardonic humor. He paced the little room, shrugging his shoulders, offering no explanation. Sally appeared about ready to collapse and I could not have told Sally's lie to Miss Sampson to save my life.

"Diane, your father and I broke in on a little Romeo and Juliet scene," said George Wright with a leer. Then Miss Sampson's dark gaze swept from George to her father, then to Sally's attire and her shamed face, and finally to me. What effect the magnificent wrath and outraged trust in her eyes had upon me!

"Russ, do they dare insinuate you came to Sally's room?" For myself I could keep silent, but for Sally I began to feel a hot clamoring outburst swelling in my throat.

"Sally confessed it, Diane," replied Wright.

"Sally!" A shrinking, shuddering disbelief filled Miss Sampson's voice.

"Diane, I told you I loved him—didn't I?" replied Sally. She managed to hold up her head with a ghost of her former defiant spirit.

"Miss Sampson, it's a—" I burst out.

Then Sally fainted. It was I who caught her. Miss Sampson hurried to her side with a little cry of distress.

"Russ, your hand's called," said Sampson. "Of course you'll swear the moon's green cheese. And I like you the better for it. But we know now, and you can save your breath. If Sally hadn't stuck up so gamely for you I'd have shot you. But at that I wasn't looking for you. Now clear out of here." I picked up my gun from the bureau and dropped it in its sheath. For the life of me I could not leave without another look at Miss Sampson. The scorn in her eyes did not wholly hide the sadness. She who needed friends was experiencing the bitterness of misplaced trust. That came out in the scorn, but the sadness— I knew what hurt her most was her sorrow.

I dropped my head and stalked out.

Chapter 10

A SLAP IN THE FACE

When I got out into the dark, where my hot face cooled in the wind, my relief equaled my other feelings. Sampson had told me to clear out, and although I did not take that as a dismissal I considered I would be wise to leave the ranch at once. Daylight might disclose my footprints between the walls, but even if it did not, my work there was finished. So I went to my room and packed my few belongings.

The night was dark, windy, stormy, yet there was no rain. I hoped as soon as I got clear of the ranch to lose something of the pain I felt. But long after I had tramped out into the open there was a lump in my throat and an ache in my breast. And all my thought centered round Sally.

What a game and loyal little girl she had turned out to be! I was absolutely at a loss concerning what the future held in store for us. I seemed to have a vague but clinging hope that, after the trouble was over, there might be—there *must* be—something more between us.

Steele was not at our rendezvous among the rocks. The hour was too late. Among the few dim lights flickering on the outskirts of town I picked out the one of his little adobe house but I knew almost to a certainty that he was not there. So I turned my way into the darkness, not with any great hope of finding Steele out there, but with the intention of seeking a covert for myself until morning.

There was no trail and the night was so black that I could see only the lighter sandy patches of ground. I stumbled over the little clumps of brush, fell into washes, and pricked myself on cactus. By and by mesquites and rocks began to make progress still harder for me. I wandered around, at last getting on higher ground and here in spite of the darkness, felt some sense of familiarity with things. I was probably near Steele's hiding place.

I went on till rocks and brush barred further progress, and then I ventured to whistle. But no answer came. Whereupon I spread my blanket in as sheltered a place as I could find and lay down. The coyotes were on noisy duty, the wind moaned and rushed through the mesquites. But despite these sounds and worry about Steele, and the never-absent haunting thought of Sally, I went to sleep.

A little rain had fallen during the night, as I discovered upon waking; still it was not enough to cause me any discomfort. The morning was bright and beautiful, yet somehow I hated it. I had work to do that did not go well with that golden wave of grass and brush on the windy open.

I climbed to the highest rock of that ridge and looked about. It was a wild spot, some three miles from town. Presently I recognized landmarks given to me by Steele and knew I was near his place. I whistled, then halloed, but got no reply. Then by working back and forth across the ridge I found what appeared to be a faint trail. This I followed, lost and found again, and eventually, still higher up on another ridge, with a commanding outlook, I found Steele's hiding place. He had not been there for perhaps forty-eight hours. I wondered where he had slept.

Under a shelving rock I found a pack of food, carefully protected by a heavy slab. There was also a canteen full of water. I lost no time getting myself some breakfast, and then, hiding my own pack, I set off at a rapid walk for town.

But I had scarcely gone a quarter of a mile, had, in fact, just reached a level, when sight of two horsemen halted me and made me take to cover. They appeared to be cowboys hunting for a horse or a steer. Under the circumstances, however, I was suspicious, and I watched them closely, and followed them a mile or so round the base of the ridges, until I had thoroughly satisfied myself they were not tracking Steele. They were a long time working out of sight, which further retarded my venturing forth into the open.

Finally I did get started. Then about half-way to town more horsemen in the flat caused me to lie low for a while, and make a wide detour to avoid being seen.

Somewhat to my anxiety it was afternoon before I arrived in town. For my life I could not have told why I knew something had happened since my last visit, but I certainly felt it; and was proportionately curious and anxious.

The first person I saw whom I recognized was Dick, and he handed me a note from Sally. She seemed to take it for granted that I had been wise to leave the ranch. Miss Sampson had softened somewhat when she learned Sally and I were engaged, and she had forgiven my deceit. Sally asked me to come that night after eight, down among the trees and shrubbery, to a secluded spot we knew. It was a brief note and all to the point. But there was something in it that affected me strangely. I had imagined the engagement an invention for the moment. But after danger to me was past Sally would not have carried on a pretense, not even to win back Miss Sampson's respect. The fact was, Sally meant that engagement. If I did the right thing now I would not lose her.

But what was the right thing?

I was sorely perplexed and deeply touched. Never had I a harder task than that of the hour—to put her out of my mind. I went boldly to Steele's house.

He was not there. There was nothing by which I could tell when he had been there. The lamp might have been turned out or might have burned out. The oil was low. I saw a good many tracks round in the sandy walks. I did not recognize Steele's.

As I hurried away I detected more than one of Steele's nearest neighbors peering at me from windows and doors. Then I went to Mrs. Hoden's. She was up and about and cheerful. The children were playing, manifestly well cared for and content. Mrs. Hoden had not seen Steele since I had. Miss Samson had sent her servant. There was a very decided change in the atmosphere of Mrs. Hoden's home, and I saw that for her the worst was past, and she was bravely, hopefully facing the future.

From there, I hurried to the main street of Linrock and to that section where violence brooded, ready at any chance moment to lift its hydra head. For that time of day the street seemed unusually quiet. Few pedestrians were abroad and few loungers. There was a row of saddled horses on each side of the street, the full extent of the block.

I went into the big barroom of the Hope So. I had never seen the place so full, nor had it ever seemed so quiet. The whole long bar was lined by shirt-sleeved men, with hats slouched back and vests flapping wide. Those who were not drinking were talking low. Half a dozen tables held as many groups of dusty, motley men, some silent, others speaking and gesticulating, all earnest.

At first glance I did not see any one in whom I had especial interest. The principal actors of my drama did not appear to be present. However, there were rough characters more in evidence than at any other time I had visited the saloon. Voices were too low for me to catch, but I followed the direction of some of the significant gestures. Then I saw that these half dozen tables were rather closely grouped and drawn back from the center of the big room. Next my quick sight took in a smashed table and chairs, some broken bottles on the floor, and then a dark sinister splotch of blood.

I had no time to make inquiries, for my roving eye caught Frank Morton in the doorway, and evidently he wanted to attract my attention. He turned away and I followed. When I got outside, he was leaning against the hitching-rail. One look at this big rancher was enough for me to see that he had been told my part in Steele's game, and that he himself had roused to the Texas fighting temper. He had a clouded brow. He looked somber and thick. He seemed slow, heavy, guarded.

"Howdy, Russ," he said. "We've been wantin' you."

"There's ten of us in town, all scattered round, ready. It's goin' to start to-day."

"Where's Steele?" was my first query.

"Saw him less'n hour ago. He's somewhere close. He may show up any time."

"Is he all right?"

"Wal, he was pretty fit a little while back," replied Morton significantly.

"What's come off? Tell me all."

"Wal, the ball opened last night, I reckon. Jack Blome came swaggerin' in here askin' for Steele. We all knew what he was in town for. But last night he came out with it. Every man in the saloons, every man on the streets heard Blome's loud an' longin' call for the Ranger. Blome's pals took it up and they all enjoyed themselves some."

"Drinking hard?" I queried.

"Nope—they didn't hit it up very hard. But they laid foundations." Of course, Steele was not to be seen last night. This morning Blome and his gang were out pretty early. But they traveled alone. Blome just strolled up and down by himself. I watched him walk up this street on one side and then down the other, just a matter of thirty-one times. I counted them. For all I could see maybe Blome did not take a drink. But his gang, especially Bo Snecker, sure looked on the red liquor.

"By eleven o'clock everybody in town knew what was coming off. There was no work or business, except in the saloons. Zimmer and I were together, and the rest of our crowd in pairs at different places. I reckon it was about noon when Blome got tired parading up and down. He went in the Hope So, and the crowd followed. Zimmer stayed outside so to give Steele a hunch in case he came along. I went in to see the show.

"Wal, it was some curious to me, and I've lived all my life in Texas. But I never before saw a gunman on the job, so to say. Blome's a handsome fellow, an' he seemed different from what I expected. Sure, I thought he'd yell an' prance round like a drunken fool. But he was cool an' quiet enough. The blowin' an' drinkin' was done by his pals. But after a little while it got to me that Blome gloried in this situation. I've seen a man dead-set to kill another, all dark, sullen, restless. But Blome wasn't that way. He didn't seem at all like a bloody devil. He was vain, cocksure. He was revelin' in the effect he made. I had him figured all right.

"Blome sat on the edge of a table an' he faced the door. Of course, there was a pard outside, ready to pop in an' tell him if Steele was comin'. But Steele didn't come in that way. He wasn't on the street just before that time, because Zimmer told me afterward. Steele must have been in the Hope So somewhere. Any way, just like he dropped from the clouds he came through the door near the bar. Blome didn't see him come. But most of the gang did, an' I want to tell you that big room went pretty quiet.

"'Hello Blome, I hear you're lookin' for me,' called out Steele.

"I don't know if he spoke ordinary or not, but his voice drew me up same as it did the rest, an' damn me! Blome seemed to turn to stone. He didn't start or jump. He turned gray. An' I could see that he was tryin' to think in a moment when thinkin' was hard. Then Blome turned his head. Sure he expected to look into a six-shooter. But Steele was standin' back there in his shirt sleeves, his hands on his hips, and he looked more man than any one I ever saw. It's easy to remember the look of him, but how he made me feel, that isn't easy.

"Blome was at a disadvantage. He was half sittin' on a table, an' Steele was behind an' to the left of him. For Blome to make a move then would have been a fool trick. He saw that. So did everybody. The crowd slid back without noise, but Bo Snecker an' a rustler named March stuck near Blome. I figured this Bo Snecker as dangerous as Blome, an' results proved I was right.

"Steele didn't choose to keep his advantage, so far as position in regard to Blome went. He just walked round in front of the rustler. But this put all the crowd in front of Steele, an' perhaps he had an eye for that.

"'I hear you've been looking for me,' repeated the Ranger.

"Blome never moved a muscle but he seemed to come to life. It struck me that Steele's presence had made an impression on Blome which was new to the rustler.

"'Yes, I have,' replied Blome.

"'Well, here I am. What do you want?'

"When everybody knew what Blome wanted and had intended, this question of Steele's seemed strange on one hand. An' yet on the other, now that the Ranger stood there, it struck me as natural enough.

"'If you heard I was lookin' for you, you sure heard what for,' replied Blome.

"'Blome, my experience with such men as you is that you all brag one thing behind my back an' you mean different when I show up. I've called you now. What do you mean?'

"'I reckon you know what Jack Blome means.'

"'Jack Blome! That name means nothin' to me. Blome, you've been braggin' around that you'd meet me—kill me! You thought you meant it, didn't you?'

"'Yes—I did mean it.'

"'All right. Go ahead!'

"The barroom became perfectly still, except for the slow breaths I heard. There wasn't any movement anywhere. That queer gray came to Blome's face again. He might again have been stone. I thought, an' I'll gamble every one else watchin' thought, Blome would draw an' get killed in the act. But he never moved. Steele had cowed him. If Blome had been heated by drink, or mad, or anythin' but what he was just then, maybe he might have throwed a gun. But he didn't. I've heard of really brave men gettin' panicked like that, an' after seein' Steele I didn't wonder at Blome.

"'You see, Blome, you don't want to meet me, for all your talk,' went on the Ranger. 'You thought you did, but that was before you faced the man you intended to kill. Blome, you're one of these dandy, cock-of-the-walk four-flushers. I'll tell you how I know. Because I've met the real gun-fighters, an' there never was one of them yet who bragged or talked. Now don't you go round blowin' any more.'

"Then Steele deliberately stepped forward an' slapped Blome on one side of his face an' again on the other.

"'Keep out of my way after this or I'm liable to spoil some of your dandy looks.'

"Blome got up an' walked straight out of the place. I had my eyes on him, kept me from seein' Steele. But on hearin' somethin', I don't know what, I turned back an' there Steele had got a long arm on Bo Snecker, who was tryin' to throw a gun.

"But he wasn't quick enough. The gun banged in the air an' then it went spinnin' away, while Snecker dropped in a heap on the floor. The table was overturned, an' March, the other rustler, who was on that side, got up, pullin' his gun. But somebody in the crowd killed him before he could get goin'. I didn't see who fired that shot, an' neither did anybody else. But the crowd broke an' run. Steele dragged Bo Snecker down to jail an' locked him up."

Morton concluded his narrative, and then evidently somewhat dry of tongue, he produced knife and tobacco and cut himself a huge quid. "That's all, so far, to-day, Russ, but I reckon you'll agree with me on the main issue— Steele's game's opened."

I had felt the rush of excitement, the old exultation at the prospect of danger, but this time there was something lacking in them. The wildness of the boy that had persisted in me was gone.

"Yes, Steele has opened it and I'm ready to boost the game along. Wait till I see him! But Morton, you say someone you don't know played a hand in here and killed March."

"I sure do. It wasn't any of our men. Zimmer was outside. The others were at different places."

"The fact is, then, Steele has more friends than we know, perhaps more than he knows himself."

"Right. An' it's got the gang in the air. There'll be hell to-night."

"Steele hardly expects to keep Snecker in jail, does he?"

"I can't say. Probably not. I wish Steele had put both Blome and Snecker out of the way. We'd have less to fight."

"Maybe. I'm for the elimination method myself. But Steele doesn't follow out the gun method. He will use one only when he's driven. It's hard to make him draw. You know, after all, these desperate men aren't afraid of guns or fights. Yet they are afraid of Steele. Perhaps it's his nerve, the way he faces them, the things he says, the fact that he has mysterious allies."

"Russ, we're all with him, an' I'll gamble that the honest citizens of Linrock will flock to him in another day. I can see signs of that. There were twenty or more men on Hoden's list, but Steele didn't want so many."

"We don't need any more. Morton, can you give me any idea where Steele is?"

"Not the slightest."

"All right. I'll hunt for him. If you see him tell him to hole up, and then you come after me. Tell him I've got our men spotted."

"Russ, if you Ranger fellows ain't wonders!" exclaimed Morton, with shining eyes.

Steele did not show himself in town again that day. Here his cunning was manifest. By four o'clock that afternoon Blome was drunk and he and his rustlers went roaring up and down the street. There was some shooting, but I did not see or hear that any one got hurt. The lawless element, both native to Linrock and the visitors, followed in Blome's tracks from saloon to saloon. How often had I seen this sort of procession, though not on so large a scale, in many towns of wild Texas!

The two great and dangerous things in Linrock at the hour were whisky and guns. Under such conditions the rustlers were capable of any mad act of folly.

Morton and his men sent word flying around town that a fight was imminent and all citizens should be prepared to defend their homes against possible violence. But despite his warning I saw many respectable citizens abroad whose quiet, unobtrusive manner and watchful eyes and hard faces told me that when trouble began they wanted to be there. Verily Ranger Steele had built his house of service upon a rock. It did not seem too much to say that the next few days, perhaps hours, would see a great change in the character and a proportionate decrease in number of the inhabitants of this corner of Pecos County.

Morton and I were in the crowd that watched Blome, Snecker, and a dozen other rustlers march down to Steele's jail. They had crowbars and they had cans of giant powder, which they had appropriated from a hardware store. If Steele had a jailer he was not in evidence. The door was wrenched off and Bo Snecker, evidently not wholly recovered, brought forth to his cheering comrades. Then some of the rustlers began to urge back the pressing circle, and the word given out acted as a spur to haste. The jail was to be blown up.

The crowd split and some men ran one way, some another. Morton and I were among those who hurried over the vacant ground to a little ridge that marked the edge of the open country. From this vantage point we heard several rustlers yell in warning, then they fled for their lives.

It developed that they might have spared themselves such headlong flight. The explosion appeared to be long in coming. At length we saw the lifting of the roof in a cloud of red dust, and then heard an exceedingly heavy but low detonation. When the pall of dust drifted away all that was left of Steele's jail was a part of the stone walls. The building that stood nearest, being constructed of adobe, had been badly damaged.

However, this wreck of the jail did not seem to satisfy Blome and his followers, for amid wild yells and huzzahs they set to work with crowbars and soon laid low every stone. Then with young Snecker in the fore they set off up town; and if this was not a gang in fit mood for any evil or any ridiculous celebration I greatly missed my guess.

It was a remarkable fact, however, and one that convinced me of deviltry afoot, that the crowd broke up, dispersed, and actually disappeared off the streets of Linrock. The impression given was that they were satisfied. But this impression did not remain with me. Morton was scarcely deceived either. I told him that I would almost certainly see Steele early in the evening and that we would be out of harm's way. He told me that we could trust him and his men to keep sharp watch on the night doings of Blome's gang. Then we parted.

It was almost dark. By the time I had gotten something to eat and drink at the Hope So, the hour for my meeting with Sally was about due. On the way out I did not pass a lighted house until I got to the end of the street; and then strange to say, that one was Steele's. I walked down past the place, and though I was positive he would not be there I whistled low. I halted and waited. He had two lights lit, one in the kitchen, and one in the big room.

The blinds were drawn. I saw a long, dark shadow cross one window and then, a little later, cross the other. This would have deceived me had I not remembered Steele's device for casting the shadow. He had expected to have his house attacked at night, presumably while he was at home; but he had felt that it was not necessary for him to stay there to make sure. Lawless men of this class were sometimes exceedingly simple and gullible.

Then I bent my steps across the open, avoiding road and path, to the foot of the hill upon which Sampson's house stood. It was dark enough under the trees. I could hardly find my way to the secluded nook and bench where I had been directed to come. I wondered if Sally would be able to find it. Trust that girl! She might have a few qualms and come shaking a little, but she would be there on the minute.

I had hardly seated myself to wait when my keen ears detected something, then slight rustlings, then soft steps, and a dark form emerged from the blackness into the little starlit glade. Sally came swiftly towards me and right into my arms. That was sure a sweet moment. Through the excitement and dark boding thoughts of the day, I had forgotten that she would do just this thing. And now I anticipated tears, clingings, fears. But I was agreeably surprised.

"Russ, are you all right?" she whispered.

"Just at this moment I am," I replied.

Sally gave me another little hug, and then, disengaging herself from my arms, she sat down beside me.

"I can only stay a minute. Oh, it's safe enough. But I told Diane I was to meet you and she's waiting to hear if Steele is—is—"

"Steele's safe so far," I interrupted.

"There were men coming and going all day. Uncle Roger never appeared at meals. He didn't eat, Diane said. George tramped up and down, smoking, biting his nails, listening for these messengers. When they'd leave he'd go in for another drink. We heard him roar some one had been shot and we feared it might be Steele."

"No," I replied, steadily.

"Did Steele shoot anybody?"

"No. A rustler named March tried to draw on Steele, and someone in the crowd killed March."

"Someone? Russ, was it you?"

"It sure wasn't. I didn't happen to be there."

"Ah! Then Steele has other men like you around him. I might have guessed that."

"Sally, Steele makes men his friends. It's because he's on the side of justice."

"Diane will be glad to hear that. She doesn't think only of Steele's life. I believe she has a secret pride in his work. And I've an idea what she fears most is some kind of a clash between Steele and her father."

"I shouldn't wonder. Sally, what does Diane know about her father?"

"Oh, she's in the dark. She got hold of papers that made her ask him questions. And his answers made her suspicious. She realizes he's not what he has pretended to be all these years. But she never dreams her father is a rustler chief. When she finds that out—" Sally broke off and I finished the sentence in thought.

"Listen, Sally," I said, suddenly. "I've an idea that Steele's house will be attacked by the gang to-night, and destroyed, same as the jail was this afternoon. These rustlers are crazy. They'll expect to kill him while he's there. But he won't be there. If you and Diane hear shooting and yelling to-night don't be frightened. Steele and I will be safe."

"Oh, I hope so. Russ, I must hurry back. But, first, can't you arrange a meeting between Diane and Steele? It's her wish. She begged me to. She must see him."

"I'll try," I promised, knowing that promise would be hard to keep.

"We could ride out from the ranch somewhere. You remember we used to rest on the high ridge where there was a shady place—such a beautiful outlook? It was there I—I—"

"My dear, you needn't bring up painful memories. I remember where."

Sally laughed softly. She could laugh in the face of the gloomiest prospects. "Well, to-morrow morning, or the next, or any morning soon, you tie your red scarf on the dead branch of that high mesquite. I'll look every morning with the glass. If I see the scarf, Diane and I will ride out."

"That's fine. Sally, you have ideas in your pretty little head. And once I thought it held nothing but—" She put a hand on my mouth. "I must go now," she said and rose. She stood close to me and put her arms around my neck. "One thing more, Russ. It—it was dif—difficult telling Diane we—we were engaged. I lied to Uncle. But what else could I have told Diane? I—I—Oh—was it—" She faltered.

"Sally, you lied to Sampson to save me. But you must have accepted me before you could have told Diane the truth."

"Oh, Russ, I had—in my heart! But it has been some time since you asked me—and—and—"

"You imagined my offer might have been withdrawn. Well, it stands."

She slipped closer to me then, with that soft sinuousness of a woman, and I believed she might have kissed me had I not held back, toying with my happiness.

"Sally, do you love me?"

"Ever so much. Since the very first."

"I'm a marshal, a Ranger like Steele, a hunter of criminals. It's a hard life. There's spilling of blood. And any time I—I might—All the same, Sally—will you be my wife?"

"Oh, Russ! Yes. But let me tell you when your duty's done here that I will have a word to say about your future. It'll be news to you to learn I'm an orphan. And I'm not a poor one. I own a plantation in Louisiana. I'll make a planter out of you. There!"

"Sally! You're rich?" I exclaimed.

"I'm afraid I am. But nobody can ever say you married me for my money."

"Well, no, not if you tell of my abject courtship when I thought you a poor relation on a visit. My God! Sally, if I only could see this Ranger job through safely and to success!"

"You will," she said softly.

Then I took a ring from my little finger and slipped it on hers. "That was my sister's. She's dead now. No other girl ever wore it. Let it be your engagement ring. Sally, I pray I may somehow get through this awful Ranger deal to make you happy, to become worthy of you!"

"Russ, I fear only one thing," she whispered.

"And what's that?"

"There will be fighting. And you—oh, I saw into your eyes the other night when you stood with your hands up. You would kill anybody, Russ. It's awful! But don't think me a baby. I can conceive what your work is, what a man you must be. I can love you and stick to you, too. But if you killed a blood relative of mine I would have to give you up. I'm a Southerner, Russ, and blood is thick. I scorn my uncle and I hate my cousin George. And I love you. But don't you kill one of my family, I—Oh, I beg of you go as far as you dare to avoid that!"

I could find no voice to answer her, and for a long moment we were locked in an embrace, breast to breast and lips to lips, an embrace of sweet pain.

Then she broke away, called a low, hurried good-by, and stole like a shadow into the darkness.

An hour later I lay in the open starlight among the stones and brush, out where Steele and I always met. He lay there with me, but while I looked up at the stars he had his face covered with his hands. For I had given him my proofs of the guilt of Diane Sampson's father.

Steele had made one comment: "I wish to God I'd sent for some fool who'd have bungled the job!"

This was a compliment to me, but it showed what a sad pass Steele had come to. My regret was that I had no sympathy to offer him. I failed him there. I had trouble of my own. The feel of Sally's clinging arms around my neck, the warm, sweet touch of her lips remained on mine. What Steele was enduring I did not know, but I felt that it was agony.

Meanwhile time passed. The blue, velvety sky darkened as the stars grew brighter. The wind grew stronger and colder. I heard sand blowing against the stones like the rustle of silk. Otherwise it was a singularly quiet night. I wondered where the coyotes were and longed for their chorus. By and by a prairie wolf sent in his lonely lament from the distant ridges. That mourn was worse than the silence. It made the cold shudders creep up and down my back. It was just the cry that seemed to be the one to express my own trouble. No one hearing that long-drawn, quivering wail could ever disassociate it from tragedy. By and by it ceased, and then I wished it would come again. Steele lay like the stone beside him. Was he ever going to speak? Among the vagaries of my mood was a petulant desire to have him sympathize with me.

I had just looked at my watch, making out in the starlight that the hour was eleven, when the report of a gun broke the silence.

I jumped up to peer over the stone. Steele lumbered up beside me, and I heard him draw his breath hard.

Chapter 11

THE FIGHT IN THE HOPE SO

I could plainly see the lights of his adobe house, but of course, nothing else was visible. There were no other lighted houses near. Several flashes gleamed, faded swiftly, to be followed by reports, and then the unmistakable jingle of glass.

"I guess the fools have opened up, Steele," I said. His response was an angry grunt. It was just as well, I concluded, that things had begun to stir. Steele needed to be roused.

Suddenly a single sharp yell pealed out. Following it came a huge flare of light, a sheet of flame in which a great cloud of smoke or dust shot up. Then, with accompanying darkness, burst a low, deep, thunderous boom. The lights of the house went out, then came a crash. Points of light flashed in a half-circle and the reports of guns blended with the yells of furious men, and all these were swallowed up in the roar of a mob.

Another and a heavier explosion momentarily lightened the darkness and then rent the air. It was succeeded by a continuous volley and a steady sound that, though composed of yells, screams, cheers, was not anything but a hideous roar of hate. It kept up long after there could have been any possibility of life under the ruins of that house. It was more than hate of Steele. All that was wild and lawless and violent hurled this deed at the Ranger Service.

Such events had happened before in Texas and other states; but, strangely, they never happened more than once in one locality. They were expressions, perhaps, that could never come but once.

I watched Steele through all that hideous din, that manifestation of insane rage at his life and joy at his death, and when silence once more reigned and he turned his white face to mine, I had a sensation of dread. And dread was something particularly foreign to my nature.

"So Blome and the Sneckers think they've done for me," he muttered.

"Pleasant surprise for them to-morrow, eh, old man?" I queried.

"To-morrow? Look, Russ, what's left of my old 'dobe house is on fire. The ruins can't be searched soon. And I was particular to fix things so it'd look like I was home. I just wanted to give them a chance. It's incomprehensible how easy men like them can be duped. Whisky-soaked! Yes, they'll be surprised!"

He lingered a while, watching the smoldering fire and the dim columns of smoke curling up against the dark blue. "Russ, do you suppose they heard up at the ranch and think I'm—"

"They heard, of course," I replied. "But the girls know you're safe with me."

"Safe? I—I almost wish to God I was there under that heap of ruins, where the rustlers think they've left me."

"Well, Steele, old fellow, come on. We need some sleep." With Steele in the lead, we stalked away into the open.

Two days later, about the middle of the forenoon, I sat upon a great flat rock in the shade of a bushy mesquite, and, besides enjoying the vast, clear sweep of gold and gray plain below, I was otherwise pleasantly engaged. Sally sat as close to me as she could get, holding to my arm as if she never intended to let go. On the other side Miss Sampson leaned against me, and she was white and breathless, partly from the quick ride out from the ranch, partly from agitation. She had grown thinner, and there were dark shadows under her eyes, yet she seemed only more beautiful. The red scarf with which I had signaled the girls waved from a branch of the mesquite. At the foot of the ridge their horses were halted in a shady spot.

"Take off your sombrero," I said to Sally. "You look hot. Besides, you're prettier with your hair flying." As she made no move, I took it off for her. Then I made bold to perform the same office for Miss Sampson. She faintly smiled her thanks. Assuredly she had forgotten all her resentment. There were little beads of perspiration upon her white brow. What a beautiful mass of black-brown hair, with strands of red or gold! Pretty soon she would be bending that exquisite head and face over poor Steele, and I, who had schemed this meeting, did not care what he might do to me.

Pretty soon, also, there was likely to be an interview that would shake us all to our depths, and naturally, I was somber at heart. But though my outward mood of good humor may have been pretense, it certainly was a pleasure to be with the girls again way out in the open. Both girls were quiet, and this made my task harder, and perhaps in my anxiety to ward off questions and appear happy for their own sakes I made an ass of myself with my silly talk and familiarity. Had ever a Ranger such a job as mine?

"Diane, did Sally show you her engagement ring?" I went on, bound to talk.

Miss Sampson either did not notice my use of her first name or she did not object. She seemed so friendly, so helplessly wistful. "Yes. It's very pretty. An antique. I've seen a few of them," she replied.

"I hope you'll let Sally marry me soon."

"*Let* her? Sally Langdon? You haven't become acquainted with your fiancee. But when—"

"Oh, next week, just as soon—"

"Russ!" cried Sally, blushing furiously.

"What's the matter?" I queried innocently.

"You're a little previous."

"Well, Sally, I don't presume to split hairs over dates. But, you see, you've become extremely more desirable—in the light of certain revelations. Diane, wasn't Sally the deceitful thing? An heiress all the time! And I'm to be a planter and smoke fine cigars and drink mint juleps! No, there won't be any juleps."

"Russ, you're talking nonsense," reproved Sally. "Surely it's no time to be funny."

"All right," I replied with resignation. It was no task to discard that hollow mask of humor. A silence ensued, and I waited for it to be broken.

"Is Steele badly hurt?" asked Miss Sampson presently.

"No. Not what he or I'd call hurt at all. He's got a scalp wound, where a bullet bounced off his skull. It's only a scratch. Then he's got another in the shoulder; but it's not bad, either."

"Where is he now?"

"Look across on the other ridge. See the big white stone? There, down under the trees, is our camp. He's there."

"When may—I see him?" There was a catch in her low voice.

"He's asleep now. After what happened yesterday he was exhausted, and the pain in his head kept him awake till late. Let him sleep a while yet. Then you can see him."

"Did he know we were coming?"

"He hadn't the slightest idea. He'll be overjoyed to see you. He can't help that. But he'll about fall upon me with harmful intent."

"Why?"

"Well, I know he's afraid to see you."

"Why?"

"Because it only makes his duty harder."

"Ah!" she breathed.

It seemed to me that my intelligence confirmed a hope of hers and gave her relief. I felt something terrible in the balance for Steele. And I was glad to be able to throw them together. The catastrophe must fall, and now the sooner it fell the better. But I experienced a tightening of my lips and a tugging at my heart-strings.

"Sally, what do you and Diane know about the goings-on in town yesterday?" I asked.

"Not much. George was like an insane man. I was afraid to go near him. Uncle wore a sardonic smile. I heard him curse George—oh, terribly! I believe he hates George. Same as day before yesterday, there were men riding in and out. But Diane and I heard only a little, and conflicting statements at that. We knew there was fighting. Dick and the servants, the cowboys, all brought rumors. Steele was killed at least ten times and came to life just as many.

"I can't recall, don't want to recall, all we heard. But this morning when I saw the red scarf flying in the wind—well, Russ, I was so glad I could not see through the glass any more. We knew then Steele was all right or you wouldn't have put up the signal."

"Reckon few people in Linrock realize just what *did* come off," I replied with a grim chuckle.

"Russ, I want you to tell me," said Miss Sampson earnestly.

"What?" I queried sharply.

"About yesterday—what Steele did—what happened."

"Miss Sampson, I could tell you in a few short statements of fact or I could take two hours in the telling. Which do you prefer?"

"I prefer the long telling. I want to know all about him."

"But why, Miss Sampson? Consider. This is hardly a story for a sensitive woman's ears."

"I am no coward," she replied, turning eyes to me that flashed like dark fire.

"But why?" I persisted. I wanted a good reason for calling up all the details of the most strenuous and terrible day in my border experience. She was silent a moment. I saw her gaze turn to the spot where Steele lay asleep, and it was a pity he could not see her eyes then. "Frankly, I don't want to tell you," I added, and I surely would have been glad to get out of the job.

"I want to hear—because I glory in his work," she replied deliberately.

I gathered as much from the expression of her face as from the deep ring of her voice, the clear content of her statement. She loved the Ranger, but that was not all of her reason.

"His work?" I echoed. "Do you want him to succeed in it?"

"With all my heart," she said, with a white glow on her face.

"My God!" I ejaculated. I just could not help it. I felt Sally's small fingers clutching my arm like sharp pincers. I bit my lips to keep them shut. What if Steele had heard her say that? Poor, noble, justice-loving, blind girl! She knew even less than I hoped. I forced my thought to the question immediately at hand. She gloried in the Ranger's work. She wanted with all her heart to see him succeed in it. She had a woman's pride in his manliness. Perhaps, with a woman's complex, incomprehensible motive, she wanted Steele to be shown to her in all the power that made him hated and feared by lawless men. She had finally accepted the wild life of this border as something terrible and inevitable, but passing. Steele was one of the strange and great and misunderstood men who were making that wild life pass.

For the first time I realized that Miss Sampson, through sharpened eyes of love, saw Steele as he really was—a wonderful and necessary violence. Her intelligence and sympathy had enabled her to see through defamation and the false records following a Ranger; she had had no choice but to love him; and then a woman's glory in a work that freed men, saved women, and made children happy effaced forever the horror of a few dark deeds of blood.

"Miss Sampson, I must tell you first," I began, and hesitated—"that I'm not a cowboy. My wild stunts, my drinking and gaming—these were all pretense."

"Indeed! I am very glad to hear it. And was Sally in your confidence?"

"Only lately. I am a United States deputy marshal in the service of Steele."

She gave a slight start, but did not raise her head.

"I have deceived you. But, all the same, I've been your friend. I ask you to respect my secret a little while. I'm telling you because otherwise my relation to Steele yesterday would not be plain. Now, if you and Sally will use this blanket, make yourselves more comfortable seats, I'll begin my story."

Miss Sampson allowed me to arrange a place for her where she could rest at ease, but Sally returned to my side and stayed there. She was an enigma to-day—pale, brooding, silent—and she never looked at me except when my face was half averted.

"Well," I began, "night before last Steele and I lay hidden among the rocks near the edge of town, and we listened to and watched the destruction of Steele's house. It had served his purpose to leave lights burning, to have shadows blow across the window-blinds, and to have a dummy in his bed. Also, he arranged guns to go off inside the house at the least jar. Steele wanted evidence against his enemies. It was not the pleasantest kind of thing to wait there listening to that drunken mob. There must have been a hundred men. The disturbance and the intent worked strangely upon Steele. It made him different. In the dark I couldn't tell how he looked, but I felt a mood coming in him that fairly made me dread the next day.

"About midnight we started for our camp here. Steele got in some sleep, but I couldn't. I was cold and hot by turns, eager and backward, furious and thoughtful. You see, the deal was such a complicated one, and to-morrow certainly was nearing the climax. By morning I was sick, distraught, gloomy, and uncertain. I had breakfast ready when Steele awoke. I hated to look at him, but when I did it was like being revived.

"He said: 'Russ, you'll trail alongside me to-day and through the rest of this mess.'

"That gave me another shock. I want to explain to you girls that this was the first time in my life I was backward at the prospects of a fight. The shock was the jump of my pulse. My nerve came back. To line up with Steele against Blome and his gang—that would be great!

"'All right, old man,' I replied. 'We're going after them, then?'

"He only nodded.

"After breakfast I watched him clean and oil and reload his guns. I didn't need to ask him if he expected to use them. I didn't need to urge upon him Captain Neal's command.

"'Russ,' said Steele, 'we'll go in together. But before we get to town I'll leave you and circle and come in at the back of the Hope So. You hurry on ahead, post Morton and his men, get the lay of the gang, if possible, and then be at the Hope So when I come in.'

"I didn't ask him if I had a free hand with my gun. I intended to have that. We left camp and hurried toward town. It was near noon when we separated.

"I came down the road, apparently from Sampson's ranch. There was a crowd around the ruins of Steele's house. It was one heap of crumbled 'dobe bricks and burned logs, still hot and smoking. No attempt had been made to dig into the ruins. The curious crowd was certain that Steele lay buried under all that stuff. One feature of that night assault made me ponder. Daylight discovered the bodies of three dead men, rustlers, who had been killed, the report went out, by random shots. Other participants in the affair had been wounded. I believed Morton and his men, under cover of the darkness and in the melee, had sent in some shots not calculated upon the program.

"From there I hurried to town. Just as I had expected, Morton and Zimmer were lounging in front of the Hope So. They had company, disreputable and otherwise. As yet Morton's crowd had not come under suspicion. He was wild for news of Steele, and when I gave it, and outlined the plan, he became as cool and dark and grim as any man of my kind could have wished. He sent Zimmer to get the others of their clique. Then he acquainted me with a few facts, although he was noncommittal in regard to my suspicion as to the strange killing of the three rustlers.

"Blome, Bo Snecker, Hilliard, and Pickens, the ringleaders, had painted the town in celebration of Steele's death. They all got gloriously drunk except old man Snecker. He had cold feet, they said. They were too happy to do any more shooting or mind what the old rustler cautioned. It was two o'clock before they went to bed.

"This morning, after eleven, one by one they appeared with their followers. The excitement had died down. Ranger Steele was out of the way and Linrock was once more wide open, free and easy. Blome alone seemed sullen and spiritless, unresponsive to his comrades and their admirers. And now, at the time of my arrival, the whole gang, with the exception of old Snecker, were assembled in the Hope So.

"'Zimmer will be clever enough to drift his outfit along one or two at a time?' I asked Morton, and he reassured me. Then we went into the saloon.

"There were perhaps sixty or seventy men in the place, more than half of whom were in open accord with Blome's gang. Of the rest there were many of doubtful repute, and a few that might have been neutral, yet all the time were secretly burning to help any cause against these rustlers. At all events, I gathered that impression from the shadowed faces, the tense bodies, the too-evident indication of anything but careless presence there. The windows were open. The light was clear. Few men smoked, but all had a drink before them. There was the ordinary subdued hum of conversation. I surveyed the scene, picked out my position so as to be close to Steele when he entered, and sauntered round to it. Morton aimlessly leaned against a post.

"Presently Zimmer came in with a man and they advanced to the bar. Other men entered as others went out. Blome, Bo Snecker, Hilliard, and Pickens had a table full in the light of the open windows. I recognized the faces of the two last-named, but I had not, until Morton informed me, known who they were. Pickens was little, scrubby, dusty, sandy, mottled, and he resembled a rattlesnake. Hilliard was big, gaunt, bronzed, with huge mustache and hollow, fierce eyes. I never had seen a grave-robber, but I imagined one would be like Hilliard. Bo Snecker was a sleek, slim, slender, hard-looking boy, marked dangerous, because he was too young and too wild to have caution or fear. Blome, the last of the bunch, showed the effects of a bad night.

"You girls remember how handsome he was, but he didn't look it now. His face was swollen, dark, red, and as it had been bright, now it was dull. Indeed, he looked sullen, shamed, sore. He was sober now. Thought was written on his clouded brow. He was awakening now to the truth that the day before had branded him a coward and sent him out to bolster up courage with drink. His vanity had begun to bleed. He knew, if his faithful comrades had not awakened to it yet, that his prestige had been ruined. For a gunman, he had suffered the last degradation. He had been bidden to draw and he had failed of the nerve.

"He breathed heavily; his eyes were not clear; his hands were shaky. Almost I pitied this rustler who very soon must face an incredibly swift and mercilessly fatal Ranger. Face him, too, suddenly, as if the grave had opened to give up its dead.

"Friends and comrades of this center group passed to and fro, and there was much lazy, merry, though not loud, talk. The whole crowd was still half-asleep. It certainly was an auspicious hour for Steele to confront them, since that duty was imperative. No man knew the stunning paralyzing effect of surprise better than Steele. I, of course, must take my cue from him, or the sudden development of events.

"But Jack Blome did not enter into my calculations. I gave him, at most, about a minute to live after Steele entered the place. I meant to keep sharp eyes all around. I knew, once with a gun out, Steele could kill Blome's comrades at the table as quick as lightning, if he chose. I rather thought my game was to watch his outside partners. This was right, and as it turned out, enabled me to save Steele's life.

"Moments passed and still the Ranger did not come. I began to get nervous. Had he been stopped? I scouted the idea. Who could have stopped him, then? Probably the time seemed longer than it really was. Morton showed the strain, also. Other men looked drawn, haggard, waiting as if expecting a thunderbolt. Once in my roving gaze I caught Blandy's glinty eye on me. I didn't like the gleam. I said to myself I'd watch him if I had to do it out of the back of my head. Blandy, by the way, is—was—I should say, the Hope So bartender." I stopped to clear my throat and get my breath.

"Was," whispered Sally. She quivered with excitement. Miss Sampson bent eyes upon me that would have stirred a stone man.

"Yes, he was once," I replied ambiguously, but mayhap my grimness betrayed the truth. "Don't hurry me, Sally. I guarantee you'll be sick enough presently.

"Well, I kept my eyes shifty. And I reckon I'll never forget that room. Likely I saw what wasn't really there. In the excitement, the suspense, I must have made shadows into real substance. Anyway, there was the half-circle of bearded, swarthy men around Blome's table. There were the four rustlers— Blome brooding, perhaps vaguely, spiritually, listening to a knock; there was Bo Snecker, reckless youth, fondling a flower he had, putting the stem in his glass, then to his lips, and lastly into the buttonhole of Blome's vest; there was Hilliard, big, gloomy, maybe with his cavernous eyes seeing the hell where I expected he'd soon be; and last, the little dusty, scaly Pickens, who looked about to leap and sting some one.

"In the lull of the general conversation I heard Pickens say: 'Jack, drink up an' come out of it. Every man has an off day. You've gambled long enough to know every feller gits called. An' as Steele has cashed, what the hell do you care?

"Hilliard nodded his ghoul's head and blinked his dead eyes. Bo Snecker laughed. It wasn't any different laugh from any other boy's. I remembered then that he killed Hoden. I began to sweat fire. Would Steele ever come?

"'Jim, the ole man hed cold feet an' he's give 'em to Jack,' said Bo. 'It ain't nothin' to lose your nerve once. Didn't I run like a scared jack-rabbit from Steele? Watch me if he comes to life, as the ole man hinted!'

"'About mebbe Steele wasn't in the 'dobe at all. Aw, thet's a joke! I seen him in bed. I seen his shadder. I heard his shots comin' from the room. Jack, you seen an' heerd same as me.'

"'Sure. I know the Ranger's cashed,' replied Blome. 'It's not that. I'm sore, boys.'

"'Deader 'n a door-nail in hell!' replied Pickens, louder, as he lifted his glass. 'Here's to Lone Star Steele's ghost! An' if I seen it this minnit I'd ask it to waltz with me!'

"The back door swung violently, and Steele, huge as a giant, plunged through and leaped square in front of that table.

"Some one of them let out a strange, harsh cry. It wasn't Blome or Snecker— probably Pickens. He dropped the glass he had lifted. The cry had stilled the room, so the breaking of the glass was plainly heard. For a space that must have been short, yet seemed long, everybody stood tight. Steele with both hands out and down, leaned a little, in a way I had never seen him do. It was the position of a greyhound, but that was merely the body of him. Steele's nerve, his spirit, his meaning was there, like lightning about to strike. Blome maintained a ghastly, stricken silence.

"Then the instant was plain when he realized this was no ghost of Steele, but the Ranger in the flesh. Blome's whole frame rippled as thought jerked him out of his trance. His comrades sat stone-still. Then Hilliard and Pickens dived without rising from the table. Their haste broke the spell.

"I wish I could tell it as quick as it happened. But Bo Snecker, turning white as a sheet, stuck to Blome. All the others failed him, as he had guessed they would fail. Low curses and exclamations were uttered by men sliding and pressing back, but the principals were mute. I was thinking hard, yet I had no time to get to Steele's side. I, like the rest, was held fast. But I kept my eyes sweeping around, then back again to that center pair.

"Blome slowly rose. I think he did it instinctively. Because if he had expected his first movement to start the action he never would have moved. Snecker sat partly on the rail of his chair, with both feet square on the floor, and he never twitched a muscle. There was a striking difference in the looks of these two rustlers. Snecker had burning holes for eyes in his white face. At the last he was staunch, defiant, game to the core. He didn't think. But Blome faced death and knew it. It was infinitely more than the facing of foes, the taking of stock, preliminary to the even break. Blome's attitude was that of a trapped wolf about to start into savage action; nevertheless, equally it was the pitifully weak stand of a ruffian against ruthless and powerful law.

"The border of Pecos County could have had no greater lesson than this— Blome face-to-face with the Ranger. That part of the border present saw its most noted exponent of lawlessness a coward, almost powerless to go for his gun, fatally sure of his own doom.

"But that moment, seeming so long, really so short, had to end. Blome made a spasmodic upheaval of shoulder and arm. Snecker a second later flashed into movement.

"Steele blurred in my sight. His action couldn't be followed. But I saw his gun, waving up, flame red once—twice—and the reports almost boomed together.

"Blome bent forward, arm down, doubled up, and fell over the table and slid to the floor.

"But Snecker's gun cracked with Steele's last shot. I heard the bullet strike Steele. It made me sick as if it had hit me. But Steele never budged. Snecker leaped up, screaming, his gun sputtering to the floor. His left hand swept to his right arm, which had been shattered by Steele's bullet.

"Blood streamed everywhere. His screams were curses, and then ended, testifying to a rage hardly human. Then, leaping, he went down on his knees after the gun.

"Don't pick it up," called Steele; his command would have checked anyone save an insane man. For an instant it even held Snecker. On his knees, right arm hanging limp, left extended, and face ghastly with agony and fiendish fury, he was certainly an appalling sight.

"'Bo, you're courtin' death,' called a hard voice from the crowd.

"'Snecker, wait. Don't make me kill you!' cried Steele swiftly. 'You're still a boy. Surrender! You'll outlive your sentence many years. I promise clemency. Hold, you fool!'

"But Snecker was not to be denied the last game move. He scrabbled for his gun. Just then something, a breathtaking intuition—I'll never know what— made me turn my head. I saw the bartender deliberately aim a huge gun at Steele. If he had not been so slow, I would have been too late. I whirled and shot. Talk about nick of time! Blandy pulled trigger just as my bullet smashed into his head.

"He dropped dead behind the bar and his gun dropped in front. But he had hit Steele.

"The Ranger staggered, almost fell. I thought he was done, and, yelling, I sped to him.

"But he righted himself. Then I wheeled again. Someone in the crowd killed Bo Snecker as he wobbled up with his gun. That was the signal for a wild run for outdoors, for cover. I heard the crack of guns and whistle of lead. I shoved Steele back of the bar, falling over Blandy as I did so.

"When I got up Steele was leaning over the bar with a gun in each hand. There was a hot fight then for a minute or so, but I didn't fire a shot. Morton and his crowd were busy. Men ran everywhere, shooting, ducking, cursing. The room got blue with smoke till you couldn't see, and then the fight changed to the street.

"Steele and I ran out. There was shooting everywhere. Morton's crowd appeared to be in pursuit of rustlers in all directions. I ran with Steele, and did not observe his condition until suddenly he fell right down in the street. Then he looked so white and so bloody I thought he'd stopped another bullet and—"

Here Miss Sampson's agitation made it necessary for me to halt my story, and I hoped she had heard enough. But she was not sick, as Sally appeared to me; she simply had been overcome by emotion. And presently, with a blaze in her eyes that showed how her soul was aflame with righteous wrath at these rustlers and ruffians, and how, whether she knew it or not, the woman in her loved a fight, she bade me go on. So I persevered, and, with poor little Sally sagging against me, I went on with the details of that fight.

I told how Steele rebounded from his weakness and could no more have been stopped than an avalanche. For all I saw, he did not use his guns again. Here, there, everywhere, as Morton and his squad cornered a rustler, Steele would go in, ordering surrender, promising protection. He seemed to have no thoughts of bullets. I could not hold him back, and it was hard to keep pace with him. How many times he was shot at I had no idea, but it was many. He dragged forth this and that rustler, and turned them all over to Morton to be guarded. More than once he protected a craven rustler from the summary dealing Morton wanted to see in order.

I told Miss Sampson particularly how Steele appeared to me, what his effect was on these men, how toward the end of the fight rustlers were appealing to him to save them from these new-born vigilantes. I believed I drew a picture of the Ranger that would live forever in her heart of hearts. If she were a hero-worshiper she would have her fill.

One thing that was strange to me—leaving fight, action, blood, peril out of the story—the singular exultation, for want of some better term, that I experienced in recalling Steele's look, his wonderful cold, resistless, inexplicable presence, his unquenchable spirit which was at once deadly and merciful. Other men would have killed where he saved. I recalled this magnificent spiritual something about him, remembered it strongest in the ring of his voice as he appealed to Bo Snecker not to force him to kill. Then I told how we left a dozen prisoners under guard and went back to the Hope So to find Blome where he had fallen. Steele's bullet had cut one of the petals of the rose Snecker had playfully put in the rustler's buttonhole. Bright and fatal target for an eye like Steele's! Bo Snecker lay clutching his gun, his face set rigidly in that last fierce expression of his savage nature. There were five other dead men on the floor, and, significant of the work of Steele's unknown allies, Hilliard and Pickens were among them.

"Steele and I made for camp then," I concluded. "We didn't speak a word on the way out. When we reached camp all Steele said was for me to go off and leave him alone. He looked sick. I went off, only not very far. I knew what was wrong with him, and it wasn't bullet-wounds. I was near when he had his spell and fought it out.

"Strange how spilling blood affects some men! It never bothered me much. I hope I'm human, too. I certainly felt an awful joy when I sent that bullet into Blandy's bloated head in time. And I'll always feel that way about it. But Steele's different."

Chapter 12

TORN TWO WAYS

Steele lay in a shady little glade, partly walled by the masses of upreared rocks that we used as a lookout point. He was asleep, yet far from comfortable. The bandage I had put around his head had been made from strips of soiled towel, and, having collected sundry bloody spots, it was an unsightly affair. There was a blotch of dried blood down one side of Steele's face. His shirt bore more dark stains, and in one place was pasted fast to his shoulder where a bandage marked the location of his other wound. A number of green flies were crawling over him and buzzing around his head. He looked helpless, despite his giant size; and certainly a great deal worse off than I had intimated, and, in fact, than he really was.

Miss Sampson gasped when she saw him and both her hands flew to her breast.

"Girls, don't make any noise," I whispered. "I'd rather he didn't wake suddenly to find you here. Go round behind the rocks there. I'll wake him, and call you presently."

They complied with my wish, and I stepped down to Steele and gave him a little shake. He awoke instantly.

"Hello!" I said, "Want a drink?"

"Water or champagne?" he inquired.

I stared at him. "I've some champagne behind the rocks," I added.

"Water, you locoed son of a gun!"

He looked about as thirsty as a desert coyote; also, he looked flighty. I was reaching for the canteen when I happened to think what pleasure it would be to Miss Sampson to minister to him, and I drew back. "Wait a little." Then with an effort I plunged. "Vaughn, listen. Miss Sampson and Sally are here."

I thought he was going to jump up, he started so violently, and I pressed him back.

"She—Why, she's been here all the time—Russ, you haven't double-crossed me?"

"Steele!" I exclaimed. He was certainly out of his head.

"Pure accident, old man."

He appeared to be half stunned, yet an eager, strange, haunting look shone in his eyes. "Fool!" he exclaimed.

"Can't you make the ordeal easier for her?" I asked.

"This'll be hard on Diane. She's got to be told things!"

"Ah!" breathed Steele, sinking back. "Make it easier for her—Russ, you're a damned schemer. You have given me the double-cross. You have and she's going to."

"We're in bad, both of us," I replied thickly. "I've ideas, crazy enough maybe. I'm between the devil and the deep sea, I tell you. I'm about ready to show yellow. All the same, I say, see Miss Sampson and talk to her, even if you can't talk straight."

"All right, Russ," he replied hurriedly. "But, God, man, don't I look a sight! All this dirt and blood!"

"Well, old man, if she takes that bungled mug of yours in her lap, you can be sure you're loved. You needn't jump out of your boots! Brace up now, for I'm going to bring the girls." As I got up to go I heard him groan. I went round behind the stones and found the girls. "Come on," I said. "He's awake now, but a little queer. Feverish. He gets that way sometimes. It won't last long." I led Miss Sampson and Sally back into the shade of our little camp glade.

Steele had gotten worse all in a moment. Also, the fool had pulled the bandage off his head; his wound had begun to bleed anew, and the flies were paying no attention to his weak efforts to brush them away. His head rolled as we reached his side, and his eyes were certainly wild and wonderful and devouring enough. "Who's that?" he demanded.

"Easy there, old man," I replied. "I've brought the girls." Miss Sampson shook like a leaf in the wind.

"So you've come to see me die?" asked Steele in a deep and hollow voice. Miss Sampson gave me a lightning glance of terror.

"He's only off his head," I said. "Soon as we wash and bathe his head, cool his temperature, he'll be all right."

"Oh!" cried Miss Sampson, and dropped to her knees, flinging her gloves aside. She lifted Steele's head into her lap. When I saw her tears falling upon his face I felt worse than a villain. She bent over him for a moment, and one of the tender hands at his cheeks met the flow of fresh blood and did not shrink. "Sally," she said, "bring the scarf out of my coat. There's a veil too. Bring that. Russ, you get me some water—pour some in the pan there."

"Water!" whispered Steele.

She gave him a drink. Sally came with the scarf and veil, and then she backed away to the stone, and sat there. The sight of blood had made her a little pale and weak. Miss Sampson's hands trembled and her tears still fell, but neither interfered with her tender and skillful dressing of that bullet wound.

Steele certainly said a lot of crazy things. "But why'd you come—why're you so good—when you don't love me?"

"Oh, but—I do—love you," whispered Miss Sampson brokenly.

"How do I know?"

"I am here. I tell you."

There was a silence, during which she kept on bathing his head, and he kept on watching her. "Diane!" he broke out suddenly.

"Yes—yes."

"That won't stop the pain in my head."

"Oh, I hope so."

"Kiss me—that will," he whispered. She obeyed as a child might have, and kissed his damp forehead close to the red furrow where the bullet cut.

"Not there," Steele whispered.

Then blindly, as if drawn by a magnet, she bent to his lips. I could not turn away my head, though my instincts were delicate enough. I believe that kiss was the first kiss of love for both Diane Sampson and Vaughn Steele. It was so strange and so long, and somehow beautiful. Steele looked rapt. I could only see the side of Diane's face, and that was white, like snow. After she raised her head she seemed unable, for a moment, to take up her task where it had been broken off, and Steele lay as if he really were dead. Here I got up, and seating myself beside Sally, I put an arm around her. "Sally dear, there are others," I said.

"Oh, Russ—what's to come of it all?" she faltered, and then she broke down and began to cry softly. I would have been only too glad to tell her what hung in the balance, one way or another, had I known. But surely, catastrophe! Then I heard Steele's voice again and its huskiness, its different tone, made me fearful, made me strain my ears when I tried, or thought I tried, not to listen.

"Diane, you know how hard my duty is, don't you?"

"Yes, I know—I think I know."

"You've guessed—about your father?"

"I've seen all along you must clash. But it needn't be so bad. If I can only bring you two together—Ah! please don't speak any more. You're excited now, just not yourself."

"No, listen. We must clash, your father and I. Diane, he's not—"

"Not what he seems! Oh, I know, to my sorrow."

"What do you know?" She seemed drawn by a will stronger than her own. "To my shame I know. He has been greedy, crafty, unscrupulous—dishonest."

"Diane, if he were only that! That wouldn't make my duty torture. That wouldn't ruin your life. Dear, sweet girl, forgive me—your father's—"

"Hush, Vaughn. You're growing excited. It will not do. Please—please—"

"Diane, your father's—chief of this—gang that I came to break up."

"My God, hear him! How dare you—Oh, Vaughn, poor, poor boy, you're out of your mind! Sally, Russ, what shall we do? He's worse. He's saying the most dreadful things! I—I can't bear to hear him!"

Steele heaved a sigh and closed his eyes. I walked away with Sally, led her to and fro in a shady aisle beyond the rocks, and tried to comfort her as best I could. After a while, when we returned to the glade, Miss Sampson had considerable color in her cheeks, and Steele was leaning against the rock, grave and sad. I saw that he had recovered and he had reached the critical point. "Hello, Russ," he said. "Sprung a surprise on me, didn't you? Miss Sampson says I've been a little flighty while she bandaged me up. I hope I wasn't bad. I certainly feel better now. I seem to—to have dreamed."

Miss Sampson flushed at his concluding words. Then silence ensued. I could not think of anything to say and Sally was dumb. "You all seem very strange," said Miss Sampson.

When Steele's face turned gray to his lips I knew the moment had come. "No doubt. We all feel so deeply for you," he said.

"Me? Why?"

"Because the truth must no longer be concealed."

It was her turn to blanch, and her eyes, strained, dark as night, flashed from one of us to the other.

"The truth! Tell it then." She had more courage than any of us.

"Miss Sampson, your father is the leader of this gang of rustlers I have been tracing. Your cousin George Wright, is his right-hand man."

Miss Sampson heard, but she did not believe.

"Tell her, Russ," Steele added huskily, turning away. Wildly she whirled to me. I would have given anything to have been able to lie to her. As it was I could not speak. But she read the truth in my face. And she collapsed as if she had been shot. I caught her and laid her on the grass. Sally, murmuring and crying, worked over her. I helped. But Steele stood aloof, dark and silent, as if he hoped she would never return to consciousness.

When she did come to, and began to cry, to moan, to talk frantically, Steele staggered away, while Sally and I made futile efforts to calm her. All we could do was to prevent her doing herself violence. Presently, when her fury of emotion subsided, and she began to show a hopeless stricken shame, I left Sally with her and went off a little way myself. How long I remained absent I had no idea, but it was no inconsiderable length of time. Upon my return, to my surprise and relief, Miss Sampson had recovered her composure, or at least, self-control. She stood leaning against the rock where Steele had been, and at this moment, beyond any doubt, she was supremely more beautiful than I had ever seen her. She was white, tragic, wonderful. "Where is Mr. Steele?" she asked. Her tone and her look did not seem at all suggestive of the mood I expected to find her in—one of beseeching agony, of passionate appeal to Steele not to ruin her father.

"I'll find him," I replied turning away.

Steele was readily found and came back with me. He was as unlike himself as she was strange. But when they again faced each other, then they were indeed new to me.

"I want to know—what you must do," she said. Steele told her briefly, and his voice was stern.

"Those—those criminals outside of my own family don't concern me now. But can my father and cousin be taken without bloodshed? I want to know the absolute truth." Steele knew that they could not be, but he could not tell her so. Again she appealed to me. Thus my part in the situation grew harder. It hurt me so that it made me angry, and my anger made me cruelly frank.

"No. It can't be done. Sampson and Wright will be desperately hard to approach, which'll make the chances even. So, if you must know the truth, it'll be your father and cousin to go under, or it'll be Steele or me, or any combination luck breaks—or all of us!"

Her self-control seemed to fly to the four winds. Swift as light she flung herself down before Steele, against his knees, clasped her arms round him. "Good God! Miss Sampson, you mustn't do that!" implored Steele. He tried to break her hold with shaking hands, but he could not.

"Listen! Listen!" she cried, and her voice made Steele, and Sally and me also, still as the rock behind us. "Hear me! Do you think I beg you to let my father go, for his sake? No! No! I have gloried in your Ranger duty. I have loved you because of it. But some awful tragedy threatens here. Listen, Vaughn Steele. Do not you deny me, as I kneel here. I love you. I never loved any other man. But not for my love do I beseech you.

"There is no help here unless you forswear your duty. Forswear it! Do not kill my father—the father of the woman who loves you. Worse and more horrible it would be to let my father kill you! It's I who make this situation unnatural, impossible. You must forswear your duty. I can live no longer if you don't. I pray you—" Her voice had sunk to a whisper, and now it failed. Then she seemed to get into his arms, to wind herself around him, her hair loosened, her face upturned, white and spent, her arms blindly circling his neck. She was all love, all surrender, all supreme appeal, and these, without her beauty, would have made her wonderful. But her beauty! Would not Steele have been less than a man or more than a man had he been impervious to it? She was like some snow-white exquisite flower, broken, and suddenly blighted. She was a woman then in all that made a woman helpless—in all that made her mysterious, sacred, absolutely and unutterably more than any other thing in life. All this time my gaze had been riveted on her only. But when she lifted her white face, tried to lift it, rather, and he drew her up, and then when both white faces met and seemed to blend in something rapt, awesome, tragic as life—then I saw Steele.

I saw a god, a man as beautiful as she was. They might have stood, indeed, they did stand alone in the heart of a desert—alone in the world—alone with their love and their agony. It was a solemn and profound moment for me. I faintly realized how great it must have been for them, yet all the while there hammered at my mind the vital thing at stake. Had they forgotten, while I remembered? It might have been only a moment that he held her. It might have been my own agitation that conjured up such swift and whirling thoughts. But if my mind sometimes played me false my eyes never had. I thought I saw Diane Sampson die in Steele's arms; I could have sworn his heart was breaking; and mine was on the point of breaking, too.

How beautiful they were! How strong, how mercifully strong, yet shaken, he seemed! How tenderly, hopelessly, fatally appealing she was in that hour of her broken life! If I had been Steele I would have forsworn my duty, honor, name, service for her sake. Had I mind enough to divine his torture, his temptation, his narrow escape? I seemed to feel them, at any rate, and while I saw him with a beautiful light on his face, I saw him also ghastly, ashen, with hands that shook as they groped around her, loosing her, only to draw her convulsively back again. It was the saddest sight I had ever seen. Death was nothing to it. Here was the death of happiness. He must wreck the life of the woman who loved him and whom he loved. I was becoming half frantic, almost ready to cry out the uselessness of this scene, almost on the point of pulling them apart, when Sally dragged me away. Her clinging hold then made me feel perhaps a little of what Miss Sampson's must have been to Steele.

How different the feeling when it was mine! I could have thrust them apart, after all my schemes and tricks, to throw them together, in vague, undefined fear of their embrace. Still, when love beat at my own pulses, when Sally's soft hand held me tight and she leaned to me—that was different. I was glad to be led away—glad to have a chance to pull myself together. But was I to have that chance? Sally, who in the stife of emotion had been forgotten, might have to be reckoned with. Deep within me, some motive, some purpose, was being born in travail. I did not know what, but instinctively I feared Sally. I feared her because I loved her. My wits came back to combat my passion. This hazel-eyed girl, soft, fragile creature, might be harder to move than the Ranger. But could she divine a motive scarcely yet formed in my brain? Suddenly I became cool, with craft to conceal.

"Oh, Russ! What's the matter with you?" she queried quickly. "Can't Diane and Steele, you and I ride away from this bloody, bad country? Our own lives, our happiness, come first, do they not?"

"They ought to, I suppose," I muttered, fighting against the insidious sweetness of her. I knew then I must keep my lips shut or betray myself.

"You look so strange. Russ, I wouldn't want you to kiss me with that mouth. Thin, shut lips—smile! Soften and kiss me! Oh, you're so cold, strange! You chill me!"

"Dear child, I'm badly shaken," I said. "Don't expect me to be natural yet. There are things you can't guess. So much depended upon—Oh, never mind! I'll go now. I want to be alone, to think things out. Let me go, Sally."

She held me only the tighter, tried to pull my face around. How intuitively keen women were. She felt my distress, and that growing, stern, and powerful thing I scarcely dared to acknowledge to myself. Strangely, then, I relaxed and faced her. There was no use trying to foil these feminine creatures. Every second I seemed to grow farther from her. The swiftness of this mood of mine was my only hope. I realized I had to get away quickly, and make up my mind after that what I intended to do. It was an earnest, soulful, and loving pair of eyes that I met. What did she read in mine? Her hands left mine to slide to my shoulders, to slip behind my neck, to lock there like steel bands. Here was my ordeal. Was it to be as terrible as Steele's had been? I thought it would be, and I swore by all that was rising grim and cold in me that I would be strong. Sally gave a little cry that cut like a blade in my heart, and then she was close-pressed upon me, her quivering breast beating against mine, her eyes, dark as night now, searching my soul.

She saw more than I knew, and with her convulsive clasp of me confirmed my half-formed fears. Then she kissed me, kisses that had no more of girlhood or coquetry or joy or anything but woman's passion to blind and hold and tame. By their very intensity I sensed the tiger in me. And it was the tiger that made her new and alluring sweetness fail of its intent. I did not return one of her kisses. Just one kiss given back—and I would be lost.

"Oh, Russ, I'm your promised wife!" she whispered at my lips. "Soon, you said! I want it to be soon! To-morrow!" All the subtlety, the intelligence, the cunning, the charm, the love that made up the whole of woman's power, breathed in her pleading. What speech known to the tongue could have given me more torture? She chose the strongest weapon nature afforded her. And had the calamity to consider been mine alone, I would have laughed at it and taken Sally at her word. Then I told her in short, husky sentences what had depended on Steele: that I loved the Ranger Service, but loved him more; that his character, his life, embodied this Service I loved; that I had ruined him; and now I would forestall him, do his work, force the issue myself or die in the attempt.

"Dearest, it's great of you!" she cried. "But the cost! If you kill one of my kin I'll—I'll shrink from you! If you're killed—Oh, the thought is dreadful! You've done your share. Let Steele—some other Ranger finish it. I swear I don't plead for my uncle or my cousin, for their sakes. If they are vile, let them suffer. Russ, it's you I think of! Oh, my pitiful little dreams! I wanted so to surprise you with my beautiful home—the oranges, the mossy trees, the mocking-birds. Now you'll never, never come!"

"But, Sally, there's a chance—a mere chance I can do the job without—"

Then she let go of me. She had given up. I thought she was going to drop, and drew her toward the stone. I cursed the day I ever saw Neal and the service. Where, now, was the arch prettiness, the gay, sweet charm of Sally Langdon? She looked as if she were suffering from a desperate physical injury. And her final breakdown showed how, one way or another, I was lost to her.

As she sank on the stone I had my supreme wrench, and it left me numb, hard, in a cold sweat. "Don't betray me! I'll forestall him! He's planned nothing for to-day," I whispered hoarsely. "Sally—you dearest, gamest little girl in the world! Remember I loved you, even if I couldn't prove it your way. It's for his sake. I'm to blame for their love. Some day my act will look different to you. Good-by!"

Chapter 13

RUSS SITTELL IN ACTION

I ran like one possessed of devils down that rough slope, hurdling the stones and crashing through the brush, with a sound in my ears that was not all the rush of the wind. When I reached a level I kept running; but something dragged at me. I slowed down to a walk. Never in my life had I been victim of such sensation. I must flee from something that was drawing me back. Apparently one side of my mind was unalterably fixed, while the other was a hurrying conglomeration of flashes of thought, reception of sensations. I could not get calm.

By and by, almost involuntarily, with a fleeting look backward as if in expectation of pursuit, I hurried faster on. Action seemed to make my state less oppressive; it eased the weight upon me. But the farther I went on, the harder it was to continue. I was turning my back upon love, happiness, success in life, perhaps on life itself. I was doing that, but my decision had not been absolute. There seemed no use to go on farther until I was absolutely sure of myself. I received a clear warning thought that such work as seemed haunting and driving me could never be carried out in the mood under which I labored. I hung on to that thought. Several times I slowed up, then stopped, only to tramp on again.

At length, as I mounted a low ridge, Linrock lay bright and green before me, not faraway, and the sight was a conclusive check. There were mesquites on the ridge, and I sought the shade beneath them. It was the noon hour, with hot, glary sun and no wind. Here I had to have out my fight. If ever in my varied life of exciting adventure I strove to think, to understand myself, to see through difficulties, I assuredly strove then. I was utterly unlike myself; I could not bring the old self back; I was not the same man I once had been. But I could understand why. It was because of Sally Langdon, the gay and roguish girl who had bewitched me, the girl whom love had made a woman— the kind of woman meant to make life beautiful for me.

I saw her changing through all those weeks, holding many of the old traits and graces, acquiring new character of mind and body, to become what I had just fled from—a woman sweet, fair, loyal, loving, passionate.

Temptation assailed me. To have her to-morrow—my wife! She had said it. Just twenty-four little hours, and she would be mine—the only woman I had ever really coveted, the only one who had ever found the good in me. The thought was alluring. I followed it out, a long, happy stage-ride back to Austin, and then by train to her home where, as she had said, the oranges grew and the trees waved with streamers of gray moss and the mocking-birds made melody. I pictured that home. I wondered that long before I had not associated wealth and luxury with her family. Always I had owned a weakness for plantations, for the agricultural life with its open air and freedom from towns.

I saw myself riding through the cotton and rice and cane, home to the stately old mansion, where long-eared hounds bayed me welcome and a woman looked for me and met me with happy and beautiful smiles. There might—there *would* be children. And something new, strange, confounding with its emotion, came to life deep in my heart. There would be children! Sally their mother; I their father! The kind of life a lonely Ranger always yearned for and never had! I saw it all, felt it keenly, lived its sweetness in an hour of temptation that made me weak physically and my spirit faint and low.

For what had I turned my back on this beautiful, all-satisfying prospect? Was it to arrest and jail a few rustlers? Was it to meet that mocking Sampson face to face and show him my shield and reach for my gun? Was it to kill that hated Wright? Was it to save the people of Linrock from further greed, raids, murder? Was it to please and aid my old captain, Neal of the Rangers? Was it to save the Service to the State?

No—a thousand times no. It was for the sake of Steele. Because he was a wonderful man! Because I had been his undoing! Because I had thrown Diane Sampson into his arms! That had been my great error. This Ranger had always been the wonder and despair of his fellow officers, so magnificent a machine, so sober, temperate, chaste, so unremittingly loyal to the Service, so strangely stern and faithful to his conception of the law, so perfect in his fidelity to duty. He was the model, the inspiration, the pride of all of us. To me, indeed, he represented the Ranger Service. He was the incarnation of that spirit which fighting Texas had developed to oppose wildness and disorder and crime. He would carry through this Linrock case; but even so, if he were not killed, his career would be ruined. He might save the Service, yet at the cost of his happiness. He was not a machine; he was a man. He might be a perfect Ranger; still he was a human being.

The loveliness, the passion, the tragedy of a woman, great as they were, had not power to shake him from his duty. Futile, hopeless, vain her love had been to influence him. But there had flashed over me with subtle, overwhelming suggestion that not futile, not vain was *my* love to save him! Therefore, beyond and above all other claims, and by reason of my wrong to him, his claim came first.

It was then there was something cold and deathlike in my soul; it was then I bade farewell to Sally Langdon. For I knew, whatever happened, of one thing I was sure—I would have to kill either Sampson or Wright. Snecker could be managed; Sampson might be trapped into arrest; but Wright had no sense, no control, no fear. He would snarl like a panther and go for his gun, and he would have to be killed. This, of all consummations, was the one to be calculated upon. And, of course, by Sally's own words, that contingency would put me forever outside the pale for her.

I did not deceive myself; I did not accept the slightest intimation of hope; I gave her up. And then for a time regret, remorse, pain, darkness worked their will with me.

I came out of it all bitter and callous and sore, in the most fitting of moods to undertake a difficult and deadly enterprise. Miss Sampson completely slipped my mind; Sally became a wraith as of some one dead; Steele began to fade. In their places came the bushy-bearded Snecker, the olive-skinned Sampson with his sharp eyes, and dark, evil faced Wright. Their possibilities began to loom up, and with my speculation returned tenfold more thrilling and sinister the old strange zest of the man-hunt.

It was about one o'clock when I strode into Linrock. The streets for the most part were deserted. I went directly to the hall where Morton and Zimmer, with their men, had been left by Steele to guard the prisoners. I found them camping out in the place, restless, somber, anxious. The fact that only about half the original number of prisoners were left struck me as further indication of Morton's summary dealing. But when I questioned him as to the decrease in number, he said bluntly that they had escaped. I did not know whether or not to believe him. But that didn't matter. I tried to get in some more questions, only I found that Morton and Zimmer meant to be heard first. "Where's Steele?" they demanded.

"He's out of town, in a safe place," I replied. "Too bad hurt for action. I'm to rush through with the rest of the deal."

"That's good. We've waited long enough. This gang has been split, an' if we hurry they'll never get together again. Old man Snecker showed up to-day. He's drawin' the outfit in again. Reckon he's waitin' for orders. Sure he's ragin' since Bo was killed. This old fox will be dangerous if he gets goin'."

"Where is he now?" I queried.

"Over at the Hope So. Must be a dozen of the gang there. But he's the only leader left we know of. If we get him, the rustler gang will be broken for good. He's sent word down here for us to let our prisoners go or there'd be a damn bloody fight. We haven't sent our answer yet. Was hopin' Steele would show up. An' now we're sure glad you're back."

"Morton, I'll take the answer," I replied quickly. "Now there're two things. Do you know if Sampson and Wright are at the ranch?"

"They were an hour ago. We had word. Zimmer saw Dick."

"All right. Have you any horses handy?"

"Sure. Those hitched outside belong to us."

"I want you to take a man with you, in a few moments, and ride round the back roads and up to Sampson's house. Get off and wait under the trees till you hear me shoot or yell, then come fast."

Morton's breast heaved; he whistled as he breathed; his neck churned. "God Almighty! So *there* the scent leads! We always wondered—half believed. But no one spoke—no one had any nerve." Morton moistened his lips; his face was livid; his big hands shook. "Russ, you can gamble on me."

"Good. Well, that's all. Come out and get me a horse."

When I had mounted and was half-way to the Hope So, my plan, as far as Snecker was concerned, had been formed. It was to go boldy into the saloon, ask for the rustler, first pretend I had a reply from Morton and then, when I had Snecker's ear, whisper a message supposedly from Sampson. If Snecker was too keen to be decoyed I could at least surprise him off his guard and kill him, then run for my horse. The plan seemed clever to me. I had only one thing to fear, and that was a possibility of the rustlers having seen my part in Steele's defense the other day. That had to be risked. There were always some kind of risks to be faced.

It was scarcely a block and a half to the Hope So. Before I arrived I knew I had been seen. When I dismounted before the door I felt cold, yet there was an exhilaration in the moment. I never stepped more naturally and carelessly into the saloon. It was full of men. There were men behind the bar helping themselves. Evidently Blandy's place had not been filled. Every face near the door was turned toward me; dark, intent, scowling, malignant they were, and made me need my nerve.

"Say, boys, I've a word for Snecker," I called, quite loud. Nobody stirred. I swept my glance over the crowd, but did not see Snecker. "I'm in some hurry," I added.

"Bill ain't here," said a man at the table nearest me. "Air you comin' from Morton?"

"Nit. But I'm not yellin' this message."

The rustler rose, and in a few long strides confronted me.

"Word from Sampson!" I whispered, and the rustler stared. "I'm in his confidence. He's got to see Bill at once. Sampson sends word he's quit—he's done—he's through. The jig is up, and he means to hit the road out of Linrock."

"Bill'll kill him surer 'n hell," muttered the rustler. "But we all said it'd come to thet. An' what'd Wright say?"

"Wright! Why, he's cashed in. Didn't you-all hear? Reckon Sampson shot him."

The rustler cursed his amaze and swung his rigid arm with fist clenched tight. "When did Wright get it?"

"A little while ago. I don't know how long. Anyway, I saw him lyin' dead on the porch. An' say, pard, I've got to rustle. Send Bill up quick as he comes. Tell him Sampson wants to turn over all his stock an' then light out."

I backed to the door, and the last I saw of the rustler he was standing there in a scowling amaze. I had fooled him all right. If only I had the luck to have Snecker come along soon. Mounting, I trotted the horse leisurely up the street. Business and everything else was at a standstill in Linrock these days. The doors of the stores were barricaded. Down side streets, however, I saw a few people, a buckboard, and stray cattle.

When I reached the edge of town I turned aside a little and took a look at the ruins of Steele's adobe house. The walls and debris had all been flattened, scattered about, and if anything of, value had escaped destruction it had disappeared. Steele, however, had left very little that would have been of further use to him. Turning again, I continued on my way up to the ranch. It seemed that, though I was eager rather than backward, my mind seized avidly upon suggestion or attraction, as if to escape the burden of grim pondering. When about half-way across the flat, and perhaps just out of gun-shot sound of Sampson's house, I heard the rapid clatter of hoofs on the hard road. I wheeled, expecting to see Morton and his man, and was ready to be chagrined at their coming openly instead of by the back way. But this was only one man, and it was not Morton. He seemed of big build, and he bestrode a fine bay horse. There evidently was reason for hurry, too. At about one hundred yards, when I recognized Snecker, complete astonishment possessed me.

Well it was I had ample time to get on my guard! In wheeling my horse I booted him so hard that he reared. As I had been warm I had my sombrero over the pommel of the saddle. And when the head of my horse blocked any possible sight of movement of my hand, I pulled my gun and held it concealed under my sombrero. This rustler had bothered me in my calculations. And here he came galloping, alone. Exultation would have been involuntary then but for the sudden shock, and then the cold settling of temper, the breathless suspense. Snecker pulled his huge bay and pounded to halt abreast of me. Luck favored me. Had I ever had anything but luck in these dangerous deals?

Snecker seemed to fume; internally there was a volcano. His wide sombrero and bushy beard hid all of his face except his eyes, which were deepset furnaces. He, too, like his lieutenant, had been carried completely off balance by the strange message apparently from Sampson. It was Sampson's name that had fooled and decoyed these men. "Hey! You're the feller who jest left word fer some one at the Hope So?" he asked.

"Yes," I replied, while with my left hand I patted the neck of my horse, holding him still.

"Sampson wants me bad, eh?"

"Reckon there's only one man who wants you more."

Steadily, I met his piercing gaze. This was a rustler not to be long victim to any ruse. I waited in cold surety.

"You thet cowboy, Russ?" he asked.

"I was—and I'm not!" I replied significantly.

The violent start of this violent outlaw was a rippling jerk of passion. "What'n hell!" he ejaculated.

"Bill, you're easy."

"Who're you?" he uttered hoarsely.

I watched Snecker with hawk-like keenness. "United States deputy marshal. Bill, you're under arrest!"

He roared a mad curse as his hand clapped down to his gun. Then I fired through my sombrero. Snecker's big horse plunged. The rustler fell back, and one of his legs pitched high as he slid off the lunging steed. His other foot caught in the stirrup. This fact terribly frightened the horse. He bolted, dragging the rustler for a dozen jumps. Then Snecker's foot slipped loose. He lay limp and still and shapeless in the road. I did not need to go back to look him over.

But to make assurance doubly sure, I dismounted, and went back to where he lay. My bullet had gone where it had been aimed. As I rode up into Sampson's court-yard and turned in to the porch I heard loud and angry voices. Sampson and Wright were quarrelling again. How my lucky star guided me! I had no plan of action, but my brain was equal to a hundred lightning-swift evolutions. The voices ceased. The men had heard the horse. Both of them came out on the porch. In an instant I was again the lolling impudent cowboy, half under the influence of liquor.

"It's only Russ and he's drunk," said George Wright contemptuously.

"I heard horses trotting off there," replied Sampson. "Maybe the girls are coming. I bet I teach them not to run off again—Hello, Russ."

He looked haggard and thin, but seemed amiable enough. He was in his shirt-sleeves and he had come out with a gun in his hand. This he laid on a table near the wall. He wore no belt. I rode right up to the porch and, greeting them laconically, made a show of a somewhat tangle-footed cowboy dismounting. The moment I got off and straightened up, I asked no more. The game was mine. It was the great hour of my life and I met it as I had never met another. I looked and acted what I pretended to be, though a deep and intense passion, an almost ungovernable suspense, an icy sickening nausea abided with me. All I needed, all I wanted was to get Sampson and Wright together, or failing that, to maneuver into such position that I had any kind of a chance. Sampson's gun on the table made three distinct objects for me to watch and two of them could change position.

"What do you want here?" demanded Wright. He was red, bloated, thick-lipped, all fiery and sweaty from drink, though sober on the moment, and he had the expression of a desperate man in his last stand. It *was* his last stand, though he was ignorant of that.

"Me—Say, Wright, I ain't fired yet," I replied, in slow-rising resentment.

"Well, you're fired now," he replied insolently.

"Who fires me, I'd like to know?" I walked up on the porch and I had a cigarette in one hand, a match in the other. I struck the match.

"I do," said Wright.

I studied him with apparent amusement. It had taken only one glance around for me to divine that Sampson would enjoy any kind of a clash between Wright and me. "Huh! You fired me once before an' it didn't go, Wright. I reckon you don't stack up here as strong as you think."

He was facing the porch, moody, preoccupied, somber, all the time. Only a little of his mind was concerned with me. Manifestly there were strong forces at work. Both men were strained to a last degree, and Wright could be made to break at almost a word. Sampson laughed mockingly at this sally of mine, and that stung Wright. He stopped his pacing and turned his handsome, fiery eyes on me. "Sampson, I won't stand this man's impudence."

"Aw, Wright, cut that talk. I'm not impudent. Sampson knows I'm a good fellow, on the square, and I have you sized up about O.K."

"All the same, Russ, you'd better dig out," said Sampson. "Don't kick up any fuss. We're busy with deals to-day. And I expect visitors."

"Sure. I won't stay around where I ain't wanted," I replied. Then I lit my cigarette and did not move an inch out of my tracks.

Sampson sat in a chair near the door; the table upon which lay his gun stood between him and Wright. This position did not invite me to start anything. But the tension had begun to be felt. Sampson had his sharp gaze on me. "What'd you come for, anyway?" he asked suddenly.

"Well, I had some news I was asked to fetch in."

"Get it out of you then."

"See here now, Mr. Sampson, the fact is I'm a tender-hearted fellow. I hate to hurt people's feelin's. And if I was to spring this news in Mr. Wright's hearin', why, such a sensitive, high-tempered gentleman as he would go plumb off his nut." Unconcealed sarcasm was the dominant note in that speech. Wright flared up, yet he was eagerly curious. Sampson, probably, thought I was only a little worse for drink, and but for the way I rubbed Wright he would not have tolerated me at all.

"What's this news? You needn't be afraid of my feelings," said Wright.

"Ain't so sure of that," I drawled. "It concerns the lady you're sweet on, an' the ranger you ain't sweet on."

Sampson jumped up. "Russ, had Diane gone out to meet Steele?" he asked angrily.

"Sure she had," I replied.

I thought Wright would choke. He was thick-necked anyway, and the gush of blood made him tear at the soft collar of his shirt. Both men were excited now, moving about, beginning to rouse. I awaited my chance, patient, cold, all my feelings shut in the vise of my will.

"How do you know she met Steele?" demanded Sampson.

"I was there. I met Sally at the same time."

"But why should my daughter meet this Ranger?"

"She's in love with him and he's in love with her."

The simple statement might have had the force of a juggernaut. I reveled in Wright's state, but I felt sorry for Sampson. He had not outlived his pride. Then I saw the leaping thought—would this daughter side against him? Would she help to betray him? He seemed to shrivel up, to grow old while I watched him.

Wright, finding his voice, cursed Diane, cursed the Ranger, then Sampson, then me.

"You damned, selfish fool!" cried Sampson, in deep, bitter scorn. "All you think of is yourself. Your loss of the girl! Think once of me—my home—my life!"

Then the connection subtly put out by Sampson apparently dawned upon the other. Somehow, through this girl, her father and cousin were to be betrayed. I got that impression, though I could not tell how true it was. Certainly, Wright's jealousy was his paramount emotion.

Sampson thrust me sidewise off the porch. "Go away," he ordered. He did not look around to see if I came back. Quickly I leaped to my former position. He confronted Wright. He was beyond the table where the gun lay. They were close together. My moment had come. The game was mine—and a ball of fire burst in my brain to race all over me.

"To hell with you!" burst out Wright incoherently. He was frenzied. "I'll have her or nobody else will!"

"You never will," returned Sampson stridently. "So help me God, I'd rather see her Ranger Steele's wife than yours!"

While Wright absorbed that shock Sampson leaned toward him, all of hate and menace in his mien. They had forgotten the half-drunken cowboy. "Wright, you made me what I am," continued Sampson. "I backed you, protected you, finally I went in with you. Now it's ended. I quit you. I'm done!" Their gray, passion-corded faces were still as stones.

"Gentlemen," I called in clear, high, far-reaching voice, the intonation of authority, "you're both done!"

They wheeled to confront me, to see my leveled gun. "Don't move! Not a muscle! Not a finger!" I warned. Sampson read what Wright had not the mind to read. His face turned paler gray, to ashen.

"What d'ye mean?" yelled Wright fiercely, shrilly. It was not in him to obey my command, to see impending death. All quivering and strung, yet with perfect control, I raised my left hand to turn back a lapel of my open vest. The silver shield flashed brightly.

"United States deputy marshal in service of Ranger Steele!"

Wright howled like a dog. With barbarous and insane fury, with sheer, impotent folly, he swept a clawing hand for his gun. My shot broke his action as it cut short his life. Before Wright even tottered, before he loosed the gun, Sampson leaped behind him, clasped him with his left arm, quick as lightning jerked the gun from both clutching fingers and sheath. I shot at Sampson, then again, then a third time. All my bullets sped into the upheld nodding Wright. Sampson had protected himself with the body of the dead man. I had seen red flashes, puffs of smoke, had heard quick reports. Something stung my left arm. Then a blow like wind, light of sound yet shocking in impact, struck me, knocked me flat. The hot rend of lead followed the blow. My heart seemed to explode, yet my mind kept extraordinarily clear and rapid.

I raised myself, felt a post at my shoulder, leaned on it. I heard Sampson work the action of Wright's gun. I heard the hammer click, fall upon empty shells. He had used up all the loads in Wright's gun. I heard him curse as a man cursed at defeat. I waited, cool and sure now, for him to show his head or other vital part from behind his bolster. He tried to lift the dead man, to edge him closer toward the table where the gun lay. But, considering the peril of exposing himself, he found the task beyond him. He bent, peering at me under Wright's arm. Sampson's eyes were the eyes of a man who meant to kill me. There was never any mistaking the strange and terrible light of eyes like those.

More than once I had a chance to aim at them, at the top of Sampson's head, at a strip of his side. But I had only two shells left. I wanted to make sure. Suddenly I remembered Morton and his man. Then I pealed out a cry— hoarse, strange, yet far-reaching. It was answered by a shout. Sampson heard it. It called forth all that was in the man. He flung Wright's body off. But even as it dropped, before Sampson could recover to leap as he surely intended for the gun, I covered him, called piercingly to him. I could kill him there or as he moved. But one chance I gave him.

"Don't jump for the gun! Don't! I'll kill you! I've got two shells left! Sure as God, I'll kill you!"

He stood perhaps ten feet from the table where his gun lay. I saw him calculating chances. He was game. He had the courage that forced me to respect him. I just saw him measure the distance to that gun. He was magnificent. He meant to do it. I would have to kill him.

"Sampson, listen!" I cried, very swiftly. "The game's up! You're done! But think of your daughter! I'll spare your life, I'll give you freedom on one condition. For her sake! I've got you nailed—all the proofs. It was I behind the wall the other night. Blome, Hilliard, Pickens, Bo Snecker, are dead. I killed Bo Snecker on the way up here. There lies Wright. You're alone. And here comes Morton and his men to my aid.

"Give up! Surrender! Consent to demands and I'll spare you. You can go free back to your old country. It's for Diane's sake! Her life, perhaps her happiness, can be saved! Hurry, man! Your answer!"

"Suppose I refuse?" he queried, with a dark and terrible earnestness.

"Then I'll kill you in your tracks! You can't move a hand! Your word or death! Hurry, Sampson! I can't last much longer. But I can kill you before I drop. Be a man! For her sake! Quick! Another second now—By God, I'll kill you!"

"All right, Russ! I give my word," he said, and deliberately walked to the chair and fell into it, just as Morton came running up with his man.

"Put away your gun," I ordered them. "The game's up. Snecker and Wright are dead. Sampson is my prisoner. He has my word he'll be protected. It's for you to draw up papers with him. He'll divide all his property, every last acre, every head of stock as you and Zimmer dictate. He gives up all. Then he's free to leave the country, and he's never to return."

Chapter 14

THROUGH THE VALLEY

Sampson looked strangely at the great bloody blot on my breast and his look made me conscious of a dark hurrying of my mind. Morton came stamping up the steps with blunt queries, with anxious mien. When he saw the front of me he halted, threw wide his arms.

"There come the girls!" suddenly exclaimed Sampson. "Morton, help me drag Wright inside. They mustn't see him."

I was facing down the porch toward the court and corrals. Miss Sampson and Sally had come in sight, were swiftly approaching, evidently alarmed. Steele, no doubt, had remained out at the camp. I was watching them, wondering what they would do and say presently, and then Sampson and Johnson came to carry me indoors. They laid me on the couch in the parlor where the girls used to be so often.

"Russ, you're pretty hard hit," said Sampson, bending over me, with his hands at my breast. The room was bright with sunshine, yet the light seemed to be fading.

"Reckon I am," I replied.

"I'm sorry. If only you could have told me sooner! Wright, damn him! Always I've split over him!"

"But the last time, Sampson."

"Yes, and I came near driving you to kill me, too. Russ, you talked me out of it. For Diane's sake! She'll be in here in a minute. This'll be harder than facing a gun."

"Hard now. But it'll—turn out—O.K."

"Russ, will you do me a favor?" he asked, and he seemed shamefaced.

"Sure."

"Let Diane and Sally think Wright shot you. He's dead. It can't matter. And you're hard hit. The girls are fond of you. If—if you go under—Russ, the old side of my life is coming back. It's *been* coming. It'll be here just about when she enters this room. And by God, I'd change places with you if I could."

"Glad you—said that, Sampson," I replied. "And sure—Wright plugged me. It's our secret. I've a reason, too, not—that—it—matters—much—now."

The light was fading. I could not talk very well. I felt dumb, strange, locked in ice, with dull little prickings of my flesh, with dim rushing sounds in my ears. But my mind was clear. Evidently there was little to be done. Morton came in, looked at me, and went out. I heard the quick, light steps of the girls on the porch, and murmuring voices.

"Where'm I hit?" I whispered.

"Three places. Arm, shoulder, and a bad one in the breast. It got your lung, I'm afraid. But if you don't go quick, you've a chance."

"Sure I've a chance."

"Russ, I'll tell the girls, do what I can for you, then settle with Morton and clear out."

Just then Diane and Sally entered the room. I heard two low cries, so different in tone, and I saw two dim white faces. Sally flew to my side and dropped to her knees. Both hands went to my face, then to my breast. She lifted them, shaking. They were red. White and mute she gazed from them to me. But some woman's intuition kept her from fainting.

"Papa!" cried Diane, wringing her hands.

"Don't give way," he replied. "Both you girls will need your nerve. Russ is badly hurt. There's little hope for him."

Sally moaned and dropped her face against me, clasping me convulsively. I tried to reach a hand out to touch her, but I could not move. I felt her hair against my face. Diane uttered a low heart-rending cry, which both Sampson and I understood.

"Listen, let me tell it quick," he said huskily. "There's been a fight. Russ killed Snecker and Wright. They resisted arrest. It—it was Wright—it was Wright's gun that put Russ down. Russ let me off. In fact, Diane, he saved me. I'm to divide my property—return so far as possible what I've stolen—leave Texas at once and forever. You'll find me back in old Louisiana—if—if you ever want to come home."

As she stood there, realizing her deliverance, with the dark and tragic glory of her eyes passing from her father to me, my own sight shadowed, and I thought if I were dying then, it was not in vain.

"Send—for—Steele," I whispered.

Silently, swiftly, breathlessly they worked over me. I was exquisitely sensitive to touch, to sound, but I could not see anything. By and by all was quiet, and I slipped into a black void. Familiar heavy swift footsteps, the thump of heels of a powerful and striding man, jarred into the blackness that held me, seemed to split it to let me out; and I opened my eyes in a sunlit room to see Sally's face all lined and haggard, to see Miss Sampson fly to the door, and the stalwart Ranger bow his lofty head to enter. However far life had ebbed from me, then it came rushing back, keen-sighted, memorable, with agonizing pain in every nerve. I saw him start, I heard him cry, but I could not speak. He bent over me and I tried to smile. He stood silent, his hand on me, while Diane Sampson told swiftly, brokenly, what had happened.

How she told it! I tried to whisper a protest. To any one on earth except Steele I might have wished to appear a hero. Still, at that moment I had more dread of him than any other feeling. She finished the story with her head on his shoulder, with tears that certainly were in part for me. Once in my life, then, I saw him stunned. But when he recovered it was not Diane that he thought of first, nor of the end of Sampson's power. He turned to me.

"Little hope?" he cried out, with the deep ring in his voice. "No! There's every hope. No bullet hole like that could ever kill this Ranger. Russ!"

I could not answer him. But this time I did achieve a smile. There was no shadow, no pain in his face such as had haunted me in Sally's and Diane's. He could fight death the same as he could fight evil. He vitalized the girls. Diane began to hope; Sally lost her woe. He changed the atmosphere of that room. Something filled it, something like himself, big, virile, strong. The very look of him made me suddenly want to live; and all at once it seemed I felt alive. And that was like taking the deadened ends of nerves to cut them raw and quicken them with fiery current.

From stupor I had leaped to pain, and that tossed me into fever. There were spaces darkened, mercifully shutting me in; there were others of light, where I burned and burned in my heated blood. Sally, like the wraith she had become in my mind, passed in and out; Diane watched and helped in those hours when sight was clear. But always the Ranger was with me. Sometimes I seemed to feel his spirit grappling with mine, drawing me back from the verge. Sometimes, in strange dreams, I saw him there between me and a dark, cold, sinister shape.

The fever passed, and with the first nourishing drink given me I seemed to find my tongue, to gain something.

"Hello, old man," I whispered to Steele.

"Oh, Lord, Russ, to think you would double-cross me the way you did!"

That was his first speech to me after I had appeared to face round from the grave. His good-humored reproach told me more than any other thing how far from his mind was thought of death for me. Then he talked a little to me, cheerfully, with that directness and force characteristic of him always, showing me that the danger was past, and that I would now be rapidly on the mend. I discovered that I cared little whether I was on the mend or not.

When I had passed the state of somber unrealities and then the hours of pain and then that first inspiring flush of renewed desire to live, an entirely different mood came over me. But I kept it to myself. I never even asked why, for three days, Sally never entered the room where I lay. I associated this fact, however, with what I had imagined her shrinking from me, her intent and pale face, her singular manner when occasion made it necessary or unavoidable for her to be near me.

No difficulty was there in associating my change of mood with her absence. I brooded. Steele's keen insight betrayed me to him, but all his power and his spirit availed nothing to cheer me. I pretended to be cheerful; I drank and ate anything given me; I was patient and quiet. But I ceased to mend.

Then, one day she came back, and Steele, who was watching me as she entered, quietly got up and without a word took Diane out of the room and left me alone with Sally.

"Russ, I've been sick myself—in bed for three days," she said. "I'm better now. I hope you are. You look so pale. Do you still think, brood about that fight?"

"Yes, I can't forget. I'm afraid it cost me more than life."

Sally was somber, bloomy, thoughtful. "You weren't driven to kill George?" she asked.

"How do you mean?"

"By that awful instinct, that hankering to kill, you once told me these gunmen had."

"No, I can swear it wasn't that. I didn't want to kill him. But he forced me. As I had to go after these two men it was a foregone conclusion about Wright. It was premeditated. I have no excuse."

"Hush—Tell me, if you confronted them, drew on them, then you had a chance to kill my uncle?"

"Yes. I could have done it easily."

"Why, then, didn't you?"

"It was for Diane's sake. I'm afraid I didn't think of you. I had put you out of my mind."

"Well, if a man can be noble at the same time he's terrible, you've been, Russ—I don't know how I feel. I'm sick and I can't think. I see, though, what you saved Diane and Steele. Why, she's touching happiness again, fearfully, yet really. Think of that! God only knows what you did for Steele. If I judged it by his suffering as you lay there about to die it would be beyond words to tell. But, Russ, you're pale and shaky now. Hush! No more talk!"

With all my eyes and mind and heart and soul I watched to see if she shrank from me. She was passive, yet tender as she smoothed my pillow and moved my head. A dark abstraction hung over her, and it was so strange, so foreign to her nature. No sensitiveness on earth could have equaled mine at that moment. And I saw and felt and knew that she did not shrink from me. Thought and feeling escaped me for a while. I dozed. The old shadows floated to and fro.

When I awoke Steele and Diane had just come in. As he bent over me I looked up into his keen gray eyes and there was no mask on my own as I looked up to him.

"Son, the thing that was needed was a change of nurses," he said gently. "I intend to make up some sleep now and leave you in better care."

From that hour I improved. I slept, I lay quietly awake, I partook of nourishing food. I listened and watched, and all the time I gained. But I spoke very little, and though I tried to brighten when Steele was in the room I made only indifferent success of it. Days passed. Sally was almost always with me, yet seldom alone. She was grave where once she had been gay. How I watched her face, praying for that shade to lift! How I listened for a note of the old music in her voice! Sally Langdon had sustained a shock to her soul almost as dangerous as had been the blow at my life. Still I hoped. I had seen other women's deadened and darkened spirits rebound and glow once more. It began to dawn upon me, however, that more than time was imperative if she were ever to become her old self again.

Studying her closer, with less thought of myself and her reaction to my presence, I discovered that she trembled at shadows, seemed like a frightened deer with a step always on its trail, was afraid of the dark. Then I wondered why I had not long before divined one cause of her strangeness. The house where I had killed one of her kin would ever be haunted for her. She had said she was a Southerner and that blood was thick. When I had thought out the matter a little further, I deliberately sat up in bed, scaring the wits out of all my kind nurses.

"Steele, I'll never get well in this house. I want to go home. When can you take me?"

They remonstrated with me and pleaded and scolded, all to little avail. Then they were persuaded to take me seriously, to plan, providing I improved, to start in a few days. We were to ride out of Pecos County together, back along the stage trail to civilization. The look in Sally's eyes decided my measure of improvement. I could have started that very day and have borne up under any pain or distress. Strange to see, too, how Steele and Diane responded to the stimulus of my idea, to the promise of what lay beyond the wild and barren hills!

He told me that day about the headlong flight of every lawless character out of Linrock, the very hour that Snecker and Wright and Sampson were known to have fallen. Steele expressed deep feeling, almost mortification, that the credit of that final coup had gone to him, instead of me. His denial and explanation had been only a few soundless words in the face of a grateful and clamorous populace that tried to reward him, to make him mayor of Linrock. Sampson had made restitution in every case where he had personally gained at the loss of farmer or rancher; and the accumulation of years went far toward returning to Linrock what it had lost in a material way. He had been a poor man when he boarded the stage for Sanderson, on his way out of Texas forever.

Not long afterward I heard Steele talking to Miss Sampson, in a deep and agitated voice. "You must rise above this. When I come upon you alone I see the shadow, the pain in your face. How wonderfully this thing has turned out when it might have ruined you! I expected it to ruin you. Who, but that wild boy in there could have saved us all? Diane, you have had cause for sorrow. But your father is alive and will live it down. Perhaps, back there in Louisiana, the dishonor will never be known. Pecos County is far from your old home. And even in San Antonio and Austin, a man's evil repute means little.

"Then the line between a rustler and a rancher is hard to draw in these wild border days. Rustling is stealing cattle, and I once heard a well-known rancher say that all rich cattlemen had done a little stealing. Your father drifted out here, and like a good many others, he succeeded. It's perhaps just as well not to split hairs, to judge him by the law and morality of a civilized country. Some way or other he drifted in with bad men. Maybe a deal that was honest somehow tied his hands and started him in wrong.

"This matter of land, water, a few stray head of stock had to be decided out of court. I'm sure in his case he never realized where he was drifting. Then one thing led to another, until he was face to face with dealing that took on crooked form. To protect himself he bound men to him. And so the gang developed. Many powerful gangs have developed that way out here. He could not control them. He became involved with them.

"And eventually their dealings became deliberately and boldly dishonest. That meant the inevitable spilling of blood sooner or later, and so he grew into the leader because he was the strongest. Whatever he is to be judged for I think he could have been infinitely worse."

When he ceased speaking I had the same impulse that must have governed Steele—somehow to show Sampson not so black as he was painted, to give him the benefit of a doubt, to arraign him justly in the eyes of Rangers who knew what wild border life was.

"Steele, bring Diane in!" I called. "I've something to tell her." They came quickly, concerned probably at my tone. "I've been hoping for a chance to tell you something, Miss Sampson. That day I came here your father was quarreling with Wright. I had heard them do that before. He hated Wright. The reason came out just before we had the fight. It was my plan to surprise them. I did. I told them you went out to meet Steele—that you two were in love with each other. Wright grew wild. He swore no one would ever have you. Then Sampson said he'd rather have you Steele's wife than Wright's.

"I'll not forget that scene. There was a great deal back of it, long before you ever came out to Linrock. Your father said that he had backed Wright, that the deal had ruined him, made him a rustler. He said he quit; he was done. Now, this is all clear to me, and I want to explain, Miss Sampson. It was Wright who ruined your father. It was Wright who was the rustler. It was Wright who made the gang necessary. But Wright had not the brains or the power to lead men. Because blood is thick, your father became the leader of that gang. At heart he was never a criminal.

"The reason I respected him was because he showed himself a man at the last. He faced me to be shot, and I couldn't do it. As Steele said, you've reason for sorrow. But you must get over it. You mustn't brood. I do not see that you'll be disgraced or dishonored. Of course, that's not the point. The vital thing is whether or not a woman of your high-mindedness had real and lasting cause for shame. Steele says no. I say no."

Then, as Miss Sampson dropped down beside me, her eyes shining and wet, Sally entered the room in time to see her cousin bend to kiss me gratefully with sisterly fervor. Yet it was a woman's kiss, given for its own sake. Sally could not comprehend; it was too sudden, too unheard-of, that Diane Sampson should kiss me, the man she did not love. Sally's white, sad face changed, and in the flaming wave of scarlet that dyed neck and cheek and brow I read with mighty pound of heart that, despite the dark stain between us, she loved me still.

Chapter 15

CONVALESCENCE

Four mornings later we were aboard the stage, riding down the main street, on the way out of Linrock. The whole town turned out to bid us farewell. The cheering, the clamor, the almost passionate fervor of the populace irritated me, and I could not see the incident from their point of view. Never in my life had I been so eager to get out of a place. But then I was morbid, and the whole world hinged on one thing. Morton insisted on giving us an escort as far as Del Rio. It consisted of six cowboys, mounted, with light packs, and they rode ahead of the stage.

We had the huge vehicle to ourselves. A comfortable bed had been rigged up for me by placing boards across from seat to seat, and furnishing it with blankets and pillows. By some squeezing there was still room enough inside for my three companions; but Steele expressed an intention of riding mostly outside, and Miss Sampson's expression betrayed her. I was to be alone with Sally. The prospect thrilled while it saddened me. How different this ride from that first one, with all its promise of adventure and charm!

"It's over!" said Steele thickly. "It's done! I'm glad, for their sakes—glad for ours. We're out of town."

I had been quick to miss the shouts and cheers. And I had been just as quick to see, or to imagine, a subtle change in Sally Langdon's face. We had not traveled a mile before the tension relaxed about her lips, the downcast eyelids lifted, and I saw, beyond any peradventure of doubt, a lighter spirit. Then I relaxed myself, for I had keyed up every nerve to make myself strong for this undertaking. I lay back with closed eyes, weary, aching, in more pain than I wanted them to discover. And I thought and thought.

Miss Sampson had said to me: "Russ, it'll all come right. I can tell you now what you never guessed. For years Sally had been fond of our cousin, George Wright. She hadn't seen him since she was a child. But she remembered. She had an only brother who was the image of George. Sally devotedly loved Arthur. He was killed in the Rebellion. She never got over it. That left her without any family. George and I were her nearest kin.

"How she looked forward to meeting George out here! But he disappointed her right at the start. She hates a drinking man. I think she came to hate George, too. But he always reminded her of Arthur, and she could never get over that. So, naturally, when you killed George she was terribly shocked. There were nights when she was haunted, when I had to stay with her. Vaughn and I have studied her, talked about her, and we think she's gradually recovering. She loved you, too; and Sally doesn't change. Once with her is for always. So let me say to you what you said to me—do not brood. All will yet be well, thank God!"

Those had been words to remember, to make me patient, to lessen my insistent fear. Yet, what did I know of women? Had not Diane Sampson and Sally Langdon amazed and nonplused me many a time, at the very moment when I had calculated to a nicety my conviction of their action, their feeling? It was possible that I had killed Sally's love for me, though I could not believe so; but it was very possible that, still loving me, she might never break down the barrier between us. The beginning of that journey distressed me physically; yet, gradually, as I grew accustomed to the roll of the stage and to occasional jars, I found myself easier in body. Fortunately there had been rain, which settled the dust; and a favorable breeze made riding pleasant, where ordinarily it would have been hot and disagreeable.

We tarried long enough in the little hamlet of Sampson for Steele to get letters from reliable ranchers. He wanted a number of references to verify the Ranger report he had to turn in to Captain Neal. This precaution he took so as to place in Neal's hands all the evidence needed to convince Governor Smith. And now, as Steele returned to us and entered the stage, he spoke of this report. "It's the longest and the best I ever turned in," he said, with a gray flame in his eyes. "I shan't let Russ read it. He's peevish because I want his part put on record. And listen, Diane. There's to be a blank line in this report. Your father's name will never be recorded. Neither the Governor, nor the adjutant-general, nor Captain Neal, nor any one back Austin way will ever know who this mysterious leader of the Pecos gang might have been.

"Even out here very few know. Many supposed, but few knew. I've shut the mouths of those few. That blank line in the report is for a supposed and mysterious leader who vanished. Jack Blome, the reputed leader, and all his lawless associates are dead. Linrock is free and safe now, its future in the hands of roused, determined, and capable men."

We were all silent after Steele ceased talking. I did not believe Diane could have spoken just then. If sorrow and joy could be perfectly blended in one beautiful expression, they were in her face. By and by I dared to say: "And Vaughn Steele, Lone Star Ranger, has seen his last service!"

"Yes," he replied with emotion.

Sally stirred and turned a strange look upon us all. "In that case, then, if I am not mistaken, there were two Lone Star Rangers—and both have seen their last service!" Sally's lips were trembling, the way they trembled when it was impossible to tell whether she was about to laugh or cry. The first hint of her old combative spirit or her old archness! A wave of feeling rushed over me, too much for me in my weakened condition. Dizzy, racked with sudden shooting pains, I closed my eyes; and the happiness I embraced was all the sweeter for the suffering it entailed. Something beat into my ears, into my brain, with the regularity and rapid beat of pulsing blood—not too late! Not too late!

From that moment the ride grew different, even as I improved with leaps and bounds. Sanderson behind us, the long gray barren between Sanderson and the Rio Grande behind us, Del Rio for two days, where I was able to sit up, all behind us—and the eastward trail to Uvalde before us! We were the only passengers on the stage from Del Rio to Uvalde. Perhaps Steele had so managed the journey. Assuredly he had become an individual with whom traveling under the curious gaze of strangers would have been embarrassing. He was most desperately in love. And Diane, all in a few days, while riding these long, tedious miles, ordinarily so fatiguing, had renewed her bloom, had gained what she had lost. She, too, was desperately in love, though she remembered her identity occasionally, and that she was in the company of a badly shot-up young man and a broken-hearted cousin.

Most of the time Diane and Steele rode on top of the stage. When they did ride inside their conduct was not unbecoming; indeed, it was sweet to watch; yet it loosed the fires of jealous rage and longing in me; and certainly had some remarkable effect upon Sally. Gradually she had been losing that strange and somber mood she had acquired, to brighten and change more and more. Perhaps she divined something about Diane and Steele that escaped me. Anyway, all of a sudden she was transformed. "Look here, if you people want to spoon, please get out on top," she said.

If that was not the old Sally Langdon I did not know who it was. Miss Sampson tried to appear offended, and Steele tried to look insulted, but they both failed. They could not have looked anything but happy. Youth and love were too strong for this couple, whom circumstances might well have made grave and thoughtful. They were magnet and steel, powder and spark. Any moment, right before my eyes, I expected them to rush right into each other's arms. And when they refrained, merely substituting clasped hands for a dearer embrace, I closed my eyes and remembered them, as they would live in my memory forever, standing crushed together on the ridge that day, white lips to white lips, embodying all that was beautiful, passionate and tragic.

And I, who had been their undoing, in the end was their salvation. How I hugged that truth to my heart!

It seemed, following Sally's pert remark, that after an interval of decent dignity, Diane and Steele did go out upon the top of the stage. "Russ," whispered Sally, "they're up to something. I heard a few words. I bet you they're going to get married in San Antonio."

"Well, it's about time," I replied.

"But oughtn't they take us into their confidence?"

"Sally, they have forgotten we are upon the earth."

"Oh, I'm so glad they're happy!"

Then there was a long silence. It was better for me to ride lying down, in which position I was at this time. After a mile Sally took my hand and held it without speaking. My heart leaped, but I did not open my eyes or break that spell even with a whisper. "Russ, I must say—tell you—"

She faltered, and still I kept my eyes closed. I did not want to wake up from that dream. "Have I been very—very sad?" she went on.

"Sad and strange, Sally. That was worse than my bullet-holes." She gripped my hand. I felt her hair on my brow, felt her breath on my cheek.

"Russ, I swore—I'd hate you if you—if you—"

"I know. Don't speak of it," I interposed hurriedly.

"But I don't hate you. I—I love you. And I can't give you up!"

"Darling! But, Sally, can you get over it—can you forget?"

"Yes. That horrid black spell had gone with the miles. Little by little, mile after mile, and now it's gone! But I had to come to the point. To go back on my word! To tell you. Russ, you never, *never* had any sense!"

Then I opened my eyes and my arms, too, and we were reunited. It must have been a happy moment, so happy that it numbed me beyond appreciation. "Yes, Sally," I agreed; "but no man ever had such a wonderful girl."

"Russ, I never—took off your ring," she whispered.

"But you hid your hand from my sight," I replied quickly.

"Oh dear Russ, we're crazy—as crazy as those lunatics outside. Let's think a little."

I was very content to have no thought at all, just to see and feel her close to me.

"Russ, will you give up the Ranger Service for me?" she asked.

"Indeed I will."

"And leave this fighting Texas, never to return till the day of guns and Rangers and bad men and even-breaks is past?"

"Yes."

"Will you go with me to my old home? It was beautiful once, Russ, before it was let run to rack and ruin. A thousand acres. An old stone house. Great mossy oaks. A lake and river. There are bear, deer, panther, wild boars in the breaks. You can hunt. And ride! I've horses, Russ, such horses! They could run these scrubby broncos off their legs. Will you come?"

"Come! Sally, I rather think I will. But, dearest, after I'm well again I must work," I said earnestly. "I've got to have a job."

"You're indeed a poor cowboy out of a job! Remember your deceit. Oh, Russ! Well, you'll have work, never fear."

"Sally, is this old home of yours near the one Diane speaks of so much?" I asked.

"Indeed it is. But hers has been kept under cultivation and in repair, while mine has run down. That will be our work, to build it up. So it's settled then?"

"Almost. There are certain—er—formalities—needful in a compact of this kind." She looked inquiringly at me, with a soft flush. "Well, if you are so dense, try to bring back that Sally Langdon who used to torment me. How you broke your promises! How you leaned from your saddle! Kiss me, Sally!"

Later, as we drew close to Uvalde, Sally and I sat in one seat, after the manner of Diane and Vaughn, and we looked out over the west where the sun was setting behind dim and distant mountains. We were fast leaving the wild and barren border. Already it seemed far beyond that broken rugged horizon with its dark line silhouetted against the rosy and golden sky. Already the spell of its wild life and the grim and haunting faces had begun to fade out of my memory. Let newer Rangers, with less to lose, and with the call in their hearts, go on with our work 'till soon that wild border would be safe!

The great Lone Star State must work out its destiny. Some distant day, in the fulness of time, what place the Rangers had in that destiny would be history.

Milton Keynes UK
Ingram Content Group UK Ltd.
UKHW010742080324
438959UK00004B/328